STARKE NAKED DEAD

Starke Dead Mysteries

CONDA V. DOUGLAS

To my niece, Victoria Head.
Thanks Vikki, for inspiring me to create my dreams.

Acknowledgements

With thanks to: Tricia Keener Blaha, Bruce Demaree, Gilbert and Joan Douglas, Kathy McIntosh, Cynthia Reed, Diane B. Rice, Lorca Warner, Michele Winkler, and my beloved hometown of Sun Valley, Idaho.

ONE

The bell rang. My father, Wild Rupert the mountain recluse, shuffled inside the store, his shoulders hunched for a blow. I jumped up from my stool behind the checkout counter.

"Dora, I'm in trouble," Rupert whispered low and hoarse. His wet lower lip wagged and displayed the rotten stumps of his bottom teeth. A sweet stench of decay wafted my way.

First time in months I'd seen my father. He never ventured into Mad Maddie's Marvels, my aunt's store. He never dared.

Yet he stood in front of me. Backlit by the late afternoon sun streaming through the front door of Mad Maddie's Marvels, his long gray beard trailed around his shoulders.

He crept a few steps inside. "You have to help me."

A deep warmth spread in my chest. First time my father ever asked me for anything. "I'll help you, Father. Anything. I'll do anything."

Rupert slid his hand into a pocket of his ragged leather duster. Strips from the lining of the old coat hung to the floor. It gave off a faint aroma of old tanned hide, nasty, vile, but familiar and thus, comforting.

He dragged out a jeweler's velvet bag, the largest made. Covered in soot, the filthy bag once had been a deep burgundy, the color of old blood. My father loosened the drawstring and withdrew a grimy blue flannel rag.

I clutched my favorite Ohm pin, a backward three with a couple of dashed accents, which rested on my jeweler's apron. I watched, transfixed.

He opened the first corner of the rag. Silver flashed in a stray sunbeam.

"Oh, what have you got?" I breathed.

He unwrapped the rest and held out the rag on his open palm, a sacrificial offering. There, on his calloused and acid-scarred hand, lay a necklace.

I gasped, grasping my Ohm pin so tight it cut into my palm.

Twelve, two-inch, heart-shaped cabochon blood rubies, each nestled in a platinum heart setting, created the heavy collar of the necklace. A pendant of a naked woman carved in onyx and set in platinum depended from the twelve links. Worth millions.

"Sell it." Rupert thrust the rag with its valuable burden toward me.

Unbidden, my hand reached toward the necklace. The enormous piece glistened with platinum and rubies and black onyx. Oh, my.

The necklace balanced over his hand, resplendent on the dark blue flannel rag. The voluptuous woman pendant hung from his fingertips. Perfect. No, not perfect. Torn solder dangled from one tiny foot, obscene.

I wanted to pin the necklace to the glass counter and grasp all that glory. I jammed my hands into the encyclopedia-sized pockets of my jeweler's apron.

"Take it, quick," my father said. His voice quavered, his beard trembled. "Before Maddie gets back."

We both glanced around the store. If Aunt Maddie returned and found her despised brother-in-law here we faced a storm of mad Maddie trouble.

"Who's the designer?" I demanded.

I wanted, no, needed to know. The elements of the necklace screamed Art Nouveau. The design glowed unique, the work of a master jeweler. I couldn't place the necklace in an oeuvre. "Vever?"

"Sell it," Rupert said.

"Lalique?" But no, the necklace couldn't be a Lalique. In everything, including his jewelry, he always used glass. Onyx, a dyed semi-precious stone, didn't count.

"Sell it."

"A Verdura?" I asked, before my father's words at last sunk in. My head jerked up. I stared at Rupert. "What do you mean, 'sell it'?"

He gave the rag bundle a shake. "Now. Today."

My mouth hung open. "B-but, where...where did you get it?"

Even at the height of his popularity and fame, when he was renowned all over the West for his "Starke" designs, Rupert never enjoyed the resources to create such a piece. I doubted any designer did today. Platinum went for well over a thousand a troy ounce.

My father shook his head. His fringe of long gray hair flew. "If you love me you won't ask any questions."

"No questions? You've got to be kid— If I love you?"

First time he spoke of my love for him. And he used it like a club.

He looked far worse than when I'd seen him last. His clothes, always old and worn, but always clean, were gray with grime. His spirit, blue.

I gulped back bile. Good thing I'd not eaten in hours. It was tough being a vegan in Starke, Idaho.

"I've run out of time." Rupert spoke to the floor. "Sell it today."

"Today?" I glanced around at Aunt Maddie's shop, at the decades of dust and disorder. I couldn't sell the Crown Jewels in this mess. I imagined the shelf with the potato salt-and-pepper shakers, priced at three dollars a pair, and next to them the necklace. Worth millions.

"Get cash, no checks." Rupert's hands shook as he clutched the bag and the necklace with its soiled flannel.

"Cash?" I rubbed my face in disbelief. "Cash?" Nobody had that kind of cash, not even the wealthy who would flood into Starke when the ski resort would open in two weeks. Buddha willing and the snow should fly.

Rupert stuffed the necklace back into the dirty velvet bag. "Take it." He held out the bag, his hand shaking.

I took a step back and bumped into the display case of spud-based souvenirs. The case rocked. A little Spuddy Buddy fell off onto the floor and produced a poof of stale dust. "What? Where did you get it? Where did you find it?"

Where could my father have found such a treasure?

"I need—at least a—a hundred thousand."

"A hundred thousand?" My voice squeaked. "Dollars?"

"It's worth millions. Even a bit damaged. Even with a bit missing." He fingered the bag in his hand, a talisman. "And it's worthless." His chin dropped to his chest. "To me," he whispered.

"But who would have a hundred thousand?" Even as I spoke, I realized I knew one person with tons of money. She might know who created the necklace as well. She knew everything. Or so she always insisted.

"Your boss," Rupert said. He knew too.

"Nance is not my boss. Not any more. Not ever again," I said. "Now I'm my own boss." I refrained from another chaos check of the room.

"She's rich."

"Yes, but I'll bet she doesn't have a hundred thousand stashed in that battered steamer trunk she carries around as a purse." Although I believed the cash might fit into Nance's voluminous satchel.

Rupert gulped. "Dora, please, I've never asked you for anything."

And you've never given me anything either, I wanted to blurt out. Ohm, I breathed. As a practicing Buddhist, and boy did I need a lot of practice, I knew that a brutal accusation would so be not Right Speech.

"What are you going to do with a hundred thousand dollars?" I couldn't imagine why Rupert needed all that money. He never needed money before, living in a tiny cabin in the woods and selling a few of his "junk" jewelry pins every fall to buy food for the winter. His clothing he got from the Widows Brigade during their annual "Charity Party."

"No questions. I have to have the money. Now. Today."

The slanting afternoon light through the dirty front window grew dimmer. "Today is gone. I can't—"

"You have to," Rupert insisted.

"No, we have to tell Lester," I said.

Lester the Arrester, Starke's Sheriff for thirty years, would know what to do. He always knew what to do. Or had known, before his grandson's death.

"No, no, no." Rupert placed the bag next to his heart. "Promise you won't tell." He looked over his shoulder at the front door, as if checking an escape route, and then back at me. He shook his head. His never-shorn beard waved from side to side. "If you tell anyone,"—he shook harder—"or if you don't get the money now, I-I'm—dead."

"Dead?" I threw my hand out to steady myself. The display case toppled over.

Rupert and I jumped as potato-shaped salt-and-pepper shakers, butter dishes, and flower vases all with "Souvenir from Idaho" scrawled across them in flaking gold paint crashed and broke.

"Maddie will be mad," Rupert said, his voice high, threaded with fear. He glanced behind him at the front door. Perhaps he feared she would appear at the speaking of her name.

"Wait. No problem and good riddance." I didn't want him to run before I had some answers.

Rupert stared at me. "But your aunt..."

I flapped my hand at the broken junk, dismissing it. "I'll take the blame. I don't want the tacky things in Maddie's new, improved store." Aunt Maddie's renovated store would showcase my original jewelry designs.

The corroded bell above the door clanged. Another thing I'd replace. A blast of frigid air followed the bell. Too cold to snow, darn it.

A woman's voice sang out, "Hello?"

The necklace flashed as Rupert stuffed it back in the velvet bag. "Get me the money. Or I'm dead," he hissed. With a desperate nod, he tossed the bag to me.

I caught it on the fly and thrust the bag into my pocket. Even in my oversized jeweler's apron, the bag bulged the pocket. Ugh.

The woman stood behind my tall father so I peeked around him to where an even-shorter-than-short-me plump figure stood in the doorway. Unfamiliar. The woman's long, thick golden hair cascaded past her waist and obscured her features.

"Pardon me, please, if you don't mind," the woman said in a high, childlike voice.

Rupert flung his hands up and froze, a terrified statue.

"It's not Maddie," I reassured him.

I wondered how many years it'd been since he and Aunt Maddie spoke. Although my father should know that my aunt would never begin a sentence with "pardon me." She might not even say "please." And she never cared if anybody minded.

Rupert looked over his shoulder. He gasped.

The woman stared up at him. "Is it—could it be?" She flung aside her curtain of hair. Her large blue eyes widened. "Bertie?"

TWO

Bertie?

Rupert's jaw dropped. His mouth gabbled wide, his rotten teeth black flags. "No, it can't be!" he screamed. He ran for the door.

The woman grabbed at his arm as he scuttled by. "Bertie."

Bertie? Did this stranger confuse my father for someone else? Someone she knew? Someone not a mountain man. Someone not a recluse. Someone, Buddha above, gregarious?

She caught the material of his leather duster. "Wait." She tugged.

My father gave an inarticulate cry.

I grabbed the woman's grasping arm. "Let go."

"Never," she spoke in a high snarl. A mean Pomeranian growl.

I stepped between them and placed my hand on the woman's considerable bosom. My hand sunk into her abundant flesh. "Let him go. Now." I nudged. Well, pushed. Not hard. Still not Right Action.

Rupert ripped free. He ran. His battered ancient sneakers crunched over the shattered spud bits. His beard floated behind him in a gray cloud. He slammed the door behind him. The bell leapt and clanged.

"Don't run," the woman called.

We dashed to the door. The woman got there first. She flung it open. The bell jumped off its nail and clattered to the floor.

I followed her out and squinted in the late afternoon glare. The tang of the Canine Creek forest fire stung my nose. The Sleeping Gods lay deep bronze in the sun. Blue haze gathered around the bare brown southern exposed mountains. This cold, this late in the year, and still somewhere near Starke a fire burned.

A pin of the golden mountains, with smoky blue-fused glass as an overlay...a friend did gorgeous fused glass...if I asked her to provide the—

The woman waved with both arms high. "Bertie."

Bertie?

She hopped up and down. An aggravated long-haired Pomeranian.

My father scuttled toward his ancient station wagon parked behind a neon pink Cadillac.

A man slouched behind the wheel of the Cadillac. His shaved bald pate reflected the neon pink. He sat up and stared at my father.

Across Main Street, two of the Sun Dog Development Company's construction crew paused from work on the Dog's main office façade. Squeezed between Maureen's Bar and McIntosh's Drugstore, the building's front mirrored the traditional "Wild West" false two-story frontage of the other century-old buildings. Badly. The faded, worn carving on Mo's Bar's and the drugstore's windows and door frames couldn't compete with the riot of crossed skis and ski poles on the new building. The Dog's building vibrated bad taste, bad planning, and bad karma.

After staring for a moment, the two construction workers turned back to work. I snorted. Strangers. Oh, not Right Thought. Perhaps they only rushed, frantic to finish before Starke, excuse me, *Aurora* opened as Idaho's newest ski resort. In two weeks. If it ever snowed. Or maybe they feared Tony, the construction foreman for most of Starke's work.

Rupert skittered over the pine wood sidewalks and almost slipped and tumbled. Brand new, courtesy of Starke's new Town Council, the sidewalks were "authentic Wild West," which meant they were slicker than snot.

The pink Cadillac man watched. His eyebrows rose toward his non-existent hairline. He leapt out of the car, revealing himself as a barrel-shaped bear of a man who appeared to have squeezed his excess pounds into a tiny pair of exercise stretch pants. A cropped sweatshirt completed his—um—ensemble.

A cold wind skittered down the sidewalk. I stuck my hands inside my apron bib and shivered. Dressed so scantily, that guy might freeze to death.

He pointed at my father. A patch of fat white flesh rolled out between pants and top. "Hey," the man yelped.

My father yelped back. He skidded to a stop, spun around, saw me and the woman, and spun back.

"Derek," the woman called, "it's him." She pointed at Rupert.

Rupert ran.

Derek jumped onto the sidewalk into Rupert's escape path. Bad idea. My father banged into the man full force and knocked Derek off the sidewalk. Derek bounced off the Cadillac.

Rupert jumped into his station wagon. It coughed to life. He cut the wheels tight. The station wagon leapt forward. Rupert missed the fender of the Cadillac by a micro-millimeter.

"Hey," the Cadillac man yelled again. A limited vocabulary that went with his limited outfit. He shook his fist at my father.

Bald tires squealed as Rupert tore down Highway 21, also Starke's Main Street.

The man showed his teeth at the departing car. "I've got you, Bertie, at last."

With one hand, the woman scooped air. "Derek, come over here," she said, a command in every word.

The man scowled. Then he stared at the station wagon's retreating dust trail. He smiled. "I'm done taking your orders, Sis."

"It's mine, not yours," the woman answered.

"We'll see about that."

"Derek, you have to—"

The man jumped back into the Cadillac. "Finders keepers," he yelled at her.

"Wait for me!" She sprinted toward the Cadillac.

The big car purred as Derek cranked the wheel and pulled away from the curb in one smooth motion.

Inches from grabbing the car's door handle, the woman stopped and stamped her foot.

The Cadillac passed, headed fast in the same direction as Rupert's car. A magnetic sign on the driver's door showed a logo of a naked woman sitting sideways on a horse. The woman's long yellow hair preserved her modesty, or rather most of it—one tiny nipple half-peeked through a strand of hair. Purple lettering proclaimed, "Godiva, God's Naturist."

I almost wished I'd left with Rupert, or even the obese Derek. Everyone seemed determined to escape the obnoxious woman.

"Derek, come back here." The woman put her hands on her hips and muttered, "You bastard," under her breath. She turned and faced me. Her one blue eye not covered by hair narrowed. "You scared him away," she said.

"Huh? Who?"

"You know who. Bertie."

My eyes widened. Was this odd woman a threat to my father? Or did he run because she was a stranger, and strange? "Who's Bertie?"

"I needed to talk to him," the woman said.

"You did talk to him. You not only talked to him, you assaulted him. Why?"

The woman gave a laugh and a flippant flip of her hand. "Oh, he was just surprised."

"No kidding."

She raised one eyebrow at me as if I'd just farted and blamed her.

I plunged both hands into my apron pockets and held onto my temper. After all, I supposed I didn't look that threatening in my heavy-duty cotton jeweler's apron spattered with green and pink casting wax and so large it hung past my knees. Although the ball peen hammer and leather mallet hanging from the apron loops ought to help.

My hand jerked out when it touched the velvet bag.

The woman tossed her head. The ocean of ultra-blonde hair gone, her face displayed deep sun-cut grooves around her generous mouth and ultra-wide baby doll blue eyes. The hair framing her face had concealed her age. She must have been in her fifties. A pin in a far-too-familiar style perched on her generous bosom. The unmistakable mishmash of beaten bottle caps, old telephone wire, scraps of cloth, and old buttons combined into a portrayal of an old mansion in flames, somehow captured at the moment of total conflagration, ethereal, beautiful, and terrifying.

Rupert, who once worked in silver and eighteen-carat gold, now created these pins during the long winter months. Always of a burning mansion.

Was this annoying woman only an overly-enthusiastic customer, the type who always felt compelled to meet the artist? A customer who'd misheard his name?

"Did you get that pin from Nance's?" I asked.

Only two places carried my father's jewelry these days—my aunt's store and Nance's gallery in Boise. Aunt Maddie hated having Rupert's pins in her store, but I'd convinced her to sell them. We held little inventory.

Now, with the potato tourist gewgaws scattered all over the store floor even less.

The woman frowned. "Delightful person, and so knowledgeable." She gave a shake of her head. "Very, very, very knowledgeable."

This woman knew Nance all right.

Her outfit exuded wealth, she wore a simple velour sweat suit in a matching neon pink to the Cadillac. It was doubtful the heavy plush of the velour provided any real barrier against the cold.

I pointed at the grimy display window of my aunt's store. *Clean window, check. Add to list, check. Long list.* Inside, on top of a couple of Spuddy Buddies, I'd displayed my few cast pins and several of Rupert's pieces. "If you'd like more, I've several lovely pieces." I tried for a happy-helpful-salesclerk voice.

The woman crossed her arms over her large breasts. "Nance didn't know where Bertie lived." She leaned in toward me. "Do you? Whoever you are?"

Enough. I leaned forward until we almost touched noses. "What do you want with my father?" I demanded. *Do you want to kill him?* I wanted to add. Somebody must.

I stepped back at the realization and clutched my Ohm pin. What somebody?

I'd only been up to Rupert's cabin twice in my life. A third time would be added as soon as I got rid of Miss Lots of Hair for answers to the questions that reeled in my mind.

The woman put her hand up to her mouth. "You must be itty-bitty Dora MacDonald." Odd thing for a woman shorter than me to say. "All grown up."

Shocked she knew me, I blurted, "It's not MacDonald, it's Dora Starke. Born of the Starke's in Starke then always a Starke," I quoted my Aunt Maddie.

The woman ran her hand through her long hair. It took quite a while. "Whatever. You're his daughter. You know where he lives." She placed her hands on her hips. "Where?"

Why was she so vociferous in her pursuit of him? "You've already frightened him enough. Leave him alone."

The woman dropped her arms. She glanced at where her ride had taken off, as if the Cadillac might magically reappear.

I softened my voice. "Look, my father's called Wild Rupert because he's been a mountain man for years and he's gone all feral shy."

So how did he get hold of the necklace? My hand strayed to my bulging apron pocket. I ached to pull the necklace out of my pocket and examine it. I put my hand in the pocket that held the necklace and felt it through the cloth bag.

"What's that you've got there?" the woman said.

"A neck—some jewelry." Good save, Dora. I even told the truth.

"Jewelry?"

Out of the corner of my eye, I saw Lester clumping down the wooden sidewalk. My clenched stomach relaxed. When I handed over the necklace to Lester then—

"If you tell anyone, I'm dead."

I couldn't chance it. The necklace weighed leaden in my pocket.

The woman stared at Lester. "Oh no, *he's* still sheriff? Isn't he dead yet?"

THREE

I wondered at her words, but before I asked, Lester arrived. He wore a mélange of a faded uniform and an old corduroy jacket, patched at the elbows. Over six feet tall, stick thin, with his stoop he resembled an aged professor. For his thirty years as sheriff, Lester the Arrester never arrested a soul. 'Course, until Starke got declared a new ski resort, less than three hundred souls existed in town to arrest.

He stomped up to me and glared, all cop, no professor. "I heard that crazy father of yours tearing out of town all the way down the block."

The woman scurried back, away from our confrontation. She flipped her hair back over her shoulder, hiding her face.

I couldn't blame her. The rage in Lester's voice would terrify a hardened criminal.

My sour stomach roiled again. I gulped. Lester might arrest Rupert, for the fatal sin of driving fast. Lester the Arrester never arrested anyone until the tragedy, but now...who knew?

"Rupert was frightened," I said.

Lester removed his hat and ran a hand over close-cropped, silver-gray hair. His hair glinted as bright as any glittering jewel in the last rays of the late October sun.

My empty stomach burned.

"That's no excuse. And who was that maniac following Rupert?"

The woman paused mid-creep. She pulled her curtain of hair aside. "Oh, Derek was only headed to our new home, The Starke Naturist Center."

Lester's shoulders jerked. "Derek." His pronunciation of that name made it clear he knew the cropped-top man. His mouth twisted in distaste. "Godiva."

The woman widened her best feature, her large blue eyes, at Lester. "After all these years you remember me."

"The nudist." Lester's neck spasmed.

Godiva lifted her chin. "Such an old-fashioned term. We're naturists." She clasped her hands as if in prayer. "As God made us."

An image of this woman naked in a snowstorm came to me. I shivered. "In Starke? You'll freeze to death." I sighed. "Maybe. If it ever snows."

Godiva giggled, an odd, high childish laugh. "We'll be inside during the winter."

"I hope you have a good furnace," I said.

"We have fire, the greatest of the elements." Her face shone. "We'll live as our true selves, unburdened by the fake encumbrances of cloth, honest and free."

I found myself smiling and nodding. Attachment to a dream led to suffering, but such fervor delighted me. I possessed a passion for jewelry design that despite all my practice of the Way still held me fast.

Lester gave a growl, deep in his throat. "Not while Starke is still my town."

Godiva cringed.

Lester added, "We ran you out of town before."

I grimaced, hearing no appeasement in his tone, no calm and steady of the old Lester. "Lester? Sheriff?" I asked in as quiet a tone I could manage.

"Get out of Starke." Lester took a step toward Godiva.

"You can't arrest her. She's done nothing wrong," I said.

"She is everything that's wrong." Lester reached for Godiva, his hand clawed tight.

She gave a tiny yelp. "Bye," she squawked. Miss Too Long Hair trotted away, heading down Main in the same direction as my father and Derek, the driver of the pink Caddy.

Lester swore under his breath.

He'd never sworn before, not in my hearing.

I patted Lester on the elbow patch. "Lester, why are you—"

He turned to me, his face hot red.

"—so angry?" I finished. I already knew the answer and it had nothing to do with nudists.

Lester grimaced.

"Oh, Sheriff, I'm..." I struggled for something not trite to say. "You can't change or fix the Path," I managed.

Lester's eyebrows rose.

"I mean—" How to explain a Buddhist precept that I couldn't grasp myself?

Mallard, Starke's deputy, drove Starke's brand new, one and only police car up to the curb and honked. Lester's face smoothed into a cop's mask.

"Um, boss?" Mallard called out of the open side window.

Dust covered both sides of the car. Until Starke got the nod for a ski resort, only Main Street, also Highway 21, had been paved. Now two other streets could claim that distinction. Not enough.

"Mallard, get out of the car," Lester ordered.

Mallard got out. Even in the crisp air, sweat stains circled under each of his arms. His broad-nosed face bore his usual expression of a stunned duck. Ever since he arrived six months ago, he'd struggled to swim in the whirlpool of Starke.

Lester held out his hand. "Give me the keys."

"Um," Mallard said as he handed them over, "I was working on those programs on the computer, you know?"

Lester crossed his arms over his chest, an irritated professor. "I suppose that's why you drove over here? To tell me that?"

"Um," Mallard said again. A huge drop of sweat rolled down his forehead, down his nose to rest, glistening at the tip. "You didn't take your cell phone, boss."

"That piece of junk doesn't work most of the time," Lester said. "And if it's an emergency, Mallard, it's probably over by now." He moved to the police car.

I understood Lester's impatience. Mallard would act as Sheriff after Lester left for Houston.

"We got a call from Mrs. McGarrity," Mallard managed.

Mrs. McGarrity provided the Starke gossip service for the Widows Brigade, a service faster than the Internet.

"And?" Lester said.

"Mad Maddie—" Mallard began

"Hey," I said. Mallard hadn't been in town long enough to call my aunt mad.

Mallard glanced at me and gulped. "I mean Miss Maddie Starke."

"That's better," I said. "What's she done this time?" My aunt earned her sobriquet, often hourly.

"Mrs. McGarrity says that Maddie's going to shoot Henry," Mallard said in a rush.

I sighed. One catastrophe at a time.

"I'm out of time," my father had said.

Mallard held out his hand toward me, palm up. "Why is your aunt going to shoot Henry?"

"Family tradition."

"Tradition?"

"We've been blasting away at the Camerons for generations."

Why my aunt wanted to take pot-shots at Henry, I didn't know. I didn't want to know.

More sweat beads popped out on Mallard's forehead. I'd bet that when he signed up as Starke's first ever deputy, he expected boredom in an old mining town. At least until the ski resort opened.

"Ever kill anybody?" he asked.

My shoulders rose again. "Not recently. We're past due."

Mallard frowned. The sweat started to collect in the crevices of his forehead, little rivers. "So, boss," he said to Lester.

"Sheriff," Lester said. "I'm not a boss, I'm a sheriff." He grunted. "At least for a few days." He slid into the police car as if finished with the discussion and the situation.

"Um, bo—Sheriff," Mallard said. "Don't you figure you ought to head over to Maddie's and defuse the situation?"

"Defuse the situation?" I said. "You can't defuse Aunt Maddie, trust me."

Lester lifted his chin in the general direction of the Starke homestead, now occupied by the last of the Starke family, Maddie and me. "You go, Mallard," Lester said.

"Me?" Mallard wilted even more.

"Mallard?" I asked.

Lester gave a dismissive wave of his hand. "It'll be a good experience." He started the police car.

I looked at Lester's closed down face. Before his grandson died, he'd never send anyone off to an armed confrontation. And an armed confrontation with my aunt.

Mallard shrugged. "But bo—Sheriff, I'm the computer geek."

"You're sheriff in five days," Lester said.

Mallard looked about to drown in his own sweat. "But—"

"And I've got to get to Houston." With that, Lester drove off.

I took Mallard's arm and flinched at his wet shirt. "You can survive anything."

He stared down at me, his eyebrows raised.

"If you survive my Aunt Maddie," I said to make him sweat.

A line of huge sweat beads formed on Mallard's brow.

Too easy.

FOUR

"Aunt Maddie, nobody dies today." I hoped I spoke the truth.

"Family tradition to shoot Camerons," Aunt Maddie replied. She squatted next to me on our homestead's roof, in Great Grandpa's favorite spot.

The first family into Starke—not counting the Native Americans, and nobody did in those days—built our homestead for the view of Dog Face Mountain, where Great Grandpa Starke figured to find his fortune. When none of his stakes paid out—instead the Camerons discovered the rich vein of silver ore—he started sitting on the roof and glaring at the mountain. We continued the habit. Minus the glare. Below us stood Henry and next to him, Mallard. Both managed to look worried and confused at the same time.

Aunt Maddie's old, bottle green, paint-spattered gardening coat spread out around her. She resembled an enormous toadstool grown on the second story roof of our homestead. The icy wind tore her short-cropped orange hair around in a storm with no snow.

The same wind tattered the smoke of the forest fire, destroying any illusion of Japanese art. I hoped the dissipation of the smoke meant the fire fighters had succeeded and the fire was out. One catastrophe dead.

Aunt Maddie drew a bead on Henry with Great Grandpa's old .22 revolver. "'Sides, I wouldn't be pointing at him if I didn't mean to shoot him."

I made an ineffectual half-hearted grab for the gun, half-afraid it'd go off if I grappled with my aunt. "Lester taught me 'never aim to wound, only to kill,'" I said.

The wind cut past my heavy cotton apron. Shivering, I wished I could wear my old pink parka over the bulky apron. It didn't fit. And I hated not wearing the apron, the badge of my chosen profession. Besides, the coat didn't have oversized pockets.

I shifted my position on the slippery shingles and tried to get comfortable. Impossible. Should have taken off my weighty apron before I got up on the roof, but I didn't dare let the necklace out of my sight—or at least possession.

"Now, Miss Maddie, please listen to Dora," Henry called. He sweated almost as much as the deputy. His fancy pantsy cost-as-much-as-a-wedding-ring suit hung limp and wrinkled on his solid, muscular frame. Always rumpled, our Henry.

"I'll just wound him a little," Aunt Maddie said.

Henry ducked behind Mallard.

Mallard rubbed his wet face. "Does that gun work?"

"My, my, that boy is new to Idaho." Maddie didn't look away from where she sighted down the barrel.

"Yes, he's new and you're terrifying him." I shifted again and the necklace clinked.

Aunt Maddie looked down at the lump in my pocket. "What the devil have you got there?"

"Jewelry. Mallard's going to sweat to death if you don't put the gun down."

"I am not," Mallard said.

"Not until Henry stops talking crazy," Aunt Maddie said.

Henry stepped back out around Mallard. "I'm not crazy, and I'm not talking crazy, and it's not crazy." He crossed his arms.

Aunt Maddie lowered the gun. She enjoyed people standing up to her. It was as rare as Mama Chin cooking a bad meal in her café.

I breathed a little easier.

Henry spread his arms wide, resembling a supplicant appealing to a higher power. "Miss Maddie, I need you to pay the rent now."

"You know full well I'm good for every single penny, including any late fees." Aunt Maddie crouched on the roof, an Old World god, one of those crabby, vengeful ones. "Soon as the Marvel's back open and selling, you'll get your money."

He rubbed at a crease in his jacket. Didn't help. Never did. Never would. "Too late," he mumbled to the cloth, "with your back rent and the rent from the Castle, I can bring the electrical up to code, re-roof the office, put in the firewalls. Without it, I'll have to sell to the Dogs."

"Don't you threaten me with going to the Dogs. You're trying to steal the land, just like your great grandfather," Maddie said.

The word steal brought back the problem of the necklace and I jerked. My right foot slithered over the shingles. The necklace clinked in the bag.

"Is that true, sir?" Mallard said to Henry.

"No, it's my land, I mean property, I mean store," Henry said.

Mallard looked lost. I figured he'd get used to it, about the time he became a true Starker, in about fifty years. Or a hundred.

"I own Maddie's Marvel's." Aunt Maddie harrumphed.

"And you're over six months behind on the rent," Henry added.

I cringed. Most of that debt belonged to me. Over the last six months, I'd used my aunt's money to fix my kiln, buy casting wax, investment powder, and silver. If I hadn't spent her savings for my new business I'd bet she'd have plenty to pay rent. Or at least enough.

My aunt waved the old gun. I leaned back, away from the any possible line of fire. I hoped.

"Same answer," she said, "you'll get it when I've got it."

Henry hopped from foot to foot. I understood his agitation, a common experience whilst talking to my aunt.

"Look, Henry," I said, "Everybody's behind. If we open on schedule—"

As if on cue, Maddie and Henry looked up. I followed. Beyond the low-lying smoke, a clear sky, as blue as a deep, true turquoise, stretched from Dog Face Mountain across Starke Valley to the Sleeping Gods. The setting sun shadowed Dog Face and obscured the new ski runs, claw marks. Dog Face carried the scars of our ambitions.

Mallard craned his neck upward. "What's everybody looking at?"

"Nonexistent snow clouds," I said.

"Huh?" Mallard said.

"What's a ski resort without snow?" I asked Mallard.

He stared at me.

"A ghost town," I answered.

"Stupid drought," Maddie muttered. She threatened the sky with her gun. "Snow."

"Snow," I added my voice. "Put the fire out."

"The fire's miles away," Mallard said.

"The smoke and threat is right here," I explained while Maddie muttered "newcomer" under her breath. The cold helped slow the progress of any forest fire. Still, in the drought, fire could spread so fast...well, like wildfire.

"No snow. Only fire. No tourists." Henry's shoulders slumped and added several new folds in his expensive suit. "I need you to pay the back rent, Miss Maddie. If I don't get it, I'll..." He shook his head.

My aunt plonked the gun into her lap, and I hoped it didn't go off and shoot her in the leg. "Oh, Henry—"

"Or else I'll have to evict you." Henry then clamped his mouth shut. He always said a little too much.

"Henry Cameron, are you threatening me?" My aunt stood up. The gun fell out of her lap.

I snatched at the gun. My feet lost their purchase. Both the gun and I skittered down the shingles.

The gun shot off the roof and shot off.

FIVE

I caught my feet in the gutter and my hands on a loose shingle. The velvet bag tumbled out of my pocket. It slithered off the roof.

"Nobody move," Mallard said in a deep strong baritone that I could hear over the ringing of my ears. "Anybody hurt?"

The gutter groaned under my feet. I scrambled for purchase. More shingles came away. Argh.

"Dora." Mallard ran to stand underneath me.

"Dora." Henry did the same.

"Dora—" Aunt Maddie scrabbled down the roof toward me.

I slipped off. I grabbed the gutter and broke my fall.

Mallard grabbed my legs. "I've got you."

He eased me down as if I weighed less than my five-extra-pounds. Okay, Right Speech, ten. I stood on the grass and gasped, somewhat sweaty from Mallard transfer. Or maybe my own. Or both.

From where the bag lay on the grass, one gleaming ruby winked at me from the not-quite-closed mouth of the bag, a defiant tongue. Ohm.

"Let me get that for ya," Mallard said.

"No, that's okay."

He scooped up the bag, pulled it shut, and handed it to me. Thank the Buddha Mallard was a newcomer to Starke. Any Starker would have opened it, pulled out the necklace, and demanded to know everything. In detail.

"What's in the sack?" Aunt Maddie had climbed back up to her perch.

"What have you got there?" Henry reached for the bag.

I stuffed it into my pocket. "Jewelry, some old jewelry." That must be worth millions, I didn't add.

"About the money—" Henry never knew when to quit.

"Dora, get the gun and shoot Henry," my aunt ordered. "Lester taught you to not miss."

Mallard snatched it from where it lay on the grass.

"I've got the money," I heard myself say. Oh boy, not Right Speech, as I had, at most, some small change. Lying always led to suffering.

"Really?" Aunt Maddie said.

"Really?" Henry said.

"Where from?" Mallard asked.

I sensed that us Starkers might be underestimating Mallard.

"Yeah, Dora," Henry said. "It's a big chunk."

"How..." I stopped myself at the word "much." I didn't want to know. I cleared my throat. "Or, rather," I amended, "I'll have the money in the next couple of days." By then maybe manna would tumble from the sky, along with snowflakes.

Aunt Maddie glared at me from her perch. "Dor-r-a-a," my aunt put a parental threat into my name, "you look awfully guilty."

Desperation created inspiration. "I had a customer for Rupert's jewelry today," I said, surprised at my own words. "Nance will want some more of his 'outsider art.'"

"Who's Nance?" Mallard asked.

"Humph," Aunt Maddie voiced her regular opinion of my father. "That won't get you much."

I forced my face into a semblance of a smile. "I'll sell my designs to Nance." My smile drooped at the corners.

"Who's Nance?"

"Dora, don't sell Nance your designs." Aunt Maddie knew how much I wanted to sell my designs under my own imprint of "Dora's Dreams."

"You'd get enough from this Nance person to pay the back rent?" Mallard asked.

I wanted to smack the snoopy cop. Not Right Action. Besides, he might arrest me.

"I'm just asking," Mallard said at my look. "I'm a cop. I'm supposed to ask questions."

"About crimes." I swallowed, hard. What would Lester say if he found out I'd been withholding information? Withholding the necklace buried in my pocket with my jeweler's loupe? Withholding my trust?

"Hey," Henry said. "I don't care how you get the money—"

"I'll get it," I said.

"—as long as you get it by tomorrow."

"Tomorrow?"

What was it with this town and deadlines? Granted, Starke would open as a ski resort in a couple of weeks. Maybe everybody figured everything had to happen beforehand. Everything being renovation of the old buildings, finishing the new buildings and stocking up for the season.

Henry lifted his chin. "Yes, no eviction if—"

"Henry..." my aunt warned.

"Yeah, Henry, I'm a Buddhist." I made a gun with one hand. "I don't want to have to shoot you." I lowered and raised my thumb in the classic shooting motion. "Bad Karma."

Henry took one look at the storm clouds on my aunt's ferocious brow and turned crinkled tail and ran, trotting over our rickety bridge that spanned Looney Jump Creek. "Come into my office when you've got the money, Dora," he called back over his shoulder. When he reached his car parked on the other side, he added, "By tomorrow."

Must have figured he was out of range of Great Grandpa's gun.

"Don't push it, Henry. I'm a semi-Buddhist, but I'm still a better shot than my aunt."

The only answer I got was the slamming of Henry's car door.

I turned to Mallard. "Give me the gun back."

He clutched it tight. "I can't. It's evidence of a crime."

"What crime?" I asked.

Mallard's brow wrinkled and a couple of sweat drops dropped. "Uh, discharging a firearm within the city limits?"

"Don't got that law," Aunt Maddie said.

Mallard shook his head. "City council just passed it."

"Dang fool meddling dog developers," Aunt Maddie grumbled.

"Doesn't matter," I said to forestall the inevitable argument, "our homestead is past the city limits."

"It is?" Mallard looked at me as if he didn't believe me.

I flipped up a hand. "Past history. Camerons threw us out."

"Of the town you Starkes started?"

Maddie growled a loud affirmative.

"But, still," Mallard tried again, "I mean, Lester would—"

"Give the gun back," I said.

Mallard transferred the gun from one hand to another. He rubbed his sweat from the stock.

"You want to explain to Lester why you've commandeered the Starke family's prize antique gun while my aunt stands there hollering about police brutality?" I asked.

"Police brutality? What? I didn't—she wouldn't—" He looked up at my aunt who grinned back.

"You sure haven't been in Starke long," I said.

"Why does everybody keep saying that?"

"Go ahead and steal our gun. See what happens," Aunt Maddie said.

"So," I said, "you want to give it to Aunt Maddie or me?" I held out my hand.

Mallard handed me the gun.

I unloaded it and stuffed it in another apron pocket.

Mallard muttered something like, "I need to get back to my CPU."

"I heard that. Don't you use that language with me, young man," my aunt yelled.

Mallard ran. "Computer programs," he called over his shoulder, "I meant computer programs, the sanest thing in this town."

Every man I'd talked to today ran away. I hoped that didn't signal the beginning of a lifelong trend.

SIX

"Give me my gun back," my aunt said.

I jumped. She stood next to me and held out her hand.

"How'd you get down so fast?" I asked.

"Practice. Give me the gun."

"No way."

She reached for my pocket, the wrong pocket. I jerked back. Should I tell my aunt about the necklace? In the dying of the sunset, I studied my aunt's always-angry face.

"Then no dinner for you, young lady. That'll give you that much more time to pack."

"What's for dinner?" My empty stomach said *give up the gun and get dinner*.

My aunt stomped toward the baby cabin in the back, her studio, once Charles's studio. I trotted along behind. After I ate, I'd head up to Rupert's cabin and get some answers.

"Slumgullion," Aunt Maddie answered my question.

My stomach reconsidered. Slumguillion meant leftovers mixed together. It all depended on the leftovers.

My father had turned me away last time I visited his cabin, years ago. "There's nothing you can do for me," Rupert had said behind his locked door. Now he wouldn't. He couldn't. My questions weighed so heavy I feared I'd drop to my knees any second. Or maybe hunger made me weak.

"What's in it?" I asked.

"Spaghetti." My aunt's old gardening coat billowed about her. She looked thinner, diminished beneath it. Stress from re-opening Mad Maddie's Marvels? Money worries? Or something about a valuable necklace?

My stomach said it could deal with spaghetti. "Okay, what else?"

In the back yard, Maddie's miter box sat outside the baby cabin on a table made of sawhorses with a plywood top. Charles's large paintings lay stacked against the cabin wall, face down. With Charles's pieces, it was best if they always remained face down.

"And that loaf," my aunt said.

"What loaf?"

Aunt Maddie scanned the frame lengths that rested next to the paintings. "That meatloaf from the back of the freezer."

Oh no. The Freezer of Death. Where food went in and came out unrecognizable as edible, unrecognizable as organic matter, unrecognizable.

I gave my automatic reply, "I don't eat meat anymore." Thank the Buddha.

"You can't be vegan here. It's Idaho," Aunt Maddie said. Her automatic reply.

There was no way to respond to that statement. My distracted platinum-and-ruby-filled mind caught up with my stomach. "What do you mean packing?"

"Since you're leaving." My aunt picked a garish, elaborate gilded-length of frame.

Great choice, the gaudier the frame the better to detract from Charles's paintings. My aunt enjoyed a perfect artistic touch with framing.

"I'm not leaving," I said. Well, only to drive to Rupert's cabin. Though a bit remote, it didn't require I pack.

The last sliver of the sun set and the light deepened to a heavy purple punctuated by a glow in the direction of Canine Creek. The fire still burned.

Aunt Maddie flicked on the powerful outside security light. She picked up a painting and placed it on the plywood table with infinite care as if she put a beloved baby into bed.

The last of my appetite fled when I contemplated the abstract mess splattered across the front of Charles's canvas. A mixture of bilious yellow, dank green, and cramped brown, it reminded me of the aftermath of a bad bout of stomach flu.

Aunt Maddie's look softened while she scrutinized Charles's art catastrophe. She gazed at the horrid artwork as if she saw her long lost lover's face. "He'll be so pleased when he returns."

"When the store opens and his pieces sell," I said. Who to? I wondered, hoping somebody besides my aunt might find Charles's artwork attractive. Maybe. I looked at one of his "Yellow Ice" series and shuddered. Maybe not.

"This one will hang in the front window," my aunt continued.

Ugh. I imagined our customers looking in the front window and then running away, screaming.

"It'll be right where Charles can see it when he returns." She smiled.

I smiled too.

Aunt Maddie's face flowed into a deep frown. She huffed. "I suppose you can't drive down this late."

"What?" I asked.

Aunt Maddie raised her finger and shook it at me.

I hated when she did that. It always made me feel ten years old again, instead of almost twenty-five.

"You left a great job," she said and wagged. "It paid great."

I sighed. "Aunt Maddie, I'm so sorry. I spent all your money. I'll pay you back. I promise."

How? What with? I didn't say and hoped she didn't ask.

She shook her head and still wagged her finger, reminding me of a bobble-head doll. "No, no, no, you needed to spend that money for your business."

"*Our* business in *your* store," I said.

She stopped wagging and shaking. "My store..." Hunching her shoulders in her coat, Maddie looked far older than her fifty-eight years. With a start, I realized how much she'd aged since I came to live with her, eighteen long years ago.

I touched one of the ragged sleeves of her old gardening coat. "Why do you want me to leave? Why now?"

She stared at Charles's art and swallowed hard. "The rent..." My aunt rubbed her mouth.

She didn't want me to see her fail. She never failed, never faltered, not when my mom, her only sister, took off, not when Rupert ran off to find my mom, not when Charles left. Then there were just the two of us, me and my aunt.

She straightened up and shrugged my hand off. "So you made a mistake—"

"I what?"

"Easily corrected." She scrubbed her hands, case closed. "I'm sure Nance will give you your old job back."

I gulped and choked. Oh Buddha no. My worst nightmare. "Aunt Maddie, working for Nance made me crazy," I managed to say.

"You're a Starke, born and bred. You were already crazy." Aunt Maddie shrugged. "Though I do wonder about that whole Buddha bit you picked up."

"Nance introduced me to Buddhism." I hoped that would make Aunt Maddie pause.

"Nance, who always let you use her equipment to cast your designs," she shot back.

"Yes, but—"

"Nance who sold those designs in her store."

"After she 'tweaked' them." I could hear the bitterness in my voice.

"Maybe they needed tweak—" My aunt stopped when she saw my face. "Never mind." She looked down at the frame piece in her hands. "You better get packing—"

"I'm not leaving my home."

My aunt's glare made me glad I hadn't given her the gun back.

"I'm staying right here. Well, after I return from selling my designs." And after I figure out what to do about my father's death threat.

My aunt sighed. "Dora, you don't have enough to sell to pay that rent." The frame dropped from her hand. "Maybe you can ask your old boss—" She stopped and swallowed hard.

"Aunt Maddie?"

"I mean, I know that Nance has a great deal of money...and she's always been generous." My aunt swallowed again.

I stood stunned. "You mean you want me to ask Nance for a loan?"

Aunt Maddie ducked her head down. "No, no, forget it." She bent and picked up the frame.

Now I gulped. My proud, determined aunt had been about to ask me to ask Nance for a loan. I'd never seen her so desperate.

I didn't mind asking Nance, but I knew that she would reply with, "What do you have to secure the loan?" Nance stayed wealthy by smart business practice. My answer: an old car, old store stock, and an even older homestead heavily mortgaged.

Maybe I could offer Charles's paintings as collateral? I winced. In my mind, I could hear Nance's high-class nasal twang, "Charles who? I've never heard the name. I'll look him up on the 'Net and get back with you."

"You don't know what all I've got to sell," I said to my aunt to reassure her. The necklace in my pocket shifted with my words. I grimaced. "I will get the money."

My aunt kept her head down.

"Mad Maddie's Marvels will open on time," I put every ounce of conviction I could muster into every word.

"But Dora..." Aunt Maddie spoke to the wood.

"No buts." I pulled out my set of keys to our old cranky station wagon.

My aunt's head came up. "Now where are you headed?"

"I've got to get up to Rupert's cabin before it's too cold." The old station wagon, a match to my father's, hated to be driven in the cold and often complained by stalling out.

"Whyever for?"

"I need to ask about the neck—to get more of his jewelry to sell to Nance."

Aunt Maddie put her free hand on her hip. "Dora, don't you dare go up to that man's cabin."

"But—"

"No buts," Aunt Maddie echoed me, "you stay away from Rupert."

"He's my father."

"He never was a father to you. He's nothing but trouble. We'd all be better off if he'd freeze to death in that horrid cabin some winter." Her face twisted as if she contemplated helping the process.

"I have to go."

"You go, and I'll call the cops and turn you in."

"For what?" For one second, I thought she knew all about the necklace in my pocket.

"Stealing my car."

I groaned. It *was* Aunt Maddie's car. My old clunker that I drove in Boise died a mile outside Starke on my way home a scant month before. Add the smoke that decreased visibility and I could envision myself stumbling about in the cold dark. Ugh.

Aunt Maddie held out her free hand, palm up. "Hand the keys over, right now."

I stuffed the keys back into my pocket. "Lester wouldn't do anything," I said. Maybe. I couldn't predict what Lester would do, not anymore.

"I'll call the state cops."

I put my hands up, palms out. "Okay, okay, I'll just go to the store and inventory my designs and call Nance." And sneak back in a couple of hours to steal my aunt's station wagon. The car and me, we'd just have to tolerate the cold.

My aunt frowned.

"Bye." I left her there before she decided she might have missed an argument. I walked down the dusty not-yet-paved road. The necklace banged against one leg while the gun bounced against the other, my only companions.

SEVEN

I turned on the magnifying circle lamp over my workbench, one of my first purchases with Aunt Maddie's money. My heart twinged. The Buddha taught that the past didn't exist, nor did the future. I turned my attention to the moment.

The intense light created an oasis of calm, a mini-meditation. Beyond it, the broken bits of tourist trash still cluttered the floor. On my bench lay several attempts of my most recent design, a pin that symbolized the new Dog Face Mountain ski resort. I shook my head. Try as I would, I couldn't get the dog's face to stop snarling. He'd bite any tourist foolish enough to ski over his face.

The powerful light flickered. I grimaced. Since all the construction started for the new ski resort, blackouts in Starke had become common.

It didn't help that all the wiring in my aunt's store was original from 1948. Whenever a tenant complained, Henry's grandfather and then his father had always said, "Still works." Now Henry needed to replace all the electrical systems to bring his properties up to code. Soon. Yesterday. Tomorrow.

With the blackouts, I couldn't cast any of my designs in my kiln. The kiln needed to maintain a constant temperature to have a clean burn. Nance had given me her old kiln. Kilns cost thousands. I'd been awed by her generosity. Until I discovered how much it took to fix it—too much. Way too much. I couldn't cast any of my designs. Period.

Once I sold a few pieces of my jewelry, if I sold a few pieces...I glanced over at my wax designs, pinned in neat rows onto Styrofoam blocks, a trick Nance taught me, all waiting to be cast. Oh Buddha, wait. Now I needed to sell those designs to Nance. One catastrophe at a time.

I pushed the wax patterns over to the side, out of the light, and scrubbed at my face. She'd still be at work. I might as well kill—I mean, call Nance.

"The Gallery," Nance answered after I dialed the old rotary phone and it rang once.

"The Gallery" as if there could be only one. Never mind that Nance's jewelry store was a remote offshoot of her family's famous New York gallery. "Non-say speaking," she continued, in her best snob voice.

"Nance, forget it, it's just me, Dora."

"So, Dora, are you ready to give up your attachment to your dream?"

She meant my dream of my own jewelry store in Starke. I always hated it when Nance played wise, older Buddhist.

"Never," I said.

"Never say never, Dora. Time is an illusion," Nance said.

Gritting my teeth, I considered hanging up, but I couldn't do that. Not yet.

Then Nance added, "Besides, I miss you."

"Aha, a desire," I said.

Nance laughed. "There's nobody here to moo at the customers."

I sighed. I'd never live that one down. "That cow painting would've never sold," I defended myself. The vast purple cow painting had hung in the gallery for months, avoided by all. Until I spotted a rancher staring at it, sidled up beside him and mooed. He'd replied, "Sold."

"You earned every penny of that commission," Nance said.

A commission Nance paid me the minute the rancher left the gallery. I sighed again. As soon as I got a good mad on for Nance, she pulled me back onto the dharma path.

"Speaking of money..." I took a deep breath. "Want to buy my designs?"

"Don't you need your designs to establish your line?"

"I need—" The money for rent, I started to say. If I told Nance about my money woes, she'd insist I return to The Gallery. "I mean, I don't need these designs."

"Well, after I fix your designs, they do sell well."

That made me growl deep in my throat.

"What?"

"Nothing. So I'll bring them down tomorrow?"

"How many? I'll have the check ready." Nance, unlike so many unbelievably wealthy people, never used float, Buddha bless her. She paid prompt and in full.

I gulped down the bitter bile of the delay of establishing my own design line and promised all of them, except for the Dog Face pin.

At least Nance changed each wax pattern before she cast the piece and made a mold of it, so the style became hers and not mine. She lacked the originality to create a design, but—and I shuddered to admit it, even to myself—she did possess an objective eye for balance.

"And I'll bring some of Rupert's pins," I said. Together with my designs, that should net me enough for some of the back rent, at least.

"Oh no, Dora. I'm no longer selling outsider art."

"Just because he's a recluse doesn't mean my father is an outsider." The mentally disturbed produced outsider art.

"Of course not, Dora."

"He's as sane as you or I," I said.

"I didn't mean—"

"Maybe we aren't good examples, but—"

"Speak for yourself."

I grabbed my Ohm pin tight until the words behind my teeth subsided. "I had a woman today who came into the store looking for more of Rupert's pins," I said. Take that and outside it, Nance.

"Regardless, I don't think—"

"Please, Nance, I need the cash." I hated the begging tone in my voice.

"What for?"

Why did everybody demand to have a reason? I bit back a naughty word. "Okay, just my designs then."

I shifted my position on my stool. The necklace clinked. Nance, an expert on Art Nouveau of world renown, would know about the necklace, if anybody did. How to ask? Ah.

"I've been studying the Art Nouveau jewelry," I said, "and I've found a great piece but can't find the designer. It's an odd mixture of rubies and platinum. With an onyx pendant."

The highest grade of onyx was far cheaper than the other materials. Nance might be able to identify it by that alone.

"Onyx?" Nance said in a strangled tone at the back of her throat. "Found?"

"Yes…" I hesitated. How much to describe the necklace so Nance would shift into her mentor mode and not her inquisitive, take-over, controlling mode? "The mixture of precious and semi-precious stones with the carved onyx pendant of a naked woman works. It shouldn't, but it does."

A long silence followed. Had I said too much? Too little? Nance always hated to say those three little words, "I don't know."

"The Noira," she whispered.

"The who?" I asked. "Is this Noara person the designer?" I'd never heard of a Noara or a Noiré or Nora. Back in the days of Art Nouveau, the 1890's, there were few women designers. Then I remembered that great pieces of jewelry sometimes earned names. "Is that the name of the necklace?"

"It can't be," Nance said.

"You know the necklace I'm talking about?" Of course she did. Sometimes Nance did know everything.

"No, I don't," she said.

Nance admitting ignorance?

"I realize you need my help," she said. A classic Nance non sequitur. "You're not ready for your own gallery."

"I need the money for a few last minute improvements, that's all." In my desperation, I still spoke the truth, just not all of the truth.

"I'm coming up." Nance hung up.

"Ah," I screamed into the dead receiver. Nance here? Nance in the store? Nance meeting Aunt Maddie? I shuddered and called back.

I got her answering machine and left a terse message that if she did come to Starke, a three-hour drive from Boise, she'd find Mad Maddie's Marvels closed and she'd pass me on the highway, headed to her gallery. I hoped that discouraged her. I prayed that discouraged her.

Almost nothing discouraged Nance. I needed to get to Rupert's cabin and then get on the road to stop her. I started toward the door when the power died.

I imagined stumbling across the loose planks of our bridge over Looney Jump Creek. And at best, falling into the creek. At worst, alerting Aunt Maddie, who'd call the state cops. I sat back down on my stool.

In the dark, I lit a few candles. I rummaged in my pockets for my emergency breakfast bar. My hand touched the bag. I pulled it out, unwrapped the necklace, and grimaced at the dirty piece. The ash that dusted the necklace had worked its way into the crevices around the beveled settings of the cabochon rubies, the inlaid features of the naked lady pendant herself. The woman's tiny onyx face, her beauty enhanced by the thin slivers of inlaid platinum for her wide eyes and full bowed lips, looked back. She caught me in her gaze.

"Who are you?" I whispered.

Where did all the ash come from? Where had my father found the necklace? Or did he bury it in ash? If so, why?

The ash floated off as I cleaned the necklace with my softest wolf's hairbrush. I promised myself not to study the piece until ash-free. With every stroke of the brush, I broke my promise.

The polished platinum of the links shone with the depth only platinum owned. The rubies flashed dark red beneath the light. I rummaged in an apron pocket for my loupe, pulled it out, and peered at one of the heart-shaped cabochon rubies.

"Oh my Buddha," I breathed. I'd never seen such a large ruby with such depth of color and clarity and so beautifully cut and polished. I scanned the rest of the twelve gems. All true blood rubies, all perfect.

The onyx of the central figure gleamed with the refraction of intricate carving. I removed the solder from the woman's toe. What had hung there?

In the candlelight, the necklace glimmered, almost alive. It was meant to be seen in the soft glow of candles. The colors of the rubies and the onyx, offset by the platinum, flowed beneath the candle flame as it flickered.

With one fingertip, I traced the lines of the heart links. A dream of keeping the piece insinuated into my mind. No one except my father knew I had the necklace. I could spend years studying the technique and style of a masterpiece.

I picked up the necklace and placed it across the front of my apron. My fingers itched to clasp it behind my neck, to wear it now, alone, late at night with no one to see me.

After I clasped it, I drew in my breath at the blazing beauty displayed across my chest. People killed for such jewelry. Such beauty. Such glory. Now I understood why.

I'd wear it for a little while, until the lights came back on.

With my wire loop, I carved into a piece of wax. More designs for Nance to buy and then change, that's the ticket, or rather, the rent.

EIGHT

Something itched on my cheek. I brushed at it, and a gob of wax fell into my hand, jerking me upright, awake.

I'd fallen asleep at my workbench, with my head on my Dog Face Mountain design. The icy cold of the store made me shiver. If only I could fire a few patterns in my kiln, for the heat.

A heavy weight lay on my chest. I looked down at the necklace splayed there. Early morning gloom showed the rubies dark as old blood.

"Sell it or I'm a dead man."

I unclasped the necklace. It tumbled to my lap and rested there, dead and cold. With another shudder, I wrapped the necklace and stuffed it back into my apron pocket.

A stench wafted to my nose. Flux. Rouge. Investment powder. All seasoned with a tincture of day-old sweat. Ooh, I needed a shower and a change of clothes. The tiny restroom at the back of the store had a stall shower where a clean pair of black jeans and black sweatshirt waited. I always wore black under my apron, so I could whip it off and display my designs on a black background. So far, nobody had ever asked me to do so. That didn't dim my hope.

I started to take off my apron, and the necklace shifted in the pocket. No time.

Outside, fog crawled along the street. No. Not fog. Smoke. I coughed. This morning, the haze from the forest fire seemed worse. Had it moved closer to Starke? Closer to my father's cabin? No time.

I raced home.

Aunt Maddie enjoyed her morning coffee in her usual spot—on the roof. I hoped the smoke might provide a little cover, but no such luck. She hollered as I thundered across Looney Jump Creek Bridge. No time.

I jumped into the station wagon and took off for Rupert's cabin. My last view of my aunt in the rearview mirror was of her standing near the peak, shaking her fist at me. I drove faster.

In the early morning light, Rupert's station wagon crouched next to the pink Cadillac. The huge car radiated neon pink and trouble. Before I reached Rupert's place, I'd parked on an offshoot of the dirt logging road that led to my father's cabin. I didn't want him to have a chance to run, to disappear into the forest, when he heard me coming.

Or would he escape into the forest? I wondered as I walked. Where a fire still burned? Smoke lay thicker here than in Starke. Thick tendrils wove through the pine trees, long fingers presaging destruction.

No, Rupert would never go toward fire. Never.

Now I wondered what the Cadillac was doing, parked outside my father's cabin? How did a stranger find Rupert's cabin tucked away in the woods outside Starke? And why?

I ran for the front and only door.

"Rupert, it's me, Dora," I called, not loud enough to startle him.

The ice cold wind soughed through the trees as my only answer. I trembled in my heavy cotton apron and thrust my hands into its full pockets of problems.

"Father?"

The dishtowel curtains hung limp at the cabin's sole tiny window.

"Hello?" I raised my hand to bang on the warped pine door. It sprung from the frame. A scuff mark showed where someone had kicked the door open.

"...*sell it today.*" I took a deep breath. Didn't help. "...*a dead man.*" I let it out. Didn't help. "...*don't run.*" Help.

Great Grandpa's gun still resided in my left apron pocket. It filled my hand with a heavy reassurance. I knew that loading the gun constituted bad karma, but still loaded it.

Bringing the revolver up in a two-handed grip, I pushed the door open with my shoulder and stepped inside. I peered into the deep gloom just past the light cast by the window and open door.

Across the one room cabin, at my father's workbench, someone sat in the lone upholstered swivel desk chair. As my eyes adjusted, I saw a distinctive bald pate. My held breath whooshed out. I smelled a faint stench of an odd mix, something smoky, metallic, and sour. I brought the gun down to point at the pine wood floor.

"Hey." I used Derek's favorite word to catch his attention.

Nothing.

"Where's Rupert? What are you doing here? Where's my father?" I demanded in quick succession.

The hairless dome didn't move.

"Derek?"

Derek didn't twitch at the sound of his name. He sat in the chair as if glued there.

A cold knot in my chest, I crept across the battered pine floor. "Derek?" I whispered and touched the chair back with one finger tip.

The chair swung around.

Derek sat there. Stark naked dead.

I screamed.

NINE

The naked man's mouth gaped in silent mimicry of my scream.

I jerked back and bumped against the workbench. Rupert's empty alcohol lamp turned over, rolled, fell to the floor, and shattered. I yelped and froze.

For several long minutes, my ragged breathing remained the only sound in the tiny cabin. My breath puffed little clouds into the ice-cold air. The strange stink resolved into a mixture of smoke, gunpowder, and urine. I swallowed back bile and shot tiny peeks at the figure in the chair.

"Derek?" I whispered. Maybe this time he'd answer. No such luck.

I'd never seen a dead Derek before. I'd never seen a dead body before. I'd never seen a naked dead body before. And I didn't want to now. No choice.

Was I too late? Was Rupert dead too? Where was my father?

Blinking back tears I stared around the minuscule cabin. The smoke must have been bothering my eyes.

Rupert's old army cot rested upside-down, two of its four legs broken. Several of his jewelry pins lay scattered and crushed on the floor next to the workbench. The stone fireplace stood filled with logs covered with cobwebs, never to be used. I always wondered how my fire-phobic father survived the winters. Right now, that was the least of my questions.

None of the clothing pegs next to the workbench held Rupert's old leather duster. I gave a single sob of relief. Perhaps my father had run. But where to? He hadn't come back to the store. Why not? Why he hadn't taken his car, I didn't know. Wait, yes, I did. Anyone would recognize his old beater. Perhaps I still had time to save him.

Derek's battered, bloody face looked my way with an open-eyed accusatory stare. Did Rupert beat this man to death? My always-frightened father? Could he have done this, even in self-defense? Never.

Would I have prevented all this if I hadn't fallen asleep at my workbench?

The smoky frigid air of the cabin cut into my lungs. I stared at Derek as if I might force a dead man to speak and give me some answers, making certain my study remained above Derek's waist.

He provided only more questions. His clothing lay stacked in a neat pile next to his body, with his shoes on top. I imagined the dead man stripping, folding his clothes, and stacking them. I giggled and slapped my hand across my mouth, the sound as loud as a gunshot.

One small bullet hole scorched into the skin on Derek's chest.

I bent closer. So small, the bullet hole resembled a bloody bit of dirt that had adhered to his chest. A deadly bit of dirt. Bile crept up the back of my throat. I swallowed hard. I unloaded Great Grandpa's gun and pocketed it. That helped, a bit. There'd been too much violence in this cabin.

Did Rupert shoot Derek? Did he even have a gun?

Yes, there, half hidden under a rouge polishing cloth, a .38 rested on the workbench amongst my father's leather mallet and wire cutters. Almost casual, as if placed there as an afterthought.

Had Rupert walked out and left it behind? Why? And I still couldn't imagine my father blasting away. But if Rupert hadn't shot this naked man, who had?

Why was Derek naked? Was Rupert searching for something? I hated to imagine what and where.

Was Derek the threat that had made Rupert insist I sell the necklace?

The walls of the one-room cabin closed in, cold and dark, a coffin. I needed to get out. I needed to find Lester. I needed—

The crunch of a car driving over the dirt road came through the open door. Through the tiny window, I saw Lester's Jeep pull over beside the line of cars parked in front of the cabin.

My knees wobbled. I put my hand on the bench to steady myself. Had Aunt Maddie made good on her threat to call the cops?

I rubbed my forehead with the back of my hand. That might be for the best. All I needed to do was turn the necklace over to Lester and—wait—what if the necklace provided a motive for Rupert to kill Derek? I believed my father would never kill anyone on purpose, but would Lester?

Lester sat in the jeep. He shook his cell phone. Even from inside the cabin, I could see the irritated frown on his face.

If anyone had asked me yesterday if my father would ever kill anyone, for any reason, I'd have said no. However, I'd have never believed he'd hand me a necklace worth millions and demand I sell it, either. That same necklace rested in my apron pocket.

Lester got out of the Jeep.

Where to hide the necklace?

I checked the little room, now a crime scene and bound to be searched as one. Where? The chinks between the logs where the wind swept through? Too small. The pine wood floor, scuffed and marred from a century of use, rested on dirt.

Lester walked around the two cars. His shoulders stooped, as if all his thirty years of being the Arrester pressed down on him.

Where had my father hidden the necklace before?

Lester headed for the cabin door.

I stepped to the fireplace. The stone facing was set in rock-hard mortar. Buddha, help me.

Buddha did. I spotted a thin sliver of an indent in the ashes underneath the fire dog. An edge of the fireplace ash trap. The ash on the necklace must have come from the trap. Quick but careful not to disturb the old, dry, cobwebbed logs, I opened the trap door with one hand and tossed the necklace in with the other. I fluttered the ashes back over the trap.

My head thwacked on the fireplace stone. "Ow." I ducked and scuttled out of the fireplace.

Tears in my eyes, I rubbed the crown of my head and scurried back to the workbench. I dropped my hand into my pocket just as Lester appeared in the doorway. I tried to look both casual and innocent. At least as much as was possible when sharing space with a dead, naked body.

He paused, one foot raised mid-air. "Dora, what are you doing here?" He stared at the body in the chair and then at me, wide-eyed, his mouth slack. His foot came down with a thwack.

I scrunched my face tight. so wanting to blurt out the story of the necklace. Lester could make it all better, just like he did when I was little.

I bit back the words. I wasn't little anymore. Well, I was still short, but that didn't count.

"I can explain." Wait, no I couldn't.

Lester put his foot down. "You can?"

"Um." Nothing came to mind.

Lester pointed at the body. His finger shook. "Explain that?"

"It's not what it looks like. I mean, I know it looks like a—dead guy—but—"

Lester stopped pointing and used that hand to rub his face. He stalked inside.

"Rupert didn't shoot him?" I winced when I heard the question mark.

Lester ran his hand over his silver hair. "If not Rupert, then who?" He shuffled, an old man, over to Derek's body. He stared at it for a long moment then shifted his stare to me. "Dora, I asked what are you doing here?" That tone brooked no argument or equivocation. Lester's eyebrows drew together into a familiar frown. That frown had kept me out of trouble and in school while I grew up.

Think fast, Dora. Inspiration smacked me again. "I panicked when I saw you drive up, Sheriff."

"Why?" Lester asked. "And why have you got ash in your hair?"

My short curly hair, a perfect trap for ashes from the ash trap. I ruffled my hair. "Because of this." I pulled the gun out of my pocket. Not an answer to either of his questions. But a gun provided a good distraction.

Lester took a step back.

"It's okay." I held it out toward him by the grip. "It's not loaded."

"Freeze!"

TEN

I jumped and dropped my gun. Poor Great Grandpa's pistol sure got kicked around these days.

Lester turned, his hand on his holster.

"Mallard," Lester and I said.

Mallard stood outlined in the doorway, his gun out and pointed in my direction.

"Don't point that gun at me," I said.

The gun didn't move.

"Stand down, Mallard," Lester said.

Mallard lowered his gun. He lifted his chin toward Derek. "Is that guy dead?" he said, his voice squeaked on the last word.

"Yup," Lester and I said.

"And naked?" Mallard asked, his voice so high on "naked" it was almost inaudible.

"Yup," Lester and I said.

"Did you shoot him, Dora?" A single drop of sweat rolled down Mallard's cheek. How could he sweat in this freezing cold?

Lester's mouth twisted. "Dora wouldn't do that. Not Dora."

"Not me." I worked hard not to look over at the fireplace. The necklace seemed to radiate heat from its hiding place.

Mallard blinked at me.

"Really, really, really bad karma," I explained.

"But..." Mallard pointed with his gun at my dropped gun. "What about that?"

"I know Dora." Lester gave me the shadow of a smile. "I practically raised her."

I smiled back. "You and Aunt Maddie and the whole town of Starke." Everyone save my parents.

"But, boss—Sheriff, didn't you find her here? Armed?" Mallard used his gun to point at Great Grandpa's revolver.

"I'm not holding a gun." I spread my arms wide.

"It's your gun on the floor," Mallard argued.

"It's not my gun. It's Aunt Maddie's gun and it's not the only gun," I said.

Mallard blinked again. He should get that tic examined. "Well, yes, Dora, we've got guns," he said. He spaced every word in case I didn't understand.

"I meant that gun." I pointed at the gun on the work table.

It wasn't like they weren't going to find it. Odd that the cops hadn't spotted it before, save for Derek's body being a major distraction.

Mallard made a distressed sound deep in his throat. Lester sighed.

Mallard holstered his gun at last. "We need to call the state police."

Lester crossed his arms across his chest. "No."

"No?" Mallard looked at me as if I might explain.

I raised my eyebrows and shook my head.

"I'm not going whining to the state police," Lester said. "Not after thirty years as Lester the Arrester."

I could understand Lester's bitterness. For decades, he'd been the only law in Starke. A month ago, he'd been forced to accept a geeky deputy. No wonder he'd quit when the town council refused to give him a leave of absence.

"Are you questioning my ability to perform my duties?" Lester continued. "When I tried to call you, my cell didn't work. Did you follow me, Mallard?"

I wondered at Lester's flip-flop in attitude from yesterday, when it seemed he wanted Mallard to take over.

"When Godiva—weird name—told us her brother had headed this direction but hadn't returned and so you came up here to check," Mallard said.

What would a nudist want with my father? I realized a possible answer. To buy some of Rupert's jewelry. Had Derek's death just been a misunderstanding?

"You haven't answered my question, Mallard," Lester said.

Mallard rested his hand on his gun holster. "I know you've got the experience, Sheriff," he stroked the gun butt, "but this guy Rupert is a mountain recluse, so after you left, I got to thinking you might need backup." He pointed at dead Derek. "Don't you think I might've been right?"

Mallard had judged, juried, and condemned Rupert already.

If I could only find my father, I could warn him. I needed to find him to get answers. I needed to find him to save him.

ELEVEN

I wiped the fingerprint ink from my hands, or tried to. "Was all this mess necessary?" I asked Mallard. He'd insisted I follow him down to the old police station while Sheriff Lester waited for Doc Byrne at my father's cabin.

When there first was a sheriff in Starke in 1882, he operated out of his two-room home and used his fruit cellar as the cell. We now sat in that long ago sheriff's front room. A heavy plastic tarp hung between this first room and the rest of the building. The sheriff's office, same as every other place in Starke, faced major renovation and expansion. And change.

"The mess of you at your father's cabin with a murdered man, or the mess of the fingerprint test?" Mallard asked.

I glared and scrubbed harder. I needed to find where my father was. I needed answers. I didn't need Mallard's sweaty attitude.

Mallard ignored me, instead intent on scanning my prints into the system, my own piece of immortality. He worked at a steel desk pushed into the corner of the office, where three computer monitors fought for space with a scanner and two printers.

"My fingerprints will be in Rupert's cabin, anyway," I said.

"And maybe on the gun that killed that man."

I paused mid-scrub. How desperate was Mallard to find a killer and close the case? Would anybody do as the killer? Would I do?

I sat back on the old wooden office chair, the one that missed a caster. It listed hard right. I straightened up. "Hey. I passed the gun residue test."

"Maybe you wrapped that red cloth around your hand when you fired the gun," Mallard said without missing a key stroke.

"That's a rouge cloth."

"That's what I said."

"No, you said red. A rouge cloth is for polishing..." Oh boy, I was getting as bad as Nance. Her pontificating must be catching.

"You were with the body when it was found."

"Anybody could have been found that body," I said. I realized as I spoke how wrong I was. Maybe Mallard wouldn't notice my mistake.

"Who?" Mallard asked.

In answer, I reached out and touched Mallard's well-pressed, if somewhat damp, sleeve.

He paused, finger poised over a keyboard, the keys blackened by fingerprint ink. Mallard had a little trouble with the fingerprinting kit. No practice.

"You actually suspect me?" I asked.

He looked at me and sighed. "You were found in your *father's cabin*, with a gun, standing over a dead man."

I leaned away from him, took a deep breath, and sucked in the nasty ink smell. I choked. "You're not a Starker. You don't know me," I said between coughs.

Mallard got up and got me a paper cup of coffee from the coffeemaker that had stood on top of the stainless steel cabinet for as long as I could remember.

"You can't suspect me."

"Why not?" Mallard handed me the cup. "I'm not Lester. I don't remember when you were an adorable kid, although you're cute now." He blushed to the roots of his sweaty hair. Pretty cute himself.

Ohm, I saw Mallard as cute? Sweaty Mallard? I needed to meditate more.

I smiled, despite myself, and then bit my lower lip. "So, are you going to interrogate me?"

He smiled back. "Interrogate you? Where's my big rubber hose when I need it?" A fresh line of sweat broke out along his forehead. "I mean, I didn't mean, um..." He looked as if he might sweat himself to death.

I stifled a tiny giggle, amazed I could still laugh. In the cup, the coffee rolled back and forth, a tiny, oily sea. I humpfed. "I never killed and never will kill anyone." I sniffed the coffee.

The rancid stench reminded me of when, after school, I'd come here and share a cup and a cinnamon roll with Lester. Comforting.

"So you say, and so Lester says, but I say the evidence needs to speak first."

"Now you sound like a TV show."

Mallard sighed. He gestured at the monitors on his desk. "I don't want to be sheriff. I'm the techie guy. I've even written—well added to—a police program. And now there's a dead naked guy. If I only had the money to develop..." He looked at his beloved computers, every monitor with a different screen saver.

The aquarium with the swimming "dog fish," little fish bodies with dog heads, I liked the best. Hmmm, if I took my Dog Face Mountain pin and shortened the nose just a bit...

I sipped the coffee. Ugh, the taste reminded me of the muddy mire of a memory lane. I set it down on the edge of Mallard's desk.

Mallard picked up the cup and pulled me back to the moment. "Coffee spills," he said as he placed it on the cabinet. "So why did you go up to your father's cabin, Dora?"

"It's my father's cabin. Do I need a reason?"

"With a murdered man in the cabin, yes." Mallard looked at me, his face all cop.

"Um..." I clutched at my Ohm pin on my apron. "Um..."

"Why were you in the cabin?" Mallard asked again. Every ounce of sweat seemed to have dried on the man.

The pin cut into my palm. Ah. I remembered my partial true reason. "I went up to get more jewelry to sell to Nance."

"Jewelry...Nance," Mallard said. His eyebrows leapt up. "Oh, I remember, for the rent."

"That's right, that Nance." Who, I hoped, waited in Boise for me to arrive. She'd have to wait a bit longer.

Mallard pointed at Great Grandpa's gun that rested next to Rupert's .38, both sealed in evidence bags, on Lester's roll top desk. "For this you brought a gun?"

"I forgot I had it."

"You forgot you had it?" Mallard's eyebrows drew together and started sweating again.

"It was in one of my pockets." I held open one huge apron pocket to demonstrate its capacity. I gulped. That pocket recently held the necklace that now rested in the ashes, trapped.

Mallard peered inside and then looked at his center monitor. "And Starkers say I'm crazy because I find working with computers easier."

"Or maybe it's because you talk to your monitors," I let slip out.

His back stiffened. "Your excuse would be more believable—"

"It's not an excuse. It's the truth." A bit of the truth.

"—if you tell me where Rupert is," Mallard continued as if I hadn't spoken.

"How would I know where he's gone?" I answered.

"He's your father," Mallard said.

"Yes but..." My shoulders fell. "After my mom ran off..." I looked down at the floor. "Rupert went looking for her and then he came back." I blinked back a tear. "Only he didn't."

"What?" Mallard asked, his voice low.

"He changed. He—" I stopped. I remembered, too well, when Rupert returned. I'd been ten years old and bereft of both parents since I was seven. I'd so hoped to have one parent back in my life. Instead, he'd retreated to this cabin and shut the door.

Now Mallard reached out and touched my arm. "People change, Dora. Things happen to them and they change."

"Sometimes not for the better." I swallowed back bitter coffee dregs as I realized what I'd said.

"It may have been a mistake," Mallard said. "Your dad may have panicked."

He echoed my own fear that Rupert, already terrified, would blast away at an innocent.

I sniffed. The smell of fresh pine wood wafted from the absent back wall of the station from behind the heavy tarp hung there. Behind it, the old original bedroom had been torn down to expand the sheriff's office into a modern facility. I coughed again.

Mallard patted my arm as if that might help. "So, you need to tell me where he might be. Would he head into the mountains?"

"Oh no, no, no."

Mallard's expression returned to its usual confusion. "He's a mountain man, right?"

"No, he's a recluse. He couldn't survive off the land." I clutched my Ohm pin. "It could snow any day."

Mallard frowned. "I thought everybody wanted it to snow."

"Snow would be a death sentence for my father."

"Ah, so, Rupert will be hiding someplace under cover. Do you know where?"

"No. I don't know." But I'd find out. When I found Rupert I'd find my answers.

Where could Rupert run? I'd always believed his cabin was his only sanctuary. After he gave up the search for my mother, he retreated there.

Could I ask Aunt Maddie where Rupert might be? No, I didn't dare. I knew her reaction to me finding a dead body in his cabin. Not great. Not good. Not repeatable.

Mallard sat back in his chair. I noticed his had all its casters. "Are you sure, Dora?"

I sniffed again and caught a faint scent of old cinnamon roll. I realized who I could ask. Who might know where Rupert hid.

"What is it?" Mallard must have read my expression.

I opened my mouth to tell him. I shut it again. Now, if I told Mallard about the necklace, would he even believe that I wasn't involved? And I was involved.

"Dora..." Mallard said in his best cop voice.

"If that's all, Sheriff—I mean Deputy—I'll be going." That sounded lame, even to me.

"No, you—"

I hopped up. My chair toppled with a crash. "Am I under arrest?" I stepped toward the door.

"No, but—" Mallard managed in a pain-strangled voice.

"All right, then see you later." I made my getaway.

"Dora, come back here," I heard behind me. I ran faster. Now I knew how my father felt.

TWELVE

I stood and panted on the wooden sidewalk outside Mama Chin's Save On Drugstore Emporium, having run the five blocks to the restaurant on Main Street and then ran out of wind, only a block from Mad Maddie's Marvel's. I told myself that nothing remained permanent. It didn't help.

Had it been only this morning that I'd discovered Derek's body? My stomach insisted it was several millennia ago. Food and answers now were at hand, my still-inked hand. I reached to open the door when the sidewalk boards vibrated a warning.

Mrs. McGarrity stomped toward me with intense intent in all of her three hundred plus pounds. The tatted lace of her sweater set ruffled in her self-made breeze. Mrs. McGarrity tatted everything and today she resembled an enormous and elaborate filigreed wedding cake.

I had no illusion that she hadn't already heard about the murder. The Widows Brigade's gossip connection in Starke flew faster than broadband Internet. And the rumors circulated with the same degree of accuracy or inaccuracy. She'd corner me and demand to know all about the dead naked man.

Mama Chin's old glass door, patched with duct tape from when my grandfather kicked it in 1945 offered an escape. The bell over the door, a twin to Mad Maddie's Marvels', jangled when I flung open the door. I stopped and stared, one foot raised. In Mama Chin's, the display racks sat empty, boxes perched everywhere. All five milk glass globe lights lay along the countertop of the fountain. At least the ancient ceiling fan clattered away.

Traditional American cooking aromas wafted around me. My stomach growled loud and insistent. "Be quiet," I said.

Mrs. McGarrity paused in her trudge down the sidewalk. Her little dog, Bark, the Rat Terrier Terrorist, paused beside her. The dog's hair bristled. Whether at my stomach's growl or me talking to a body part, I didn't know. He barked once. The loud sound reverberated around the restaurant and demonstrated why he was named Bark.

Mrs. McGarrity glanced at her watch, the one with the antique art deco design watchband that I so coveted. She no doubt considered whether she had time enough for me before another Widows Brigade meeting. Mrs. McGarrity adored her meetings where she reigned over the Brigade, whose membership numbered three, total.

I gave my errant tummy a pat.

Her frown of perpetual disapproval softened. "Oh, Dora, you poor dear." She resumed her progress toward me, this time at a trot. She thundered the last few feet, her plump feet slapping the wood, the hand not holding the dog's leash outstretched. Maybe she feared I'd melt into sobs.

"How terrible for you, you poor little thing," Mrs. McGarrity huffed at me as she jogged.

Maybe she wanted me to sob.

I paused mid-pat.

Mrs. McGarrity might also be headed into Mama Chin's. To spread the word about a murdered man in my father's cabin. I didn't know what Mama Chin's reaction might be to the news. She might not tell me where Rupert was. She might tell the police.

My stomach clamped in fear.

Mrs. McGarrity reached me. She puffed. At almost six foot, she towered over me. She stroked my arm, the lace on her sleeve flopping. The dog sniffed my apron.

"Oh, don't worry," she said, "I'm sure they'll catch that nasty killer Rupert."

Her face sparkled. The Widows Brigade loved a good scandal. If Starke's oral history reported it right, they had adored a hanging. Although my great grandfather broke the rope and lived.

I pulled away. "Did you forget Rupert is my father?"

Mrs. McGarrity stepped back. Her dog didn't, having discovered a food spot on my apron. I wished I'd discovered it first. "Now, now, little Dora," Mrs. McGarrity purred, "I only meant that, um—"

I snorted. "You meant that you've already condemned Rupert."

Mrs. McGarrity's look of pity faded. "It was his cabin."

"That doesn't mean he kill— Quit licking my apron," I said to the dog. "And I'm not your little dear..." At Mrs. McGarrity's scowl, I hesitated. It didn't do to annoy the Widows Brigade. They possessed lots of rope.

My stomach demanded sustenance, preferably Mama Chin's cinnamon rolls. I berated myself for considering my stomach at a time like this. My stomach berated back. It threatened to denounce veganism and rip off a chunk of Mrs. McGarrity's little dog's hind leg and eat it raw.

I ducked into Mama Chin's. Mrs. McGarrity tromped on my heels. Could she tromp.

"We're closed," Mama Chin's voice came from the back.

"You're never closed," Mrs. McGarrity called back. She sounded desperate.

Oh no, that meant she needed a gossip fix.

I turned and tried to block most of Mrs. McGarrity. Not easy. "You can't bring the dog in here," I said.

Mrs. McGarrity paused, the door part open.

From inside came an indignant chittering. I ignored it. A pair of red eyes regarded us from a cardboard box. The box was tucked into a far corner, far away from the tempting kitchen.

Mrs. McGarrity huffed. Bark's ruff raised.

"Mama Chin's rules, remember?" I said.

The little dog tried to squeeze around Mrs. McGarrity's bulk.

"Some rules," Mrs. McGarrity said. "If she can have that vermin—"

"He's not vermin. He's Fat Freddy."

"Filthy—"

"Rats can be cleaner than dogs and people," Mama Chin said as she swung open one of the kitchen's double swinging doors. "And no dogs."

At Mama Chin's tone, Mrs. McGarrity stepped back onto Bark's paw. Bark yelped and Mrs. McGarrity jumped. A space opened big enough for Bark to squeeze by her.

"Bark, Bark," Mrs. McGarrity cried.

"Freddy," Mama Chin hollered.

A blur of pure white fur followed by a bigger blur of chocolate fur raced through the kitchen's swinging doors. Freddy sure moved fast for such a fat rat. Freddy raced over his owner's shoes but bigger Bark banged into Mama Chin's shins as he ran by.

"Ow!"

"Don't hurt my dog!" Mrs. McGarrity ran full tilt at Mama Chin.

Mama Chin yelped and leaped back into the kitchen.

Mrs. McGarrity banged through the swinging doors, and I followed. The doors swung wildly back and forth. I held out my hand to stop a door and got smacked. In the kitchen, silence reigned.

I managed to kill the swing and pressed the door open into the kitchen, expecting to see the remains of bloody carnage and Fat Freddy. Rat Terriers, Mrs. McGarrity had proudly told me once, were named because they hunted...well, rats. Even pet rats.

Instead, Bark crouched at the lip of a large hole cut in the middle of Mama Chin's kitchen floor. A trap door for the hole lay to one side. The tunnels. Built underneath Starke during its early days as a rip-roarer of a mining town, the tunnels connected all the old buildings.

During my childhood, the tunnel entrance in my aunt's store often provided a refuge. Aunt Maddie often stored the worst tourist junk in the small open space beneath our trap door. I'd hunker down at the entrance in the cool, damp dark and cry where no one could hear. I wanted to go hide out there now and forget all about the murder and my missing Rupert.

"Freddy, come back," Mama Chin called down into the black hole. She and Mrs. McGarrity bent over the tunnel entrance, next to Bark.

I joined the little clutch at the tunnel entrance.

Mama Chin got down on her knees and leaned forward. Her black-panted bottom pointed upward, an exclamation point. "I'll make sure that evil beast doesn't hurt you," she continued.

At "evil beast" Bark looked at her as if to say, "Who, me?" Then he gave her a big slurp of a kiss.

"Ugh," Mama Chin said.

Mrs. McGarrity made a shooing motion at her dog. "Bark, don't do that." She frowned hard. The widow must be hurt by his affection toward another. Mrs. McGarrity's husband, before his death, had also been known to freely share his affections.

Mama Chin looked up at Mrs. McGarrity. "Dogs are dirtier than rats. Freddy never kisses me."

Mrs. McGarrity's frown deepened.

"It's all your fault," Mama Chin said. "You interrupted me while I was checking the tunnel." She stood and pointed down at the hole. "Freddy's gone, he's lost. Who knows what could happen to him down there?" She gave a little sniff. "And now that the entrances are being filled..." She sniffed again.

I patted her arm. "Don't worry, Mama Chin. Rats are naturals in tunnels."

"Not pet albinos." Mama Chin moved her point to Bark. "Get that dirty mutt out of here, now."

Bark licked her finger.

"I'll have you know, he's a purebred Rat Terrier," Mrs. McGarrity said.

Mama Chin stepped close to Mrs. McGarrity until they stood chest to face. Mrs. McGarrity's generous chest to Mama Chin's pinched angry face. Mama Chin looked up at Mrs. McGarrity with the same expression I expected she had when she took a kill shot aim on her annual bear hunt. She always got her bear.

"In Asia, dog is considered a great delicacy," Mama Chin said in a quiet, low voice.

Mrs. McGarrity snatched Bark up into her arms. Bark squirmed. "You can't mean that," she said.

Mama Chin smiled a faint, determined smile. "Bamboo shoots and fresh peas."

Mrs. McGarrity turned, lace flying, Bark wriggling. "I'll shut you down," she shot over her shoulder as she banged through the swinging kitchen doors.

Bark scrambled to Mrs. McGarrity's shoulder.

"I'm already shutting down," Mama Chin shot back.

Bark stared at us as the doors swung shut, his eyes wide, head tilted to one side. He let out a single huge bark, a bark big enough to shake his sides and prove he was well named.

Mama Chin turned to me. "Did Bark know what I said?"

Bark groaned, deep in his chest. The mournful sound faded as Mrs. McGarrity left Mama Chin's.

"About eating him?" I asked.

"I didn't mean it," Mama Chin said. "I'll never cook Chinese."

I gazed around the kitchen. A catastrophe reigned here as well, with boxes of canned food, sacks of sugar, and flour scattered everywhere. "You didn't mean it about shutting down, right?"

She nodded.

I nibbled on my lips. Perhaps she meant that the café was shutting down for renovation, as Mad Maddie's Marvels had. "Really?" I asked.

Mama Chin didn't answer. She returned to the lip of the tunnel entrance and stared down it with a grief-stricken look on her face. I stood next to her and put my arm around her shoulders.

"We could go searching for Freddy," I suggested. Although the idea of crawling around in the long abandoned tunnels made my Buddhist-compassionate-so-I-offered skin crawl.

Mama Chin shook her head again. "You know what a wussy boy he is. We might frighten him further. He might run."

I sighed. "True but...he's also a stomach with legs. Why not put some food right here," I pointed with a foot, "and maybe he'll follow the scent home."

"Dora, that's a great idea." Mama Chin sounded amazed.

"I sometimes have ideas," I defended myself.

"Uh-huh." She opened the refrigerator door and looked inside. "No, Freddy hates asparagus," she said, her voice muffled.

I'd wasted way too much time dithering with various pet problems. I had to find my father. If I struck while Mama Chin was grateful and distracted, she might answer without thinking.

"If Rupert wasn't at his cabin, where would he be hiding?" I winced. Shouldn't have used the word "hiding." It implied he might have something to hide. And boy, did he.

Mama Chin pulled her head out of the fridge. "What?"

I thought fast. "Rupert's not at his cabin and I need to find him."

Mama Chin's eyes narrowed. "Why?"

I licked my lips and used the same reason I had with Lester and Mallard. "I need to get hold of some of his jewelry to sell."

Mama Chin placed one hand on her hip. "Dora, even if that's true—"

"It is true." Okay, not the whole truth, but still.

"—and even if I did know, I wouldn't tell you."

"Why not?" I feared I knew the answer.

"Mrs. McDay got here before Mrs. McGarrity." Satisfaction dripped from her every word.

I sighed, fearing the Widows Brigade had beaten me to Mama Chin.

"Rupert's gone and killed a man," Mama Chin said and confirmed my fear.

"You're as bad as the Widows Brigade. You've already convicted my father of murder. We don't know yet what happened."

Mama Chin held her hands up, palms out. "Dora, you don't know about Rupert." She ducked and turned back to the fridge.

"Tell me."

"Cinnamon rolls," Mama Chin answered.

My stomach leaped in joy. "What has that got to do with my father?" I managed around a mouth full of saliva.

Mama Chin shook her head. "Darn, no time to make them."

My stomach sank toward my toes. "Mama Chin, you have to tell me where Rupert is. Please."

Mama Chin looked at me. "Let the police deal with your father." She opened the freezer. "Besides, I make 'em with eggs, milk, and butter."

"The police?"

"No, silly, the cinnamon rolls."

My stomach gave a tiny, dismayed moan. "Oh no, the rolls are off my list." I'd always suspected that the cinnamon rolls contained eggs and milk but had never dared ask.

"That's why I never told you before."

"I'm going to be a starved-to-death vegan."

"Vegan." Mama Chin snapped her fingers. She pulled a package of patties from the fifties' avocado green refrigerator. Emblazoned across the side were the words "all natural meat substitute."

My empty tummy perked up. Yum, my favorite: fake meat.

"Mama Chin, where's my father?" I put every ounce of my childhood spent sitting at her counter eating cinnamon rolls into my voice.

Mama Chin stood, one hand grasping the industrial-sized package of pretend burgers. "Why?"

My mouth worked. I wanted to spill the beans, or the necklace. However, it was my burden. And I didn't know what Mama Chin would do with the information. Probably go right to the cops. I held out one hand, palm up, toward her.

"Dora, I don't know where he is," she said.

I believed her. I ran my hand over my mouth. "Okay." Now what could I do to save my father? Where could I go? Who could I turn to?

"Fat Freddy loves my new vegan burger." Mama Chin moved to the 1940's stove. When I'd asked why she kept the one from her mom's days, she told me with only a little cafe to run, why'd she need a new one?

"Vegan burger?" I asked.

She turned on the stove. "Yup, the new Mama Chin's Save On Drug Emporium is getting a new, expanded menu for the Aurora ski bums and that includes vegan burgers."

My stomach gurgled a cheer. Hooray, hurrah, yippee. I gestured at the scattered cans and boxes. "You're shutting down to renovate, like we're doing at Mad Maddie's, right?" I asked with a faint hope it might be true.

Mama Chin shook her head. Her tight-wrapped gray braids bobbled on her head. "Wrong. I'm moving to a new place." She slathered a hunk of thick white vegetable shortening onto an iron pan and plonked it on the stove.

"But you've been here forever. Your family has been here—well, the Chins got here third—just after us Starkes and the Camerons."

Mama Chin's mouth pursed. "And you've never let us forget how we're the newcomers."

"Newcomers?" I flailed my arms. "This place is your *new* place. Your mom rented it after the Starke fire, and that was sixty years ago."

"We're moving out to the mall." She slid the burger into the frying pan.

"You're going to the Sun Dog Mall?" I couldn't believe it.

The voracious wolf pack of developers was building the monstrous mall that crouched at the end of Main Street. The mall resembled mining shafts pressed together. The tall planked wood structures, not yet completed, already looked tacky.

"Don't know why those durn-fool dogs went building mine shafts, not after the fire that shut Starke's real ones down forever and killed those men," Mama Chin said, echoing my thoughts.

The mines were petering out before the fire, but afterward the Cameron Mining Company shut down. And Starke's population plummeted. Until now.

"Doesn't make no never mind, however. First place to open is going to be mine." Mama Chin picked up the pan and flipped the burger. "And Henry can take his hole and shove..." With quick, deft motions, she spread the vegetable shortening on the two halves of a hamburger bun and placed them face down in the pan.

"Hole? What hole?" I asked.

Mama Chin slid the bun from pan onto the plate. "The tunnel entrance, of course." She eased the burger onto the bun and added mustard, tomato, and lettuce.

I loved my burgers made that way, back when I ate meat.

"Henry's not getting his hole filled in, not on our dime." Mama Chin's head raised. "That didn't sound quite right."

"I can kinda see where Henry might expect you to fill up the tunnel. After all, the Chins built them."

Mama Chin paused from where she cut the burger in half. "No. Great Grandma Chin only built the first one."

"For an opium den."

Mama Chin sliced so hard that half the burger scooted off the plate. "And Great Grandpa Chin died because of it."

I gulped. The only time we Starkers succeeded in hanging a man. "That was a long time ago," was all I could think of to say.

Mama Chin gave an unconvincing shrug. "Besides, it was your great grandfather built all the connecting tunnels."

Great Grandpa had made certain the sheriff didn't know about the tunnels either. I wondered if Lester knew they existed. Or that one existed under the sheriff's office.

A tunnel entrance existed at Mad Maddie's too. Did Henry expect us to pay to fill it in too?

Mama Chin placed half of the burger down in front of the tunnel entrance.

"No wonder Freddy's so fat," I said without thinking.

Mama Chin paused from where she held out the plate to me. "Are you saying my rat is overweight?"

I picked up the burger and took a bite. Nirvana exploded in my mouth. Sweet and juicy and meaty. "Mama Chin, he's wider than he is long," I said around a mouthful of joy.

Mama Chin snatched the plate from me.

"Hey," I protested. My stomach gave a rumble in agreement.

"If he is fat, and I'm not saying he is, it's because..." Mama Chin pointed at the container of vegetable shortening. "I use that bear fat to fry everything."

"Bear fat? From a bear? Your bear?" I glanced at a photo of Mama Chin standing over a dead bear with her rifle cradled in her arms, stuck to the fridge with a magnet that said, "Every day without a smile is a day without love."

"No, from the bear fat store. Yes, from my annual bear kill." Mama Chin placed the plate next to the other half of the hamburger next to the tunnel entrance.

"If you move to the Sun Dog Mall, you won't have time to hunt bear."

Mama Chin lifted her chin.

I stepped back, away from the pain in her face.

"Doesn't matter. Henry ran us out." A century of fear of reprisals for being Chinese in the West echoed in Mama Chin's voice.

The anger roiled up from my belly and burned into my throat. "Ran you out?" My voice reverberated, raw with anger.

Mama Chin's face shut down. She stared down at her iron pan. "Henry figured he could up the rent and insist we close off the tunnel."

Henry was acting like his greedy great-grandfather. How dare he put money ahead of us Starkers?

"That's it." I snatched my half of burger off the plate on the floor, bear fat be damned. "I'll be at Henry's." I stormed out of the kitchen, double doors swinging.

"You sound just like your aunt," Mama Chin called after me.

"There's no reason to be insulting," I called back. "I'm going to fix this."

I stomped and chomped down the sidewalk toward Cameron Realty. Once I told off Henry, I'd... I paused and chewed the last bite. I'd what? I didn't know where Rupert might hide. I stood on the wooden sidewalk. At least my stomach lay silent, filled and fulfilled. The only part of me that was quiescent.

My mind spun. I needed to save my father. I needed answers. So who to ask?

A flash of bright pink captured my gaze.

Across Main Street, construction workers crawled over the Sun Dog office, one of them, Dusty, I'd babysat years ago. Now, he stood over six feet tall and seemed confident enough to wear a bright pink bandana around his red hair.

Pink. Pink Cadillac. Godiva's car. So who was this nudie chocolate lady, Godiva? What did she want with my father? Why was her brother dead in my father's cabin? If I knew where she lived, I could ask. Aha.

I gobbled the last bite of burger and resumed my stomp. I knew where to find out. Hmmm, two goals with one scold, I liked that.

THIRTEEN

The bay door rolled open on oiled hinges and spoiled the illusion of Cameron's Real Estate Office.

Henry jumped where he stood at a filing cabinet. "Dora?" Today he wore another designer suit in heavy gray wool, even more rumpled than yesterday's.

Was it only yesterday that my life was filled with the normal catastrophes of desperately designing jewelry and worrying about snow? I longed for the simple suffering before Rupert showed up at Mad Maddie's.

I pushed the door all the way open. Even oiled, the door squealed in protest. The metal, over the decades of use, had warped.

A powerful smell of petrol permeated the old garage. Now, even carpeted with an expensive deep pile in tasteful beige, the space retained all the earmarks of its original purpose. A suspicious oily gray showed in one spot on the carpet.

Henry slammed the file shut. "You've brought the back rent?" he asked, his face as eager as Fat Freddy's at mealtime.

I strode into the office. "Henry, how dare you?" I thumped my fist on his highly-polished new desk.

Henry jumped. "You sound like your aunt. Are you going to shoot me?"

"Good thing I don't have my gun. I might forget all my Buddhist teachings and do just that."

"Your aunt does owe the back rent, Dora. If you can't pay..." Henry ran his hand through hair already a collection of cowlicks "You can pay, right?"

"It's not about that. You ran Mama Chin out."

"Out where?" Henry looked behind me as if Mama Chin might be standing in the middle of Main Street.

"Out to the Sun Dog Mall."

"What?"

"She's moving the Save On there."

"Oh no, she's really leaving?" Henry covered his face with his hands.

My ire faded, a tiny bit. "Of course, she's leaving."

"But Mama Chin's has been in that same spot since the fire."

My anger dampened more. However, I reminded myself, being a Cameron, Henry might be faking his dismay. "You charged her extra rent because she's Chinese American," I said.

Henry stopped scrubbing and looked at me. "Mama Chin believes that?"

I nodded.

"Mama Chin isn't Chinese American. She's a Starker," Henry said as if the two were mutually exclusive.

"When you charged her extra, what else was she supposed to think?"

"But her mom's Mrs. McChin now that she's a member of the Widows Brigade. How can Mama Chin think that?" He plunked down in the leather office chair behind the desk. "Besides, I'm charging your aunt the same—"

I whimpered. "You are?"

"It's part of your back rent too. Miss Maddie didn't tell you?"

No, no, of course not. Aunt Maddie wouldn't want me to worry. She'd figure she could find a way to pay. She figured wrong.

I grabbed my Ohm pin and stood up straight. "You can't do that to us or Mama Chin, Henry. You can't expect us to pay before the ski resort opens," I said with all the force I could muster.

"But that crazy town council insisted those tunnel entrances need to be sealed, too dangerous, so I need—" He slumped in the chair, a little boy playing big important developer. "Oh God, I've fucked it all up."

"Henry?" Us Starkers never swore. The Widows Brigade made sure of that, unless we swore over a true catastrophe. "What's wrong?"

Instead of answering, he stared around the garage. "This place doesn't even look like a real estate office."

I followed his gaze. The ceiling showed stains from old leaks. Built in the thirties, the garage had a flat roof behind its traditional false front. Not good in snow country.

"It's not. It's Cam's Auto Repair, always has been, always will be," I said.

"Man, I worked so hard for my dad." Henry glanced at the oil stain and his mouth quirked in a half-smile.

I pointed at his fancy suit. "You can dress up the mechanic, but oil still runs through your veins, Henry."

"Used to be gold."

"Huh? Oh yeah, you mean Cameron's Assay." I crossed my arms. "Good thing that was before Maddie's time or she'd have killed the lot of you after you stole the town from us Starkes."

The Camerons always succeeded, no matter what. Even when the Starke mines closed along with most of the businesses, Henry's father kept Cam's Auto Repair successful. People still needed to get their cars fixed.

He snorted a laugh. "Now it's dirt."

"Dirt, you mean land, your real estate business?"

After Henry graduated from high school he'd headed to Boise and hadn't come back until he could make a profit from owning most of Main Street.

Henry hung his head. "Just worthless dirt."

"What do you mean?"

His head drooped farther. "If only the ski resort had opened last year...if the town council hadn't insisted on fixing those tunnels and the wiring. If those sons of bitches—"

I jumped at his use of another swear word. Oh, dear.

"Those Dog Face Developers didn't want to condemn my properties..." Henry's chin rested on his chest.

The vegan burger roiled in my stomach. Like everyone else in Starke, Henry needed money. That's why he demanded all that rent.

All us Starkers had jumped with joy—except for Fat Freddy, who was too fat to jump—when Starke got the go ahead to be Idaho's newest ski resort. I wondered if anybody jumped anymore.

My ohm pin rested cold under my fingers and offered no comfort. Did Henry demand payment because he knew Rupert possessed a necklace worth millions? Did Henry know about the necklace and about how much it could bring, even if it was stolen?

"I wanted to save Starke," Henry continued.

"Oh, Henry." I went around his huge desk, bigger than some of the cars he once worked on, and patted his arm. His bicep muscle moved under my hand, still large and powerful even after a decade as a developer desk jockey. Yum. I leaned closer. "Oh, Henry," I said in a different tone altogether.

Henry raised his head. I smiled. He sat up straight and grinned back. "Hey, Dora, remember after the senior prom when we—"

"We most certainly do, young man," Mrs. McGarrity said from the open bay door.

Henry and I leaped in opposite directions. Henry toppled off his chair while I banged my hip hard on the desk corner.

"God da—Shii—Ow," I said.

"We weren't doing anything." Henry scrambled to his feet.

"Exactly what you said the last time," Mrs. McGarrity said. Behind her bulk, her dog Bark, Mrs. McDay, and Mrs. McChin all fluttered.

Mrs. McDay wore her signature straw boater, a black monstrosity from the forties. The straw hat, with the weave unraveling, was decorated with a cluster of once-red, now faded, wooden cherries.

Henry tugged on his waistcoat. If he attempted to smooth out its myriad wrinkles, he failed. "Which was eight years ago," he muttered.

"There you were with Dora in that stolen car—"

"Borrowed from my dad's shop," Henry protested.

"Both of you almost naked."

The heat rushed into my face. "I only had my dress top down." I blushed harder at my own words.

"Freeze your nipples off, being middle of March and all." Mrs. McChin patted the pure white braids wrapped around her skull, a white-haired version of the hairstyle worn by her daughter, Mama Chin. And for all I knew, once worn by Mrs. McChin's mom. Family tradition.

As I recalled, my nipples had been cold. But other portions of me had compensated by being quite warm. Until the Widows Brigade showed up and froze both Henry and me.

"That's why we're here, naked nipples." Mrs. McDay nodded her head and the faded cherries on her ancient black straw hat bobbed up and down.

"Dora's naked nipples?" Henry stared over at my chest and gave another faint smile. I smiled back.

"Anybody's naked anything. Where's Godiva staying?" Mrs. McGarrity said. Always to the point, or two points, was Mrs. McGarrity.

Yay. My next question to Henry. With the Widows Brigade asking, I'd get an answer.

"What?" Henry looked at his desk as if he expected to find pieces of chocolate scattered over it.

"She's the nudie lady," Mrs. McChin said.

"She said they call themselves naturists now," I said.

"Nothing natural about it," Mrs. McGarrity said. Bark wriggled his curly tail as if he agreed, even though he was naked.

"Oh, that Godiva." Henry gazed at the open bay door as if contemplating a run for it. I understood how he felt, a common emotion when dealing with the Widows Brigade.

"It has to be stopped," Mrs. McGarrity said.

"Yes, before it spreads," Mrs. McChin said.

"And somebody's nipples freeze off," I couldn't help adding. That earned me a communal scowl from the Widows Brigade.

Henry ran both hands through his hair. "Um, why do you think I'd know?"

Mrs. McGarrity shook her finger at Henry. "Now, Henry, where else would she come to find a place in Starke to—"

"Go starkers," I said and grinned.

Another communal scowl and this time Mrs. McDay shook her head at me. Cherries bobbed.

"—open her den of iniquity," Mrs. McGarrity finished her sentence.

I remembered the short, somewhat plump and middle-aged woman I'd met. "Iniquity? Have you met Godiva?" I asked.

"Thanks to those goddamn Dog Developers." Henry clamped his lips shut.

Too late. "Henry," the Widows Brigade and I said in unison.

"Your father, Henry," Mrs. McGarrity said, "didn't let that crazy woman and her brother settle in, not for no reason, no way, no how. So why did you?"

Henry shot a determined look at me. "She's my only paying renter. You said you'd have the back rent today, Dora. Where's my money?"

I sighed. "You have no idea how busy" —talk about an understatement—"my day has been. I haven't had a chance to drive to Boise." Somehow, some way, I needed to do that and real soon. Nance never possessed patience.

One catastrophe at a time, I told myself. It didn't help.

"That was our agreement. You need to pay today," Henry said.

I looked at him. He stood ramrod straight, his knees locked back. He'd turned all professional businessman on me.

"You'll get what's coming to you," I said.

Mrs. McGarrity tapped one plump foot. Dust jumped from the carpet. "Henry, where is that immoral, naked Godiva?" Her tone brooked no argument.

Henry gazed down at his expensive carpet. "Good thing she arrived in town early," he said as if to himself. "I wonder if it's too soon to go to the Castle and get a check from her." His head jerked up. His eyes popped open wide when he stared at Mrs. McGarrity. He must have realized he'd told the Widows Brigade where Godiva was. And me.

"To the Castle," cried Mrs. McGarrity.

Bark yodeled his agreement, or excitement, at Mrs. McGarrity's tone.

"No, wait," Henry said over Bark's woo-woo.

"To the Castle," echoed Mrs. McDay and Mrs. McChin.

"Her brother got murdered by Rupert," Henry said.

"He did not," I said.

"The brother's not dead?" Mrs. McDay asked.

"Yes, but you don't know that my father killed him."

Mrs. McGarrity dismissed my protest with a wave of her hand. "Even more reason. Obviously this nude woman is a bad influence in Starke."

"Because her brother is dead?" Henry asked.

"We already covered that, Henry." Mrs. McGarrity whirled in a flurry of frills and headed to the bay doors.

"You can't go there," Henry cried. "She's in mourning."

"That sort of thing happens when you're naked," Mrs. McDay said.

We all looked at her. Mrs. McGarrity shook her head. Mrs. McChin sighed.

Mrs. McDay widened her eyes. "What? I meant being a bad influence."

Mrs. McGarrity paused one foot over the threshold, Bark at her side. "Henry's right."

"He is?" the rest of the Brigade chorused.

"First, we need a banner," Mrs. McGarrity said. "After the party, we can use Lester's."

Lester's? "Oh, no, you're not going to..." I stopped dead at the idea.

Mrs. McGarrity puffed out her considerable chest. "Of course, after all, those dogs wouldn't give him a leave of absence—"

"There's no justice," Mrs. McDay said.

"—and now he hasn't got a dime of pension."

"No justice," Mrs. McChin echoed.

"And they can't find who ran his poor grandson down." Mrs. McGarrity nodded. "No justice at all. Least we should give the man is a party. Come, ladies."

"We'll need more of Mrs. McChin's cookies." Mrs. McDay licked her lips. I did too. She trotted after Mrs. McGarrity.

Mrs. McChin followed. "If I'm bringing cookies then you need to bring—"

"Ladies, please." Henry took up the rear in a mini-parade after them.

I was last out and shut the bay door behind me. I trotted to my aunt's station wagon. I had to get to Godiva before the Widows Brigade got to her. After that she might be speechless or worse.

FOURTEEN

I pulled up the graveled circular drive to the Cameron Castle. Set back from Main Street by the long drive, the hotel rotted away out of sight. Renovation efforts on one corner of the huge wraparound porch highlighted the old hotel's decay. The round tower, added as an afterthought by Henry's grandfather and almost a third as big as the whole hotel, unbalanced the entire structure.

The Castle's one huge tower stood almost half-hidden by an enormous fir tree. The tree looked to be the only thing that held the whole hotel up. Branches crawled across the roof and years worth of pinecones and needles lay deep on one porch corner, a fire danger.

I grimaced. Last year Henry planned to renovate and re-open the Castle as a signature hotel for the ski resort. Henry had fallen far and hard.

Another too-pink Cadillac, this one a SUV, sat alongside Starke's only police car next to the front porch steps. I crouched as I drove around in case Mallard or Lester came out and looked. Like they wouldn't recognize the station wagon.

Now what? If only I could be a fly on the wall while the police interviewed Godiva.

Wait, I knew how to be a fly. Ew.

A sneeze threatened my nose, making me rub the offending proboscis. My shoulders scratched across the roots that hung from the side of the four-foot-tall and one skinny person wide tunnel. It'd been years since I crawled into the tunnel entrance at my aunt's store, long enough to forget the big yuck factor.

I'd bet that a hundred years ago, when the tunnels were used every day, they remained clear. With the number of people who had escaped from the cellar jail cell to Chin's opium den and then on to the Cameron Castle—a whorehouse in those days, although those Camerons would never admit it—and back to jail, the plants, bugs, and other vermin, ohm, ugh, eek, got discouraged and moved elsewhere.

I even caught a glimpse of a rat. Okay, the rat seemed to be rather obese and quite white and when I called out "Freddy?" I could have sworn the rat glanced over his shoulder. Maybe Freddy was visiting his not-so-domestic relatives. I hoped maybe not.

With huge rough-hewn logs supporting the ceiling and walls, the old tunnels seemed built to last forever, despite the town council's fears. The century old, hand-painted signs still hung from the support beams and directed me. On my way, I'd passed an interrupted poker game from long ago. The cards still lay face down on a tiny table as if the players might return at any moment. I shivered in the cold air and kept walking, half-hunched over.

I found the hundred-year-old cracked wooden "Cameron Castle" sign, with an arrow pointing upward. I climbed. Halfway up the ladder rungs, half-buried into the side of the tunnel, I shone my flashlight at the trap door that led into the Castle. I hovered. Cobwebs draped between the trap door and the long roots of what had to be the huge fir tree outside. First, Mallard's voice droned and then came the higher tones of Godiva, both indistinct.

Needing to hear what they said, I climbed higher. An inch at a time, my hand barely touching the wood, I opened the trap door. Maybe Mallard and Godiva were in another room, but I couldn't tell. It wouldn't do to fling open the door and yell "Surprise!"

No feet greeted me from my vantage point as I peeked through the crack. I grew bolder and opened the door wider.

The room stood empty. It looked almost as full of cobwebs as the tunnel. Pegs ran all along one side, and bars with wooden hangers hung from the other. One hanger sported a lone, dusty duster. The room must have been a large coatroom a century ago when the Cameron Castle boomed along with Starke. It must have been quite convenient for those who visited the Castle ladies.

A faint scent of tobacco and sweat, horses' and men's, lingered in the room, a ghost of good times past.

The voices grew louder.

"Oh, my poor, sweet, dear brother," Godiva wailed.

Hmmm, yesterday she'd sworn at that poor sweet dear brother, in an altogether different tone.

"I never thought that Wild Rupert person could possibly be that wild, but I'm sure there's an explanation for why he killed my brother, who was only up there to buy me some of that wild man's jewelry." Godiva gave a sniveling sob.

Was she calling my father a killer? Why did everyone except me already condemn him?

Rupert's jewelry. He made more of his bottle cap pins than anything else. Where would Godiva pin them? In her hair? Why would she want jewelry she never wore?

Mallard's much deeper voice rumbled. I raised the trap door as far as possible and strained to hear.

Another dramatic sob from Godiva answered.

"Yes, so you've said a number of times, Miss Godiva," Mallard's voice came much clearer. "And as I've said before" —a number of times, I heard implied in his voice—"I'm most sorry for your loss. But I need to ask these questions. I need to know why your brother—"

"Derek, oh dear Derek, how will I bury him, now that he's returned to his natural state?"

"Natural state? You knew he was naked?" Suspicion crawled through his words.

"Naked? In this cold?" Godiva answered.

Mallard must have nodded, for Godiva said, "A prejudiced person perhaps stripped my brother's poor dead body to cast aspersions on naturists everywhere."

"You mean cause more suspicion of you, his closest relative?" Mallard asked.

"Perhaps his naturist beliefs were why he was killed," Godiva continued as if Mallard hadn't spoken of suspicion of murder. "We are a persecuted people." Her voice rang with piety.

"Um, maybe, but, to get back to a simpler question, why did your brother bother to go all the way up to Wild Rupert's cabin? Why not buy Rupert's pins from Dora?"

Good questions. I leaned forward. A long rope of something alive and wriggling dropped down in front of me. I gave a tiny yelp.

"Did you hear something?" Mallard said.

I froze. The earthworm dangled in front of my nose. A sneeze snuffled at the back of my nose, trying to express itself.

"What?" Godiva said.

"It sounded like a squeal."

I don't squeal. That was a yelp, Mallard.

"Huh," Mallard said after a moment. "I don't hear anything now."

I let out my breath a whisper at a time.

"And I didn't even know until I'd been here for months where Rupert resided," Mallard continued, "and you've been here..."

I crawled out of the tunnel.

"A couple of days, wonderful days, until now," Godiva said.

"So," through the cloakroom door I heard the strained patience in Mallard's voice, "how did your brother even know where Rupert lived?"

I paused, the trap door in my hands as I realized I knew the answer to that question. Derek must have followed my father up to his cabin. Did Derek pursue my father only for a few bits of tin and wire?

"Who can say? And we can't ask my dear, beloved brother." A new wail erupted from Godiva.

"Please, ma'am, this is as hard for me as it is for you." Embarrassment tinged Mallard's every word.

I'd bet he sweated now.

"But, *why* would your brother go to Rupert's cabin?" Mallard persisted. Good for him. "You've already bought Rupert's jewelry somewhere else. Why not go back there? Why pursue a recluse?"

Excellent questions. Mallard, for all his reluctance to be anything but a computer cop, knew what to ask. Why had Godiva been so relentless in finding Rupert? Why had Derek followed my father all the way to his cabin?

Something tickled on the back of my right hand. I glanced down and saw a spider the size of a chipmunk picking his way across. I squealed, yes, squealed and dropped the trap door.

In the reverberating slam, the cloakroom door opened.

"Dora?" Mallard said. A blast of heat followed his words.

I turned to where Mallard and Godiva stood in the doorway, almost shoulder to shoulder.

FIFTEEN

From behind Mallard and Godiva hot air roiled.

"What the hay, Dora?" Mallard demanded, his hand drifting toward his gun holster. Rivulets of sweat ran down his red face. He held his uniform hat clutched in his moist hands.

Godiva pressed her hand her brilliant pink summer dress. Could be worse, she could be naked. "How did you get inside?"

"Did you break in?" The sweating sheriff's deputy asked, or rather accused.

"That's trespassing," Godiva growled. She turned to Mallard. "Arrest her."

"You can't arrest me, because ..." Searching for inspiration, I looked past Mallard and Godiva.

The cloakroom opened onto the old reception room. Enormous dead animal heads, most of the glassy-eyed beasts were elk, hung around an immense stone fireplace. The mahogany reception desk that stood against the far wall looked cobweb-covered and the floor deep with dust. The air reeked of old dead things. And smoke.

On the far side of the lobby a gigantic blazing fire roared in the immense stone fireplace and created the summer-like heat.

A log sparked and sent flashes up the chimney. I wondered how long it had been since the chimney had been swept. And how close the sparks flew to the fir tree, an old tree, full of pine oil, an excellent flammable fuel.

The taste of my past repast of vegan burger roiled in my mouth. The necklace rested in the ashes of my father's fireplace trap. It called to me from its cold stone bed. What if someone, Mallard or Lester maybe, decided to heat up Rupert's freezing cabin with a fire in the fireplace? I needed to get the necklace back in my apron pocket. Soon.

Ah, Lester—a diversion or at least a possible distraction from Godiva's insistence on my jail time for trespass. "Where's Lester?" I said.

Mallard sweated. "He had something at the office. You know there's been a murder."

Godiva gave a sob that sounded forced. She teared up, big globs of water forming in her eyes.

Mallard looked skyward. A fresh drop of sweat formed on the tip of his nose. He looked frantic that she might erupt into waterworks again.

He turned to me and adopted an arms-across-the-chest cop stance. "How did you break in?"

Oops, my rather lame tactic didn't work. I took a step away from the closed tunnel door, again flush to the floor. I hoped he wouldn't notice the door. If I broke the tradition of the police not knowing about the tunnels, suspecting, yes, but knowing, no, then I'd have more upset Starkers on my overfull hands. Plus my access to the Castle would be destroyed.

"I didn't break in," I said. "I don't break in. That would be so not Right Action."

"Right action?" Mallard asked.

I figured now wasn't the time for a lecture in Buddhist principles. *Don't look down*, I wanted to say to Mallard. "I came in the back way," I said instead. "It was unlocked." There, I spoke the truth. Then I peeked at the cloakroom back door. A bar ran across it. Cobwebs strung from the bar to the door. Uh-oh.

Godiva followed my glance. And before Mallard did too, she threw her arms around me and hugged me to her bosom. "Oh, you poor, poor dear."

"Thanks," I said to her because she'd distracted Mallard. "It's okay," I said around a mouthful of blonde hair. Something scratched at my face.

"It must be as awful for you as it is for me," she continued. "Him being your father and all."

"How did you know Rupert was—" Mallard started to ask.

"No really, I'm fine." Now that she'd diverted Mallard, I wanted nothing more than to disentangle myself from her hairy bosomy embrace. Otherwise, I might suffer a hairy bosomy death of suffocation.

I pulled away from her iron grasp. I scratched my cheek again. Godiva wore a different pin on top of one generous breast, a tiny one difficult to see under all that hair.

"You," Godiva said to Mallard, "you awful man, how could you?"

"Could I what?" Mallard asked.

"Torturing two grieving, vulnerable women."

Torturing? Grieving? Vulnerable? I gave Godiva a wide-eyed look. She gave a tiny shake of her head in warning. Then she shook her finger at Mallard. "You should be out finding out who killed my brother."

Mallard took several steps back.

"What kind of a policeman are you?" Godiva demanded.

Mallard glanced behind as if checking an escape route.

"I'll tell you what kind of policeman you are." Godiva took a step toward him.

He stumbled back, away from the irate nudist.

"You're a policeman trespassing on private property."

Mallard blinked at her. "I came here at your request instead of you coming to the Sheriff's—"

Godiva pointed at the main doors. "Get out."

"But ma'am—"

"I'm too young to be a ma'am." Godiva stamped her foot. Decades of dust jumped. "Out. Now."

Mallard strode across the wide, hot expanse of the reception room and flung open one of the double main doors. It squealed, much louder than me, and then slammed shut behind him.

I didn't blame him. I wanted to flee, too, but Godiva blocked the cloakroom door. And I hadn't gotten any of the answers I'd come for, either. Not yet.

"Now we can talk." Godiva grabbed my arm and tugged me into the main room.

Yay, I almost said. At long last, someone wanted to talk to me and give me some answers. Myriad questions tumbled through my mind, each fighting for expression. As I opened my mouth to ask—something, anything—Godiva grabbed my arm and demanded, "Where's your dad?"

The force of her grab made me stagger into the fireplace. A poster-sized photo of Godiva and Derek tumbled from its perch on the mantelpiece. The two peered from behind a white pillar, Derek above Godiva, both showing only skin. The pillar covered most of Godiva's and all of Derek's naughty bits.

Godiva must have realized attacking me wasn't the way to get answers. She released me gave a wistful, half-smile. "Us sibs in better times." Sorrow resonated in those five words.

This time, I believed her grief. If she had killed her brother, for whatever reason, she hadn't meant to.

"That seems so long ago," Godiva continued, "back when I was only plain Mary Jane."

"Mary Jane?" I couldn't imagine the woman before me being called a normal, regular, boring name.

"Before I took my true name in honor of a woman of courage," she finished. She brushed at the corner of one eyelid. "Uncle never understood what we naturists are all about."

Huh? "Uncle?" I asked.

Godiva didn't answer. She walked over to the fireplace on a little trail, Godiva foot-size, through the dust. How could she stay here? Why would she want to?

She stopped right before I believed she would step into the flames. Godiva stared into the fire. "He always thought being as God made us, in our true state, meant only lewd and lascivious behavior." Her mouth twisted. "Especially women, or 'little bit of nothing' as he called me. In fact, it's clothing that provides the cover for such behavior."

"Well, clothing does sometimes get in the way of lewd and lascivious," I said, remembering prom night.

She clutched her hands to her breast in a classic victim pose. The firelight glinted off the small pin on her sweatshirt. "Now, poor dear Derek has been martyred to such wrong thinking."

That seemed a little extreme until I remembered Derek's naked murdered body. "Not martyred by my father," I said.

"That's why I need to know where Bertie is," Godiva said to the fire.

The dam of my questions broke. "How do you know my father? Why do you keep calling him Bertie? Why didn't you tell Mallard you knew him?" I fired off.

Godiva flipped a hand in my direction. "I confess."

"Confess?" My heart raced.

"Yes, dear Dora." She giggled. "I confess to reading that delightful article about the new Starke ski resort that dear, sweet Henry wrote."

Curse Henry. He'd written a national magazine article which featured the "zany" characters of Starke, foremost amongst them, my father, "Wild Rupert" the reclusive artist.

"I decided it was time to return to Starke to open my naturist center in the wondrous, untamed, unsullied wilderness of Idaho," Godiva said. "No doubt attitudes have now changed."

The Widows Brigade's attitude sure hadn't, but I figured Godiva would find that out for herself, soon enough.

"That doesn't explain how you knew to come to me to ask about Rupert," I continued, determined this time to get an answer, "or even how you knew my name."

Godiva giggled. The pin glinted as it rose and fell in the folds of fabric and cleavage. "The deputy that was here said your name." She smiled at me as if she expected an A for the explanation.

Do you even know his? I wanted to ask. "No. Before, at Maddie's Marvels."

Godiva turned back to the fire. "Oh, then, that Boise woman at that jewelry place told me your name."

Nance wouldn't tell a customer where else to buy what the customer was already purchasing at her gallery. Why would Nance undercut her own sales?

"I'm cold," Godiva said. "It's so cold."

Huh?

She held out a hand that hovered only inches away from the flames.

"Careful, you'll get burned," I said.

"Oh, I never get burned. Where's Bert—Rupert?" she asked, still staring into the fire.

"Why should I tell you? You haven't answered any of my questions. You said you think he's guilty just like everybody else. He didn't kill your brother."

"Of course not," Godiva agreed. "Sweet Bertie boy could never kill anyone."

"Huh?" This time I said it out loud. "Why did you tell Mallard otherwise? Did you kill Derek?" Say yes, and solve that catastrophe.

Now she did turn and look at me wide-eyed. "Don't be ridiculous."

"They do say it's usually a relative," I said.

"I'm a devout naturist."

Huh, again. Was Godiva speaking in some sort of naked code?

"We embrace life, not destroy it."

Ah.

"I can answer your questions as soon as I talk to your father," she said and smiled. The firelight played over her face and reflected off her bright, perfect teeth. The brilliant gleam of all that white terrified me.

Nance never told anyone that Rupert was my father. "You're lying," I said.

Godiva's hand flew to her pin. "What?"

I took a close look at it for the first time and gasped.

A starburst pattern—sterling silver rays inset with garnets, radiated out from a central star garnet. The rays curved and the tiny pin represented a star being born. I knew this because the pin was one of my father's signature pieces, from when he designed jewelry for an exhibition.

"What?" Godiva asked again.

I pointed at her chest.

She looked down at the tiny new star riding on her bosom.

"That pin's from my father's Seattle exhibition."

"My pin? I got this pin years ago."

"Where?"

"I..." Godiva stared at the pin as if she'd never seen it before. Maybe the ghost of Derek had sneaked it onto her boob as a parting gift.

"You had to have gotten that pin from the Seattle exhibition." The exhibition, years ago, remained my father's one triumph.

Godiva's face brightened. "Yes, in fact, that's where I first got interested in him...his pins."

"You just said you found out about him from the article."

Her mouth pursed. "I meant that's where I found out more about him." Her face cleared. "I was so pleased that Starke had an artists' community already." She smiled at me again. "That includes you, Dora."

Oh, thanks a lot, that means so much, I now don't suspect you of anything at all, I wanted to say but my sarcasm was so not Right Speech.

What was Godiva hiding? Or did she hide nothing? Was she just thrown by her brother's death, as anyone would be? Was she always this defensive and offensive? Did I want her to be the killer because I didn't much like her?

"Where is he?" she asked again.

"I wouldn't tell you even if I knew," I said.

Her eyes narrowed. "You don't know?"

"No, do you?"

"What? Why would I ask if I already knew?"

I hesitated and then said, "Maybe you're covering up."

"I never cover up, I'm a naturist." She pointed at the front door. "You need to leave."

I didn't dismiss that easily. "I'm not leaving until you—"

"Out."

"Why are you so interested in my father?"

"If you don't leave this instant, I'll scream until that sweaty deputy returns."

I put my hands on my hips. "Good. He might able to get some answers out of you."

"All he'll be doing is arresting you."

"What for?"

Godiva smacked herself on the cheek, hard. "Oh, Officer, she attacked me." She scratched at her neck and left pink rivulets. "Help, help," she said, her voice rising on the second. "Help."

I trotted toward the main doors. "I'm going, you crazy woman," I said over my shoulder as I grabbed the elk antler handle of one of the enormous double doors.

Catching a glimpse of Henry's surprised face through the open door, I jumped back a foot.

He must have rushed to the Cameron Castle before the arrival of the Widows Brigade, hoping to get paid. Post-Widows Brigade, Godiva might not want to pay rent, she might be headed out of town with a scorched, naked behind.

"You tell Bertie I'm the only one who can save him, Dora," Godiva said in a low, flat voice.

Her words made me turn back. "From who?" Did she mean that she knew who was after Rupert? Did she know Rupert was still alive? "What do you know?"

Godiva crossed her arms over her ample chest, crushing my father's pin. She showed her teeth.

"Tell me." I took a step toward her. If she didn't, I'd add to her slap marks.

"Miss Godiva?" Behind me, Henry pressed inside. He looked from Godiva, with her red face and scratched neck, and back to me. "Dora, what have you been doing this time?"

"I will find out what you're up to. I'll be back," I said to Godiva and winced at the Schwarzenegger inflection in my voice. I left in a cloud of dust and glory. Well, maybe not glory.

SIXTEEN

As I entered the front door of the store, Aunt Maddie swept the bits of broken potato salt- and peppershakers from the floor. She'd righted the display case and placed the lone survivor, a peppershaker, back on the case's top shelf. She'd re-hung the old bell above the door, which jangled.

My aunt looked up, and her face crumpled with fury.

I reached up and yanked the bell down, sick of its betraying sound.

"I should have called the cops on you." She clutched the broom in her hands as if she held a sword.

I kept a cautious few feet between us. "They showed up anyway."

"Useless." My aunt put a world of disdain in that one word, but whether the word was for me or the police, I didn't know. "The lot of you," she clarified and turned back to her sweeping. Rage showed in every knot in the muscles of her back. "First that nudie woman shows up again after God-only-knows how many years," she grumbled into the mini-dust storm she created, "and then her brother shows up naked and dead. No sense of propriety, these nudists."

I shifted from foot to foot as I tried to come up with a way past her anger. "Sorry—"

She didn't look up. "Buddhists don't apologize."

"Yes, we do."

Aunt Maddie paused in her sweeping. "The past no longer exists and believing so only adds to our suffering."

I stood open-mouthed.

She resumed sweeping.

Bell in hand, I pointed at the broken tourist junk. "No use crying over spilled potato outhouses." I grinned. If I could make Aunt Maddie laugh... I gave the bell in my hand a little shake. It clanged a sour note. "Don't worry. I'll replace this."

My aunt swept harder. Small bits of potato-shaped outhouses flew. "That bell has hung there ever since Great Grandmother opened this store."

"Then it's high time we replaced it. We can sell it as an antique." I set the bell on the now upright display case.

Aunt Maddie pointed with the dustpan at the stacked cardboard boxes of my wax patterns. "Like you sold those pieces to Nance?"

I took the dustpan from her and held it while she swept the tourist trash bits into the pan. Decades of dust jumped from the planks as she swept. My family was never known for our housekeeping abilities. Criminal, yes, housekeeping, no.

If I started working with gold I'd need to get a powerful shop vacuum to make sure I recovered my gold dust. When I worked with gold, I amended. Which would be soon, I promised myself.

"I'll drive to Boise." When? The sun already touched Dog Face Mountain peak. And I needed to find my father. *Sell it. Now.* I wondered if Rupert had been trying to find me today. If so, I'd been with a dead man, then the police, and then looking for him too.

"I've been detain—a bit distracted today," I said.

"You mean by finding a dead body?" Aunt Maddie swept harder.

My shoulders jerked. I looked up at my aunt and coughed.

Aunt Maddie patted my shoulder. I coughed again. She thumped my back. "I'm sorry, my little one, that should never have happened," she said.

I stood up with the full dustpan in my hand. "It's just dust."

"No, I meant you finding th-that—" Aunt Maddie snorted. My shoulders sagged as I remembered the slumped, naked body. "Oh, Dora." My aunt hugged me tight.

The full dustpan slid from my fingers. Dust and potato kitsch flew. I took the broom from her, so that I could lean on it instead. I'd spent my whole life leaning on my aunt. "I'll sweep," I said. Straws flew off the end of the broom as I worked.

She crossed her arms across her chest. "It's your own fault."

"Of course, I did bump into the case and knock all this over."

"No, Dora. How could you go up to that man's cabin?" She put decades of hatred into "that man's."

I looked up from where I'd created a neat pile. I wished my life was as easily tidied.

Thunder roiled across my aunt's forehead, presaging a storm. "That horrid man."

"He's not horrid. He's misunderstood."

My aunt crossed her arms under her generous bosom. "I understand Rupert perfectly."

"Aunt Maddie, I know you blame my father for Mom's running off, but he's blameless."

"Patty didn't run off." Almost fifteen years of missing her sister resonated in my aunt's voice. "Rupert drove her away with his womanizing."

"Womanizing?" I stood frozen, the broom clutched high in my hand. "You mean my father..." An image tried to form in my mind of my father as a lady's man and failed.

My aunt grimaced. "Now, with what's happened, you need to know."

"Aunt Maddie, you're talking about my father. He doesn't even talk to women." And if he did, they'd be horrified by the rotten stumps of his teeth.

Aunt Maddie sighed. "Rupert wasn't always as he is now."

On my knees, dustpan in one hand, broom in the other, I swept and remembered my father before my mother left. My handsome father, who always walked tall and laughed and winked at all the girls, myself included. Unrecognizable in the broken man I knew now, as broken as the bits I swept.

"He went after my mom, to get her back." I repeated what I so wanted to still believe.

"Huh, that's what he said he did," Aunt Maddie said, "but he went back to Seattle, the scene of his triumphs, and I'm not talking about the exhibition."

I gulped again, the taste of that long ago burger stale in my mouth. The exhibition happened in Seattle and my father returned there when? What had happened in those months when my father pursued my mother, or so I thought?

"Who?" I asked.

"Who what?"

"The woman?"

"That loser had a whole string of them," Aunt Maddie said.

I stood up as I realized the depth of my aunt's animosity. So, if Aunt Maddie had discovered that Rupert had the necklace...would she force him to sell it? For the money to pay the rent? Would she threaten him with death? If so, why do so now?

Squeezing the dustpan handle tight to keep my anger centered, I said, "That loser is my father."

"He abandoned you a long time ago."

"No, he came back. My father came back." If she would show some leniency, I might not suspect her.

"Rupert had no place else to go. I'd forgive him for a lot, but not how he acted when he returned."

"Why not? I have."

"You're his daughter, you'd forgive him anything."

Would I?

Aunt Maddie shook her head. "Now he's a killer."

"You mean like Charles?" I couldn't help myself.

Her face clouded. "What are you saying?"

"He left and abandoned you. Does that mean he's a killer?" I hated the rage I heard in my own voice. I acted like my aunt's own flesh and blood in the worst way.

My aunt flung her arm toward the front door and knocked the dustpan out of my hand. "You need to get out."

"I'm sorry, Aunt Maddie, I didn't mean to say that." But I lied. Yes I did. I so wanted someone besides me to believe Rupert innocent.

"You need to leave town, today. Don't come back."

"Aunt Maddie, I will get enough money from Nance for the back rent." My words sounded inadequate and hollow.

"You stay in Boise. Where you belong."

My aunt always had welcomed me home. Tears came to my eyes. Must be all the dust. "I belong here." The tears threatened to spill over. I swallowed hard.

Aunt Maddie's face softened.

"If I'm here I can help you."

She gave a tiny smile, a quirk of her lips.

"And Rupert," I added.

Oops.

Her face closed down. "You get away from the naked dead." Her lower lip trembled.

She wanted to provoke me, for us to argue. To protect me, she wanted to drive me away. Make me run.

I grasped her arm. "I'm not going to leave, not now."

She yanked her arm away. "I expect you out of here by morning," she said. My aunt shook her head again, her red and white hair flying in a raging inferno. Maddie flung open the door and slammed it behind her.

She stomped off, blind to the truth about her beloved Charles. I wondered what was my own blindness. Was I so desperate to see my father as a victim that I didn't see who he truly was? He was, if I were to believe my aunt, a womanizer at the least and perhaps far worse. Should I go to Lester and tell him everything I knew? Which was not much, not enough to save my father. Everyone except me believed him the killer.

If I sold the necklace, if Nance would buy it, then would Rupert give me enough of the proceeds to save Maddie's store? If I could ever find him and if he hadn't vanished into the mountains forever, then I could—no, I took a deep breath and let it out at a count of four.

I swept harder. If I focused on the moment in a form of meditation sometimes the path became clear. Dust floated in the last of the dusk light that filtered through the front display window. The motes reminded me of ashes on the wind. I paused and peered out the front window. Most of the smoke had dissipated, leaving only a few thin fingers creeping along the sidewalk, a good sign.

If I could look past the veil that obscured my mind... Look. Across the street, parked in front of Maureen's, was Lester's jeep. What was he doing there? Shouldn't he be at the sheriff's office?

Lester sat ramrod straight behind the wheel. He looked right at me and waved a finger in admonition.

I bent back to my task. Thoughts tumbled in my mind. Lester must be staking out Maddie's store. He must expect Rupert to come here, looking for me. If that happened, if Rupert snuck in past Lester, I might be able to get some answers from my father.

Perhaps I could even convince Rupert to turn himself over to Lester, where he'd be safe. With Rupert's help, Lester might be able to figure out who murdered Derek. Then Lester could leave on a high note. He needed one.

And I needed to stay here tonight to wait for Rupert. I promised myself to stay awake all night. I finished cleaning up the one mess I could and headed out for coffee and dinner. Then more coffee, enough to keep me alert, watching and waiting for as long as it took to capture my dad.

SEVENTEEN

My head jerked off my worktable. Ohm, I'd fallen asleep. Again. I'd broken a promise, so not Right Action. What woke me?

Silence. Not even the sound of cars passing on Main Street outside. It must be the early hours of the morning.

Potato chip crumbs adhered to my cheek. I brushed off the crumbs and peered past the bright light of the circle lamp. Darkness lay beyond. I wanted to huddle in the oasis of light forever.

After I turned off the lamp, I crept to the front of the store. My eyes adjusted to the gray light of early dawn that filtered through the front window. Nothing moved in the shadows outside. Even the smoke lay still.

Perhaps it had been only that wretched dream of finding my father in his chair, naked and dead, that had awakened me. My nightmare served me right. Through the front window I saw another nightmare. The dim outline of Lester's Jeep remained parked across the street. I wondered if Lester lasted the night awake or had fallen asleep like me. I didn't dare go outside to check.

I turned the light back on. Beneath it was my wax patterns of the new designs I'd cobbled up for Nance, including a couple of attempts at a Dog Face Mountain pin. I'd decided I'd even sell Nance that design for the ski resort symbol, if I ever got it to stop snarling.

In my mind, the necklace called to me from its bed of ashes, a black and diamond siren. I could go to my father's cabin now and bring the necklace home if not for Lester. The necklace would have to wait.

A few crumbs from my dinner of potato chips had scattered amongst the patterns. I hadn't wanted to go back to Mama Chin's for another try at vegan fare so I'd bought the chips and a Coke over at Maureen's. As a good Buddhist, I needed to honor my body by feeding it with good food. Potato chips and Coke didn't fill that order, but at least it was vegan.

I shook my head at the crumbs as I scolded myself about eating around my work. Crumbs could sneak onto a wax pattern and destroy it.

The wastebasket hid behind the front door. I pulled it out and with infinite care cleaned the crumbs off my workbench. The salty sticky crumbs joined the fake potato bits of the broken kitsch in the basket.

Kitsch. Kitsch sells.

In the cellar were items that made this junk look like classical statuary. When I'd been down there I'd seen the pieces of sixties and seventies tourist stuff—statuettes in sixties dress with arms open wide and big grins and "Groovy, Man" inscribed beneath, inspirational plaques with sayings such as "today is the best day because it is today" with big smiley faces around it, and worst of all, a bouquet of fake plastic flowers, daisies with smiley faces in the center. Ugh.

Nance could sell all of it. Nance would want to sell it, as art. She had the skill to display such horrors so that they charmed and enticed. So what if the customer got the piece home and thought "Eew, why did I buy this?"

My watch glowed with six-thirty a.m., close to dawn. I could pack up the whole lot of the tourista junk in the tunnel, drive to Boise, and get to Nance's store as she opened. I could be back in Starke with a check for Henry by early afternoon. One catastrophe averted. Maybe.

I flung open the trap door. My father's battered face looked up at me. With a scream, I dropped the trap door.

EIGHTEEN

The trap door clanged shut. My father yelped, a muffled squeal.

I yanked up the door. The tunnel ladder stood empty. "Don't run. Father, please, come back," I called into the darkness.

A bearded oval floated disembodied to the bottom of the ladder. Rupert made so little noise that he appeared disconnected from his body.

My knees wobbled with relief. My father still lived. "You came back," I said to him.

He reached out his hand. "Help me."

"Always." I hauled him out of the tunnel and into the light.

When he stood next to me, I goggled at his damaged face. Deep purple bruises spread out from a cut lip and one eye swelled almost shut. Long scabbed scratches ran across his forehead.

"Oh Buddha, you're hurt," I said. *Sell it...*

He turned toward the front window.

"Move." I gave him a little push into the shadows.

He looked at me, his good eye wide. "Dora?"

"Sorry, but Lester is—" I stopped. If he knew Lester had staked out the store, he'd bolt.

"Lester?" Rupert took a couple of steps toward the tunnel.

I shut the trap door. "I mean I wouldn't want anybody to spot you from the street." Especially Lester, I added to myself. I wanted to convince my father to turn himself in to Lester on his own, not the other way around.

Rupert stepped back into the shadows. I guided him over to my stool at my workbench at the back of the store and helped him sit down. He winced.

"How badly hurt are you?" I asked.

My father tugged at his beard and grimaced again. He dropped his hand. "I'm okay."

"Did Derek beat you?"

Rupert shuddered. "He knocked the door down."

I remembered the broken lock. Another wave of relief hit my knees and they almost buckled. Rupert must have been terrified. He must have grabbed his gun during the fight and fired without thinking. "You killed him in self-defense."

My father jumped up. He gasped and grabbed his side. Rupert stared at me, his damaged mouth gaping. A raw hole showed where one rotten tooth had been knocked out.

Good thing I stood between him and the tunnel exit. "Don't worry, I'll keep you safe, no matter what," I promised.

I hoped I could keep that promise.

Rupert's wounded lower lip trembled. "Derek's the killer, not me. I've never killed anyone."

"Except in self-defense, which doesn't count, since Derek was the one threatening your life, you're safe now. Right?" I opened my mouth to say, and you can turn the necklace over to the cops. Catastrophe solved.

"No, no, I didn't shoot him," Rupert answered.

I gulped in shock. "But—I mean—how—is that why you stripped him naked, because somebody else killed him?"

My father's eyes popped wide. "He was naked when they found him?"

I nodded.

"I didn't take off Derek's clothes." My father chewed on his lower lip, his beard flapping. "Someone must have been searching for the necklace. I knew you had it, Dora."

The necklace. The killer had been hunting for the necklace on Derek's body. Although where on Derek's body didn't bear thinking about.

Rupert tilted his head. "Wait, how did you know he was naked? The Widows Brigade?"

"I know because *I* found him." I gulped again and tasted stale potato chips.

"Oh, Dora, I'm so sorry," my father said, echoing Aunt Maddie. He reached toward me.

I stepped into the curve of his arm. He smelled of fear, sweat, tunnel dirt, and underneath, polishing rouge and solder dust. I remembered how, when I was tiny and we were a family, he always smelled of rouge and casting wax and metal dust.

He gave me one squeeze and then dropped his arm. I stepped back and tried to think of a way to get my father to tell me what was going on without scaring him away. Already he'd spoken more words in these few moments than he had in decades.

I gestured for him to sit back on the stool. He sat on the edge, ready to spring up at any moment.

"Who killed Derek?" I asked.

"How long do canned peaches last?" Rupert asked.

From a murdered man to canned peaches. Had I fallen asleep again and this was some new nightmare? "Peaches?"

"Maybe a few decades?"

"Canned fruit?"

Rupert tugged on his beard. "Do you have anything to eat?"

"Ah." I retrieved the last of the breakfast bars from my apron.

Rupert ripped into the package and snarfed down the bar. He couldn't be injured too badly, I consoled myself.

I wondered how my father managed with his bad teeth. I wondered how he'd manage out in the woods and whether that was where he had been hiding. And what, if anything, canned peaches had to do with it.

He saw me staring and covered his mouth again as he swallowed the last bite. A habitual gesture to cover his bad teeth? Tears came to my eyes as I realized I didn't know my father well enough to know his habits.

Rupert saw my tears. He dropped his hand. "Oh, Dora, I'm so sorry," he repeated. He reached into his coat pocket and then held out that hand to me.

I took his hand. It trembled beneath mine.

Underneath my fingers, the old familiar scars and calluses created by jewelry fabrication on my father's hand rubbed against mine, a reassurance. And something else that poked into my palm, sharp and hard.

"I made it last night," Rupert said. "For you."

He'd given me a pin made from bits of tin, wire, and a piece of ruby red bottle glass—a woman's silhouette scratched upon the glass above a free form in the starburst pattern my father so loved. How did he take scraps of trash and create such beauty? Could I ever hope to do the same?

I frowned as I realized the woman's form resembled the necklace's onyx fairy and the starburst in the piece Godiva wore earlier today. Into my pocket went the pin. I didn't want to consider what it might mean, not yet.

"Don't you like it?" Rupert asked. He brushed the crumbs from his beard.

I smiled at him. "I love it. It's beautiful."

My father smiled his shy, happy smile. "You sold the Noira, right?"

"Who? Nor—" I remembered what Nance had said before she hung up. "Do you mean the necklace?"

"Where'd you put the money?" Rupert pulled open my top workbench drawer. "You did get cash?"

I chewed my lower lip.

He looked up from where he rummaged in my bottom drawer and licked his split lip. "How much did you get?"

Who was this avaricious stranger?

"How can I sell the necklace when—"

"You haven't sold it?" Rupert's eyes and mouth both gaped wide.

"You haven't answered me."

"Sell it to Nance. She'll pay what you ask," Rupert said.

"You don't know that."

"Oh, Dora, you've seen the Noira. You've held it. Wouldn't you pay anything to possess it?"

I exhaled hard, remembering how I had wanted to keep the necklace forever. To keep me grounded, I squeezed the pin in my pocket tight.

He shook his head. "If you don't give me the money, I'm dead."

"Who's going to kill you? Answer me."

My dad combed his beard with his fingers. "You will have killed me."

I tipped my head to one side, not believing what I'd heard. "What?"

"I have to have the money to be free." Rupert bent his head and covered his face with his hand. "Won't you help me, Dora?"

"You're my father," I said. Perhaps both of us needed reminding. I held out my hand.

Wet glistened on my father's cheek. My heart burned. Whoever he had been, whatever he had done, now he was Wild Rupert, lonely and afraid. And for the first time he had come to me.

"If I do sell it—"

"You have to."

"Can I have some of the money?" I clapped my hand to my mouth. Oh Buddha, what had I asked? I still didn't know where he had found the necklace. I couldn't believe that it wasn't stolen, and I couldn't sell a stolen object.

My father looked down at the contents of my bottom drawer. Empty except for one of his old dapple blocks. "I never did give you much of anything, did I, Dora?"

My heart swelled and filled up my chest so much it hurt. "You taught me how to make jewelry. You gave me a love of design. That's plenty."

"No, it's not. It never was." He stroked his battered cheek. "With the missing pearl—that doesn't matter, it was added later, if you get all the—sure, I can give you some of the money," he said as if to reassure himself. "How much do you need?"

"I don't know. I don't know how much Aunt Maddie's back rent is."

My father's mouth snicked shut. "Maddie's back rent?" he asked through tight lips.

I raised my eyebrows and nodded.

"No. Not for Maddie, not now, not ever."

"Why?"

"It was that Charles of hers who took Patty away."

I made a startled gargle at the back of my throat. "But Charles left after Mom," I said when I could speak.

Rupert's mouth twisted, deep and ugly. "Patty left first and that bastard followed, like a dog after a bitch."

I moved farther away from Rupert.

He didn't seem to notice.

"Aunt Maddie says—"

"She never believed me after Seattle." His gaze shifted to far away. "Where is she?"

"Who? Maddie?"

"No, her."

"Mom?" I peered at the shadows as if my mother, gone for years, might leap out. Did he mean where had I hidden the necklace? "The necklace?"

Rupert shook his head hard and grimaced in pain. "Not the necklace." He seemed to look past me or through me. "Godiva. Where is she?"

"She's at the Castle."

I stared at my father's face. The shadows made deep hollows under his eyes, the bruised one a black hole. He looked starved for something more than food.

"How do you know her name?" My eyes burned as I stared at him and realized that he knew her before. "If you knew her, why did you run?" I took a step toward him. "Is that crazy nudist why you need to sell that *Nora* necklace?" I took another step. "Is she blackmailing you?" I took a third step. "And if she is, why? What have you done?"

He shrunk back on my stool, a much-diminished man. "I did something for love once and now it's caught up with me."

I shook my head. "No more riddles, Rupert. Who killed Derek?"

"Good question, Dora. Let's hear the answer, Rupert." Lester's voice came from behind me.

I jumped. Why hadn't the bell clanged? Oh wait. It sat on the countertop.

Lester stood so close to me that his breath touched the back of my neck. He'd snuck up on us both. Good cop.

Rupert screamed. He leaped off my workbench stool. It tumbled with a crash. Bent to one side to protect his ribs, he scuttled around a display case and down the side aisle toward the front door.

Lester ran along the central aisle. I followed.

Rupert looked behind him, yelped, and pushed over the front display case. It toppled. The last remaining potato peppershaker shattered. Rupert tore out the front door.

Lester shoved aside the case and pursued. I chased after. We all thundered down the wooden sidewalk.

Even injured, my father had longer legs than me and ten years of youth on Lester, plus a head start.

The forest fire still cast a warning glow behind Dog Face Mountain. Thick morning smoke mixed with the mist to create a low-lying, choking miasma. In the gloom, Rupert reminded me of a dream figure as he sped ahead of us. I shivered in the deep cold of the early morning. My breath plumed as I breathed, miniature ghosts.

We ran down Main Street. Rupert turned at the corner that headed up to the new mall. He squeezed through a cut in the chain link fence around the construction. Security lights flashed on. Rupert half whirled around, his face stark white in the brilliant light. He stumbled, recovered, and ran on, into the clapped together shaft-like buildings half-finished.

We followed. Only a block ahead of the sheriff, I ran first into the main entrance of the main building and blackness.

Blind, I tripped over my father and fell.

He thrust me off of him. "I'm so sorry, Dora. I'm not strong like you."

"Rupert," I said.

"Sell it and save me." He scrambled away and vanished.

I struggled to stand. I'd gotten to my knees when Lester fell on top of me.

"Oomph," Lester said. He panted and wheezed. Beneath his noisy breathing, my father's footsteps clattered away.

"Rupert, wait!" I called out as best I could from under Lester's weight. For such a thin man, Lester weighed quite a bit.

"Rupert, you're making this worse," Lester wheezed out.

No answer came, except for the fading sound of Rupert's footsteps. Was this where he had hidden? If so, then where might he hide now?

I sneezed from the sawdust.

Lester crawled off me with a groan and a "Sorry, Dora." He pulled me to my feet, his strength as much a surprise as his weight. "Take my hand until we get out of the dark," he said. His strong hand closed around mine and he led me into the light.

NINETEEN

I couldn't believe what I saw.

From the computer screen my father grinned back at me with white even teeth. Clean-shaven and with a full head of hair, he looked even more handsome than I remembered from my childhood. I looked away.

Lester tapped the computer monitor screen. "Dora, you need to see this."

He sat in his chair next to his old roll-top desk, the desk scarred by decades of sheriffs who smoked and lined smoldering cigarettes along its edge. The monitor crowded the old desk. One of Mama Chin's cinnamon rolls, half-eaten, sat atop the monitor.

I looked back at my father's face. I never remembered him appearing so happy.

"It's a picture of my father from a long time ago. So what? Is that why you hauled me in here before breakfast?" I studied the cinnamon roll. It looked to have been on the monitor for quite some time.

My coffee cup still sat perched over on Mallard's desk. I wondered if Lester would mind if I made coffee.

"Dora, pay attention." Lester leaned on his elbows next to his computer. "Watch." He clicked the mouse and another screen popped up.

A newspaper article from seventeen years ago led with a huge photo of the necklace above a headline that proclaimed "MAN KILLED IN THEFT OF CURSED 'NOIRA,' WORTH MILLIONS."

Urgh, I no longer wanted anything to eat or drink.

The necklace shone forth, glorious even in black and white newsprint. Perfect in this photo, the necklace finished with an elegant black water pearl. *The missing pearl.*

From the grainy print, the necklace woman's expression appeared serene and malicious. The resemblance to Rupert's newest pin was unmistakable. The pin lay heavy in my apron pocket.

"Noira," I whispered. "That's what he meant."

Lester gave me a sharp look. "Read it." He handed me the mouse.

I gulped.

"Read it," Lester ordered.

I scrolled down so the article filled the screen, not able to stop myself, although I wanted to. The article told of an infamous necklace made by a designer named Pietro in 1892. Pietro? I'd never heard the name and I wondered why.

The article then went on about the most recent owner, an elderly, wealthy magnate in Seattle. This tycoon purchased the Noira from the previous owner's bankrupt estate only to die a few months later in a fire at his mansion, a fire set to cover up the theft of the necklace by a well-known jeweler.

At the words "a well-known jeweler," my stomach flip-flopped. When the article was written, well-known designer Rupert created with silver and gold. Now, he made tin jewelry.

"Okay, so what?" I asked. My voice squeaked.

"Look." Lester pressed the "down" arrow.

At the bottom of the article my father's photo sat next to the picture of a well-dressed old man. The old man's mouth was pursed so tight I figured he'd never smiled.

I bit back a sob, no longer able to pretend my father didn't find the necklace somehow, someway. He'd stolen it. My father stole. What else had he done? Had he lied? Had he killed the old man?

A breeze waved the plastic tarp that blocked the construction of the new jail. Underneath the fresh pine scent lurked a smell of fresh-turned earth as if the construction workers had dug a grave. Had they broken into the tunnel that led to the original jail cell, an old converted fruit cellar beneath our feet?

"I don't even remember seeing that photo," I said. "Maybe it isn't Rupert."

Lester folded his arms, a cop stance I hated.

"It doesn't even really look like him now."

"Dora," Lester said.

"So it could be anybody." I knew I spoke a lie.

"No." Lester typed a few keys and the monitor screen began to morph. "I learned Mallard's new program." He ran a hand through his hair. "Pretty amazing—" Lester pressed "enter" and my father's face changed.

Rupert aged. He lost hair and gained wrinkles.

"It ages at-large major criminals' faces." With a single keystroke Lester added a gray beard. Except for the wide, toothy smile, my father now looked as if the photo had been taken yesterday, or the day before, when he wasn't black-eyed and beaten. "And then searches the Internet for similar facial features."

If Mallard possessed enough funds to promote his new computer program, enough funds so that he could walk away from the job of sheriff, from Starke... Naw, not the geeky, sweaty Mallard I knew. Or thought I knew.

I gestured at the screen. "How did that help you find the article?"

"Program works both ways so I ran Rupert's face from Henry's article through the program after we found, um, you found, the dead man."

"Curse Henry," I muttered under my breath, not loud enough for Lester to hear.

"Oh, Dora, I'm sorry that happened," Lester said. He reached up and pulled the cinnamon roll off the monitor. "It's a bit stale."

"Made with milk and butter and I'll take it." I grabbed it from him and took a bite. Even old, it tasted of the good times between Lester and me.

"I don't know what good knowing all this computer stuff will do me after I leave," Lester said. His shoulders hunched.

Damn the town council for not giving Lester a leave of absence. I hated the pain on his face. "You can get a job easy with any police department." I hoped Lester heard the truth in my words.

"I didn't learn it for another job. I learned it for my little Jimmy."

Jimmy? His grandson? A photo of Jimmy sat next to the monitor. Now that I looked at it, it seemed computer generated.

Lester caught my glance. "I didn't have any recent photos of him." His shoulders sagged. "My fault, I never was a father to my son or a grandfather to Jimmy. I was always too busy being the one and only Sheriff of Starke."

"Lester, that's not true." I wished I could give him more than a denial. I wished I could show him how he'd always helped me, with long talks over cinnamon buns, fresher than the one I now munched.

"Too busy taking care of Starke and now it's too late." Lester sat up and drew back his shoulders. "Well, at least now I can help my son find the son-of-a-bitch who killed my grandson."

My heart contracted. I tried to think of something to say to alleviate Lester's suffering. We all suffer in life and some of us suffer so much. I couldn't bring back his grandson, killed in a hit-and-run in Houston only a couple of years ago.

I swallowed a bit of hard bun. I couldn't save his grandson. Maybe I could save my father. "My father isn't a criminal, no matter what this article says." I flipped my hand at the monitor in a dismissive gesture. "Much less a major one. He's just old Wild Rupert, a mountain recluse."

Lester gave me one of his signature "I know you're playing hooky" looks. "Dora, I hauled you in here because you have to know Rupert is dangerous."

"Not to me."

"He's a thief and a murderer." Lester pointed a finger at my father's photo as if he pointed a gun. "He stole and killed over a thing, a stupid bit of nothing." The sheriff squeezed the trigger on his imaginary gun.

I gulped. I wanted Lester to go to Mama Chin's and buy us a fresh cinnamon roll. And while we sat and sipped cop coffee and split the roll, I wanted to tell him about the Noira necklace and my father and what little I knew and what I suspected. I wanted the heavy noose weight of the Noira off of my neck.

"Dora, once a man starts killing..."

"My father would never hurt me." I swallowed again and almost choked.

Rupert hurt me every time he stayed away. It wasn't my father who saw I got to school. It was Aunt Maddie. It wasn't Rupert who wiped away my tears when I fell. That was Maddie too. And it was Lester who taught me to stay in school and do the right thing and to shoot a gun.

I remembered the article about Dog Mountain Ski Resort and the photo of the recluse artist, Wild Rupert. Godiva mentioned it. Had she spotted my father as the thief of the Noira and blackmailed him? Or Henry? Or even Aunt Maddie? Or Derek? Is that what got him killed?

Dear Buddha, had my father lied to me? Had he really killed two men? My shoulders slumped. I shook my head. No, it couldn't be true. I so didn't want to believe it. But if Rupert stole the necklace, what else did he do? My father's tin pin weighted my pocket and my soul.

Tin. Tin that came from an old, old can.

"Canned peaches," I said. I now knew where Rupert hid, right under the noses of the law.

"Peaches?" Lester blinked. "What have canned peaches got to do with anything?"

"Nothing. I'm just hungry." I ate another bite of cinnamon bun. I didn't want Lester thinking about the old jail cell beneath our feet. My father might be there, listening.

"You're always hungry." Lester's words pulled me back to the present. "If you'd stop that Buddha nonsense and eat meat once in a while, you'd be fine." He scooted his chair closer to mine so we sat knee to knee. "Dora, you found that man's body in your father's cabin. Why won't you listen?"

I held my breath as I remembered that my father had known who Derek was and had known he was dead. Was he lying about everything else? And yet...

"He didn't take his clothes off," I said. Who had stripped the body? Who knew about the necklace besides Rupert and, I realized with a gulp, me?

"What?" Lester asked.

"My father, Rupert, he was startled when I asked him why Derek was naked. So he couldn't have killed Derek."

Lester rubbed his hand over his face. "Dora, somebody else may have come by later and stripped the body."

"Who else would know about—" Oops, I almost said necklace again. I had rubies and platinum and an onyx woman on the brain. And now a black freshwater pearl.

"Maybe Godiva found her brother and since they're nudists she wanted him to be found..." Lester waved his hand in a dismissive gesture. "Or maybe somebody wanted to cast suspicion on Godiva."

Exactly what Godiva had said.

"Why didn't she call you, then?" I asked.

"She did, remember? And maybe she didn't want to be found with her brother's body because she'd be the main suspect, as the closest relative."

I'd said the same to Godiva.

"Rupert didn't kill Derek and I'll find out who did." I realized as I spoke that I knew next to nothing about the victim. I needed to find out more.

Lester crossed his arms over his chest. "I already know who killed that man."

Even with the leather elbow patches on his jacket, he looked every inch the sheriff. The sheriff who had already tried and condemned my father and would use what I told him as further evidence against Rupert.

The last of the cinnamon roll tasted bitter in my mouth. How eager was Lester to close this, his last case and his first murder?

"I'm leaving in four days, and no matter what I have to do," —he touched the gun at his hip— "I'm not leaving an unsolved murder behind me." His chin dropped to his chest. "Maybe I never was much of a sheriff, never really had to be." His head came up. "Until now."

Ohm, eager didn't begin to describe it. Lester sounded more than determined to find Rupert. He sounded obsessed.

I hunched my shoulders. "Maybe you won't find him."

Lester sat back in his chair and regarded me. "I will and when I do, what do you think Rupert will do?"

"He'll run. He always runs." Or would he? I didn't know anymore what my father might do.

"Where will he run? To the mountains?" Lester gestured out at the window where smoky sunlight streamed in. "Into the fire? Or into a snowstorm?"

The first of the winter storms could roll in tonight and the mountains would transform from a sanctuary to a death sentence.

"He's got no money to run anywhere else," Lester continued.

My stomach churned. Rupert could have plenty of money if I sold the necklace to Nance. Would that be the only way to save him?

"What happens when he's cornered?" Lester persisted. "He's wild. What do wild animals do when cornered?"

"Fight," I whispered.

Lester dropped his voice to match mine. "What happens if he fights?"

I brought my chin up. "Will you kill him?"

If my father died during capture, who would ever know if he were truly guilty or not? Who besides me would care? I remembered Godiva's last words to me that she could save Rupert. Had that been a threat? Or an offer?

Lester scooted his chair back.

"Will you do whatever it takes to finish off your illustrious career, Sheriff?" I hated every word as I spoke them, but couldn't help myself.

"Dora." Lester's one word contained enough pain for both of us.

I stood. "If that's all, Sheriff, I'm going."

"You're not going until I say."

"You can't hold me here."

"Since you're a material witness, I can."

I gasped. "You'd arrest me?"

Lester stood.

"Fine, go ahead and toss me in the old jail cell." As I said it, I realized it might not be a good idea to open up Rupert's hiding place. I stomped my foot in case Rupert hid below to warn him.

Lester took a step toward me.

"Maybe you're right. You never were a good sheriff." I had to get out and I had to get out now.

Lester winced. Hurt showed in every seamed line of his face. Before he recovered, I walked to the door.

"Dora, wait, please," I heard behind me.

I turned and shut the door on Lester's sorrowful face.

TWENTY

I stopped on the sidewalk a couple of hundred feet from the Sun Dog Mall. If my father still hid in that mining shaft monstrosity maybe I could coax him out.

Tony worked on the torn section of the fence. Next to him sat a heavy chain and sturdy new padlock for the gate.

The mismatched quartet who stood outside the entrance ignored me. The Alpha Male and Alpha Female of the Dog Developers were shoulder to shoulder across from Mama Chin and Mrs. McGarrity. Alpha Female, rail thin, wore a gorgeous fitted suede coat with those hideous, fashionable one-ugly-leather-fits-all boots. Suede that would spot with the first snowflake and boots that would slither on ice. Not a native. A stranger.

Used to be months between "stranger sightings" in Starke, save when Old George forgot to wear his pants. Not anymore.

Mrs. McGarrity and Mama Chin stood boobs to face. Mama Chin and Mrs. McGarrity looked ready to go mano-y-mano or rather womano-y-womano, with the Dogs as referees. I backed away.

I headed to the store. There I showered and put on the lesser of two evils, the less dirty black jeans and T-shirt, hoping that'd refresh and renew. No such luck. I righted and sat on the stool that Rupert had used. Had it only been an hour or so ago? I laid my head on my crossed arms on my workbench. I'd close my eyes for five minutes...

Derek sat in the chair, naked and dead. He opened his mouth and said in Nance's voice, "Dora, you always miss the obvious."

I awoke with a yelp and tumbled off the stool.

Nance reached out and caught me.

Nance. Here in Starke. Buddha help us all.

As Nance propped me back up, I turned my head and stared at a huge red dot centered over her left nipple. I reared back and almost fell off the stool again.

"Wake up and be in the moment," Nance said.

I hated it when she spoke in Buddhist clichés. I righted myself, rubbed my sleep-numbed face. I dared another glance at Nance and her huge red circles.

She wore another one of her self-designed dresses. No matter the weather or circumstance, Nance always wore a dress.

For all her skill in jewelry design, for all her deft salesmanship and extravagant creativity, her dress designs remained a disaster. This dress, in a red and white bull's eye pattern, exacerbated Nance's gawky height. She'd cut the material so that a bull's eye centered over each breast and gave her enormous bright red nipples.

"You need one-pointed attention." Nance picked up my hot wire pen and touched the dog's too long nose of my Dog Face Mountain wax pattern. "If you take away a twitch here," she said and deftly removed the tiniest bit of wax, "and smooth this here," —she drew the pen along his jaw line— "he's not rabid anymore."

She'd transformed my Dog Face wax pattern into a friendly, tail-wagger of a dog with two touches. I hated how she could do that, or maybe how I couldn't. What else was I missing?

"Thanks, I guess." I sounded petulant, even to myself.

"You're welcome, Dorky Dora," Nance said, using one of her favorite nicknames for me.

I shook my head to clear out the sleep cobwebs. A crick in my neck made me flinch. Sometime soon, I needed to sleep in a bed, preferably mine, if Aunt Maddie didn't follow through on her threat to throw me out.

Nance turned to the countertop. "Get your stool over here," she commanded.

I opened my mouth to protest her imperious tone. And closed it again. I knew Nance.

"It took me forever to get up here," Nance said. "First ditzing with the bank and then the highway was closed because of the fire."

Oh no, a closed highway meant people would change their minds and not come up for Starke's, I mean Aurora's, grand opening.

"Who's minding your gallery, Nance?" I asked. "What if they close the highway again? Don't you think you'd better head home?" With each sentence, my voice rose with desperation.

Nance opened the first of two paper bags on the counter.

The aroma of Mama Chin's burgers wafted toward me. I drooled.

"Here's breakfast." She opened the second bag and the smell of fresh coffee followed close on the burger perfume.

I pulled my stool to the counter, resisting the urge to snatch both bags from Nance. "Are those vegan burgers from Mama Chin's?" I asked, instead of grabbing.

"Silly woman didn't want to cook them this early in the morning." Nance pulled the burgers from the bag. "But I explained to her about customer service."

I winced. I'd been the butt of many of Nance's explanations. I sometimes believed I'd become a Buddhist because Nance was. It was easier to surrender. Mama Chin must have felt the same way.

"She fries her burgers in bear fat," I said.

"The Dalai Lama eats meat," Nance said. Her response whenever she ate meat. "Besides, I'm sure it's vegetable shortening. I tasted it while that lovely lady cooked the burgers."

"You stood next to Mama Chin while she cooked?"

"Of course. I wanted to be certain she did the burgers right."

My mouth dropped open. If I'd done that, Mama Chin would have beaten me to death with her spatula. Nance never ceased to annoy, uh, amaze me. I filled my mouth with a bite of burger. Yum.

Nance jumped off her stool, burger in hand. She always stayed in motion. Maybe that was how she also stayed stick thin.

She trotted to my workbench and started pulling open drawers with her free hand.

I raised my eyebrows at Nance's new eccentricity. "What are you looking for?" I almost asked why she rummaged through my stuff, but was afraid to hear the answer. Bad enough she had invaded my world.

Nance's head jerked up from where she'd stuck it in my workbench's bottom drawer. She waved her burger around. Bits of vegetable matter flew.

"So after breakfast..." She took a big bite of burger and pointed at the counter where I sat. "You and I will move this counter," she said as she chewed, "over to here," she gestured across the room to in front of the picture window, "and see how it looks."

A muscle twitched under my left eye.

"Then that case there needs to move over here." Nance took another bite. Her eyes narrowed as she stared at the toppled case.

"Oh, Nance, no," I said through masticated vegan burger. Since the eighteen months I'd worked for Nance, I'd managed to bury the memories of her moving fetish. Good thing Aunt Maddie wasn't around or there might be another murder.

Nance ignored me. She had spotted the trap door to the tunnels. "What's in here?" Without waiting for an answer, she popped her last bite of burger into her mouth and then grabbed the door and yanked it up. "Eew," she commented as she peered down into the cellar space below, "there's all sorts of horrid trash down here."

I sighed and chewed. There went my dream of using the old tourist items as additional collateral for a loan from Nance.

"Somebody's been down there. I see footprints in the dust," Nance muttered. She looked up and glanced around the store. "Now where did I see that flashlight?"

A horrid suspicion, fueled by enough caffeine to wake up my brain, sprang into my mind. Nance mentioned the Noira when I called her, eons—a couple of nights—ago. I set my half-finished burger down and stood up. "When I called you, you knew it was the Noira just from my description."

Nance looked at me, her mouth half-open. Her teeth showed burger remnants. "What?"

"Is that what you're searching for?"

She let go of the trap door. It slammed down, and. I jumped.

With one hand Nance smoothed the fabric of her dress, which only drew attention to the bullseyes. "Shoot me here," the dress seemed to say, "or here."

"The Noira's unique." She stepped to her old, now my new, laptop.

"That computer you gave me doesn't work," I said. Like the kiln, I almost added.

"Don't be silly. I'd never give you anything broken." She turned on the old monitor, and the desktop immediately appeared. Figured it would work for Nance.

I sighed and went to look over her shoulder.

"Now where," Nance said as she connected to the Internet, "did I find those articles about Wild..." The laptop died. She straightened up and placed her hand over one bullseye. "Never mind, I know it by heart. Attachment leads to suffering," she began in a singsong voice.

I groaned. I despised Nance in her favorite Buddhist sage mode. "I know—"

She held her hand up, a Buddhist traffic cop. "Everyone who became attached to the Noira suffered death. Pietro, the twenty-three-year-old designer."

"Only twenty-three?" Admiration and envy warred in me. "He was that good that young?"

Nance nodded. "The Noira was only his third master design. And his last."

My shoulders slumped. "I can't even get a little pin right." I gestured in the direction of my corrected-by-Nance Dog Face pin.

Nance patted my shoulder. "You'll get there. You've got talent."

I smiled.

"You should be grateful you're not a prodigy, a genius like Pietro." Nance frowned at the computer screen as if remembering a personal tragedy. "He committed suicide hours after giving his ex-lover Noira the necklace." Nance shook her head. "What a waste. And such bad karma." She gave a wave. "Pietro cursed his famous actress ex-girlfriend Noira with the necklace. They say he knew Noira's vanity would force her to wear the necklace where all could see the resemblance to Noira herself."

"So?" I said. Who wouldn't want to resemble that beautiful onyx centerpiece?

"Some people saw the African features in the face of the onyx woman, a slight exaggeration of Noira's face."

I remembered the exquisite full lips of the black onyx woman.

"In 1892, Noira could no longer pass for white. That was a death knell for Noira's career," Nance continued. "When her life lay in ruins, she followed her ex-lover and killed herself. The curse continued after Noira's death and other suicides and murders followed." She jerked her head away from the computer. "Oh, Dora, I read about Wild Rupert—"

"My father never killed anybody," I said.

"People kill for a beauty as great as the Noira," Nance breathed the word Noira like a mantra. Desire flushed her cheeks, and I suspected her face resembled mine when I'd held the Noira. Nance's look intensified. "What would it be like to see the Noira, to hold such glory?"

"Magnificent, it was—" I stopped.

Nance turned her stare to me, her eyes sharp as a hawk's. "What did you say?"

"Magnificent. Breakfast."

"That wasn't it." Nance placed her hands on her hips. She resembled a bird of prey about to pounce, a hawk with a bizarre bullseye plumage. "You've held—"

"You never answered my question, Nance." I mimicked her with my own hands on my hips.

"What am I doing here?" Nance stepped out into the middle of the room and opened her arms wide. She whirled in a circle arms gesturing around the room "This is my new gallery."

I choked on the swallow of coffee I'd just taken. "Huh?" I managed.

Nance stopped mid-spin and clasped her hands to her bosom. "That's why I'm here, to fix it." With her hands in an attitude of prayer centered in mid-chest, the red bullseyes bulged even more. They seemed to be pointing right at me.

Nance fixing something meant disaster.

"This is my aunt's store," I said.

"Not for long." Nance spun again. "As soon as I buy—do the furnishings come with? Do I want these furnishings?" She paused and fingered the carved wood tree.

Life size, it dominated a back corner. Meant to display necklaces and earrings, Charles had carved it days before he left. He had been a far better sculptor than painter.

"Oh, I want this. How much?"

"You can't throw us out. You can't do that to my aunt. I won't let you."

Nance stopped again at my tone. "I'm saving her, and you. That's what I'm doing."

"The store is all Aunt Maddie has," I said. It'd destroy her to lose what my aunt believed was her last chance to get Charles back, to have love return. I understood that, but had no idea how to explain it to Nance.

Nance tilted her head. "I figured when you were selling your designs that she was selling the store."

Even in her bizarre body-position, every word she spoke sounded pure business. Born of a wealthy and famed family of jewelers in New York, she'd come out to Boise and established her own flourishing gallery. I respected her success.

I remembered how Aunt Maddie almost swallowed her pride to ask for a loan. "We need the money for rent. If you could see us a loan for a bit." I stopped at the look on Nance's face.

"What would you secure that loan with?" Nance gestured around the store. She dropped her arms and gave me a hard stare. "Or what do you have to sell?"

Sell it to Nance. She'll pay what you ask.

"The Noira's stolen." I said it to see Nance's reaction. Also to remind myself.

Nance jerked back. She recovered and flipped her hand back and forth in a dismissive gesture. "If recovered, it'd only go to a museum. Locked away, imprisoned."

"An old man died."

Nance stood frozen for a moment. She never stood so still. "That was a long time ago."

"Not this last killing." *Murders followed.*

Nance stroked her chest where the Noira might rest. "Awful. Tragic. But the Noira, the Noira..." She gave herself a little shake. "Dora, I'll need you to start this afternoon cleaning some of this stuff out. Where is your aunt? Mads, that's her name, right?"

"Mads?" I squeaked.

"Well, whatever. She'll need to clean, too. I'm sure she'll be as good an employee as you are, Dora."

I worked my jaws, unable to make a sound.

"Maybe I should make a list." Nance dived into her also custom-designed-by-Nance handbag. Made of heavy-duty bright-red carpet material, the suitcase-sized bag closed with a set of interlocking lion's jaws. Those jaws looked powerful enough to clamp down on any thief.

Nance held up a small wax pot, stared at it, then tossed it back into the bag.

"I'm not your employee."

Nance looked up from her rummage. In one hand she held a thick sheaf of bills. Twenties.

"My Aunt Maddie, and that's Miss Maddie to you, is not your employee."

"Not until she—"

"Not ever."

"Now, Dorky Dora—"

"Don't call me that."

Nance straightened up. "All right, Dora Starke, you need to adjust your attitude while you're my employee."

Heat roiled through my body. "I don't care how wealthy you are. You can't come in and take over people's lives."

Pain filled Nance's face. "You asked me to help."

I shook my head. "Oh, Nance," I said, in a much softer tone, "I asked for your help in saving the store for my aunt."

Nance smiled. "You don't know what you need. I do. Now, I'll need to move this display cabinet."

"You're not getting this store." I pointed at the front door. "Out. Now."

She looked at me, open-mouthed. "Dora, you've changed over the months you've been gone."

"I've got work to do," I said.

"I must say the change hasn't been for the better, Dorky."

"Out," I said.

"As soon as I talk to your Aunt Mads—"

"I wouldn't."

Nance harrumphed.

"Avoid Aunt Maddie."

Nance swept my half-eaten breakfast back into the brown bag. "You'll see. Once you're on the True Path, you'll see." She strode toward the front door. "Don't worry," she flung the words over her shoulder, "I'll be back."

She stomped off, her bright red nipples leading the way, listing a little to the left because of her huge handbag. Wondered what she carried in there, maybe the same assortment of jewelry equipment as I did in my apron. I wanted to go after her, to apologize for my harsh words.

My breakfast had walked out the door. As had any chance of selling my patterns to Nance. Or getting a loan from her.

One catastrophe at a time.

I might have an opportunity to retrieve one problem. I checked up and down the street. No Lester, no Mallard.

Time to run.

TWENTY-ONE

The yellow crime tape screamed *Keep out, Dora.* How could it be so specific to me? I blinked and the words changed to "Crime Scene Do Not Cross." I needed sleep.

I covered my eyes with my hands and pressed tight. I sniffed, fearing to smell that taint of death, but there was only the pungent stench of the forest fire. A lone car swooshed on the nearby highway, a whisper of sound that said *hurry.*

Whoever had strung the brilliant yellow bands that glittered festive in the sun, across Rupert's door, had been enthusiastic. I suspected Mallard. How could I get inside?

I rummaged in my apron pockets for a tool and came up with two pairs of needle-nose pliers, my next-to-favorite loupe in a plastic bag. So that's where that had gone—a tiny ball peen hammer, a small steel dappling block. No wonder my apron hung heavy; myriad silver jump rings in various sizes co-mingled with cotton lint, three screwdrivers, and two lumps of wax that were once attempts at Dog Face pins. No help there.

In the corner of the last pocket rested the remains of Rupert's newest pin, crushed by the weight of my dappling block. The tin copy of the Noira's face mocked me. When I retrieved the real necklace, I wanted to toss it into Looney Jump Creek to be lost forever. Get rid of the damned thing. I didn't want to leave it in my father's cabin to be found by someone else, someone who might be a killer.

I pried a strip of crime tape from the door. Several strands pulled free and flapped in the breeze. A brittle wind that promised a bitter winter picked up one strip and stuck it to my apron, making me jump.

Another piece of tape fluttered over and adhered to my apron. Batting at it made it stick to my hand.

I stood there. Stuck.

Prying the piece of tape from my hand made it tear. Back it went onto the doorframe. I pulled at the tape on my apron front, which held fast to the fabric and my ohm pin. The tape obscured its face, as if my beliefs were now masked.

I shivered. The cold cut to my bones. The brittle temperature meant no snow, not yet. My soul ached as well. Much of me yearned for simpler times—say, two days ago.

Unpinning the ohm pin, I pulled the tape away. That piece too went on the doorframe. Both strips were torn and mangled. I re-stuck the flapping tapes to the door as well as possible. And paused.

Did it matter that I took down the crime tape? After all, wasn't the tape to keep out criminals and to preserve evidence? Hadn't Lester and Mallard already searched the place? Should I go to the sheriff's office and confess what I knew? Turn Rupert in? Hope he didn't get killed during capture?

I couldn't betray my father.

The Noira burned with an icy fire all the lives it touched and turned them to ash. We were all trapped within its curse.

Trapped. Ash. Now I knew how I could retrieve the Noira without going inside. I turned away from the now disaster-taped door and trotted toward the back of the cabin.

Yes, there was the chimney's ash trap. I dropped to my knees and raised the little metal door and reached inside.

I sneezed. With the back of my hand I scrubbed at my nose. And sneezed again. Ash flew everywhere.

My nose itched and twitched. Ash covered my apron, my jeans, and my hands and probably my face. Tiny motes of long ago fires danced in the air, they tasted dark and rancid. Ugh.

I sighed and plunged my hand back into the ash trap. I yanked it back out again as something crawled across the back of my hand. A Daddy Long Leg. Ick, daddy-long-legs, black widows, and spiders galore, oh, my.

Although my father never had a fire, neither had he ever bothered to clean out the fireplace, the chimney, or the trap. Maybe he didn't realize the ash trap could be accessed from outside the cabin, and that a little door led into the chimney for easy disposal of the ashes. Maybe he didn't care. If he did know, maybe somehow he wished the Noira would disappear from the ash trap and his life.

My hand closed around an object too small to be the necklace. An enormous black freshwater pearl lay on my palm, the same pearl that once hung from the Noira and finished it with an echo of the woman's pendant form.

I bowed my head. In the newspaper article, the necklace had been complete. Rupert had to have stolen the necklace. There was no denial left in me.

Wrapping the pearl in my handkerchief, I put it in my pocket and rummaged in the ashes for the necklace. My hand brushed up against a square, flat metallic object, wedged in the trap.

How much of his life had my father secreted away here? I pulled out a couple of fistfuls of ashes. More motes of old fires long cold fluttered in the smoky, sunny air. I coughed. The Noira might add me to its list of victims if I died of ashy lungs. Or a spiders bite. I shuddered.

My fingers groped at the square, which didn't budge. What could it be?

Underneath the metal square, I touched the smooth cold of the Noira, the naked woman pendant sensuous beneath my fingers. The necklace must have tumbled from its bag. I snagged it out. But the cloth, caught on the woman's foot, followed. The necklace must have fallen out before. The pearl had snagged on something and been torn off.

I replaced the necklace and put it in a pocket. I fumbled around the mysterious square, determined to get it out. From inside, came the sounds of paper rustling in the fireplace.

At the sound, I froze and listened with one-pointed attention. A log thumped. Somebody was setting a fire in Rupert's cabin. Whatever was in the ash trap was about to be destroyed. Perhaps with my fingers.

I hooked said fingers under an edge of the square. Something wriggled on my hand. I whimpered and yanked hard. It scraped loose against the bricks, along with some of my skin.

The cat spider on my hand scurried off. I held a metal and glass framed photograph covered with ash. Through the ash, I saw two naked figures, both of whom I recognized, one of whom was family.

I sat back on my heels, holding an answer. Maybe not the answer I wanted. That somehow all that had happened over the past couple of days was a mistake easily explained. But an answer all the same.

A fire crackled in my father's fireplace. I could already feel the heat coming from the open ash trap and scrambled to my feet.

My car stood parked at the front of the cabin. I didn't know why someone would park next to me and just go inside my father's cabin. But that gave me an opportunity to escape with my booty, no questions asked. At the front of the cabin there was the only window and the front door. I crept around the side.

Each step crunched on the pine needles. I hoped whoever set the fire was too engrossed to notice me sneaking to my car. I couldn't imagine who had set the first fire in decades—certainly not my father. I wished for Great Grandpa's gun. Maybe I could use my dappling block as a weapon.

I peered around the corner to the front and saw Mallard crouched outside the front door, gun in one hand, the other pushing away the fallen crime tape. Aunt Maddie's car was only a hundred feet away. Parked next to it was Godiva's pink monstrosity. Next to the Cadillac was the patrol car. I must have been so focused on the contents of the trap I didn't hear either car arrive.

Mallard seemed intent on the inside of the cabin. I had to make it to my car and get away before he caught me and asked any silly little questions, such as, "What are you doing here, Dora?" and "What's that in your pocket, Dora?" Once I had the necklace secreted away I'd be happy. Well, maybe not happy, but more able to talk to Starke's deputy.

I watched him, my neck craned as I crept by the side. He pushed the door open and took a little hop into the cabin and yelled, "Freeze!"

A startled squawk from inside answered him. I took my cue and scuttled low, a stealthy crab—whose apron clattered against her knees as she went.

Mallard spun around, banging his gun on the doorframe.

I jumped back with a yelp. Reflex, in case the gun went off. Too many guns had gone off in the last few days.

"There you are," Mallard said, or accused rather, for suspicion colored his every word. "Where have you been?"

Ohm. Even more suspicion.

"Who do you have on 'Freeze' in the cabin?" I asked. Best way to avoid answering a question is to ask another question. I trotted to Mallard, trying to pretend I spent most of my time lurking—um—sneaking—um—hanging around outside my father's cabin.

I peered over his shoulder.

Godiva stood next to the fireplace, in which a large fire crackled. She wore yet another velour exercise outfit, this one in brilliant burnt orange. How many of those suits did the woman own? I supposed that being a nudist might cut down on wardrobe requirements, but still, show a little imagination.

"Dora?" Mallard asked again in a policeman's tone.

"Godiva, put out that fire." I strode to the fireplace and placed the photograph facedown on top of the mantelpiece. With both hands, I used the fireplace shovel to scoop ashes on the flames.

"Hey, stop," Godiva protested. "I'm cold."

How could she expect to survive Starke's winter if the snow ever came?

"You want a chimney fire?" I pulled the logs apart. "Another forest fire?"

"Dora, Mrs. McGarrity saw you breaking into Rupert's cabin as she drove by," Mallard accused.

"Mrs. McGarrity and her Meals on Wheels," I said and sighed. Of course, she only delivered one meal up to Gummy Annie's place, but still I should've remembered she'd go past right about the time she did indeed drive past.

"Dora—"

"I didn't break in." I pointed at Godiva. "She broke in."

"I did not. The tape was already trashed." She pointed back at me. "When I saw a car parked out front, I figured there was somebody already inside."

"Mrs. McGarrity saw *you*, Dora," Mallard said. He looked from Godiva to me. I guess he decided neither of us appeared all that dangerous so he put away his gun.

"Why did it take you so long to get here?" I asked Mallard.

Mrs. McGarrity insisted on swift justice, preferably while she was still on the scene. I wondered why she hadn't made a citizen's arrest of me while she had the chance.

Mallard shrugged. "Mrs. McGarrity's cell phone didn't work up here."

Oh no, the Widows Brigade had gone high-tech. We were all doomed.

"She had to drive to where it did," he continued.

I nodded and turned back to Godiva. "What're you doing here?"

"What are you looking for?" Mallard asked.

A better question, and I suspected I knew the answer. Godiva searched for the money, or the necklace, or both.

"Get inside and shut the door, you're letting in the cold," Godiva said, an answer that was not an answer.

Mallard put his hands on his hips in an echo of the sheriff. "Godiva, I half-figured you were the killer, returned to the scene of the crime."

"I think she is," I whispered under my breath.

"What did you say, Dora?" Mallard asked.

Maybe Godiva heard my words, for she turned to the fireplace and held her hands close to the dying embers. "I wanted to see where my dear brother died."

Mallard frowned. I suspected he didn't quite believe Godiva's glib reply.

Perhaps she caught the frown. She pointed at my apron. "That's ash." She shot me a look as suspicious as Mallard's. "From the ash trap."

I looked down. Oh, great Hotei, ash covered the front of my apron with two dark circles on my knees.

"What have you been up to this time, Dora?" Mallard sounded as if I were some hardened criminal.

I stood still and hoped the necklace didn't clink in my apron pocket. I didn't want to say "retrieving the Noira necklace from where I put it when Lester interrupted me standing over a dead body." Mallard wouldn't approve.

"Ash trap?" Mallard asked. He raised one finger. "My grandmother had one of those." He lowered his hand to rest it on his holster. "We didn't search it for evidence—"

Evidence. "Which I found." I retrieved the framed photograph.

Ash on the glass made the photo difficult to see. I didn't want Mallard or Godiva any closer to the necklace in my pocket so with a corner of my apron I scrubbed the glass.

The photo revealed a man with his arm held close around his female companion. It had been shot from the waist up, a mercy since both were naked. The woman had crossed her arms around her ample bosoms, another mercy, although flesh spilled both above and below her arms.

Although younger, it was easy to recognize the subjects. My father didn't look much different from the photo in the newspaper article. They stood in front of a large column, a column I now recognized as part of the burning mansion that Rupert compulsively re-created in his pins.

I held up the cleaned photo and shoved it in Godiva's direction. "How do you explain this?"

Godiva reared back as if I held a snake instead of metal, paper, and glass.

Mallard stared at the photo. Then he stared at Godiva, his eyebrows in a "V".

Godiva crossed the room in three steps. "Give me that."

I pulled it out of her reach.

She snatched at it, her hands claws. "It's mine."

"You said you didn't know Wild Rupert very well. That you knew him as a drifter named Bertie," Mallard said.

"A drifter who was a fellow nudist," Godiva said.

"You didn't come up here to open a nudist colony," I said.

"I did too." A petulant whine crept into Godiva's voice.

"You came up here to find my father."

"What's your relationship with Rupert?" Mallard asked.

"I don't have a relationship with Rupert."

"You're lying," I said.

From the photo, it appeared they'd once been close, in fact skin tight. Given Rupert's terrified reaction when he saw Godiva in the store, she'd hounded him, maybe blackmailed him. Had she also killed her brother, Derek, to avoid splitting the profits?

Godiva tried another grab at the photo.

"Hand it over, Dora," Mallard said.

I complied, grateful it was out of my hands and that Mallard took it as serious evidence. "What else have you lied about?" I asked Godiva.

She stood panting, her long hair over her face, all composure gone.

Mallard held out an imploring hand toward Godiva. "You know this looks bad. You're at the scene of your brother's murder. And possibly destroying evidence."

Or searching for the necklace. Or the money. Or both.

"Means, motive, and opportunity," I chimed in.

Godiva picked up a hank of hair and tossed it over a shoulder. "No motive." She flounced toward the door. "With Derek dead, I have nothing. Check the will."

"Hold on." Mallard grabbed her upper arm. Gently.

"Unhand me. I won't tolerate police brutality."

Mallard dropped her hot potato arm.

She pranced out to her car at an amazing clip. Godiva got in and roared off in pink glory.

Mallard ran his hand through his hair in an imitation of Sheriff Lester. "How that old man ever did this job for so long, I'll never know."

I almost suggested it might be an easier job without a murder to solve, but stopped myself.

"Let's go," Mallard said.

"Why me?" I asked again.

Mallard gave a small groan. "Starkers," he muttered. He gestured at the cabin door. "You need to give a statement. Out."

"I already gave a statement. To you, just now."

"Dora..."

Urp. Out I went.

TWENTY-TWO

I slumped in a hard wooden chair. Too familiar.

A few hours had transformed the sheriff's office, and not for the better. Now I knew why Mrs. McGarrity hadn't stuck around at my father's cabin. She had a party to go to, or from the looks of it, maybe a funeral.

A large bouquet of black balloons sat on Lester's desk. One had escaped and floated near the ceiling. Across the center of the ceiling a bright lavender banner with black uneven letters proclaimed: HAPPY RETIREMENT, LES. No one ever called Lester "Les." The S on the banner had been squeezed into the end. And he hadn't retired; he'd quit.

It seemed fortunate, depending on how I defined fortunate, that I had a chair, for the tiny office bulged with bodies.

Lester ignored Mallard and me. Plenty else vied for his attention. Two-thirds of the Widows Brigade flitted around Lester's desk. His monitor had been pushed aside to make room for a large cake with lavender frosting. A once large cake, all that remained was a tiny corner piece.

A cluster of construction workers stood on the office side of the wall of plastic, taking a break from working on the new jail.

Tony, the construction foreman I'd babysat years ago, seemed ubiquitous. He wore a mustache of lavender frosting over his luxuriant mustache. He gave a little wave at me and went back to his cake. His ancient jeans showed both dust and dirt.

Would the crew soon break into the tunnel? Or the jail cell?

Did my father now sit in the fruit cellar jail cell below and cower, afraid of discovery? Did he smell the sweet aroma of lavender cake while he ate ancient canned peaches? Or had he already run, again?

I balanced a plate of cake on one aproned knee, the better to disguise the bulge of the necklace in my pocket.

Mallard sat facing me, our knees almost touching. He glared around. "This party wasn't my idea."

"Of course not," I said.

"If I'd known they were cooking this up—"

"You'd have been powerless to stop it," I finished for him. "The Widows Brigade are a force unto themselves."

Mallard nodded. "An unstoppable force." He caught on quick. We'd make a Starker out of him yet.

I took a bite of cake and almost didn't care that it was made with eggs and milk. Mrs. McChin remained as good a cook as her daughter, Mama Chin. Not eating vegan was the least of my problems, I decided, and took another bite.

Where was Mrs. McChin? It wasn't like her to miss a major opportunity for compliments on her baking. I expected I wasn't the only one who wondered. Mrs. McGarrity occasionally glanced up from her hovering over Lester at the office door. Then frowned before resuming hovering.

Mallard unlocked his center drawer. When he opened it, I saw Great Grandpa's gun in a plastic bag marked with "EVIDENCE" in red. Next to it, in another evidence bag, rested a .38 that looked like the gun I found in Rupert's cabin.

"What are you doing? Shouldn't you be out arresting Godiva?" I wanted to suggest he haul her in by her long hair, but that wouldn't be Right Action, neither the suggestion nor the hauling.

Mallard ignored me. There seemed to be a lot of that going around. He booted up his now-familiar program. "There's a new saved file," he mumbled.

I leaned forward to see and Mallard shifted his shoulder to block my view.

"Dang, Lester's better with my program than I am," he continued. Angst rang in every word.

I looked at Mallard, the cake forgotten.

Mallard had created the program that led Lester to discover Rupert's long ago indiscretion. How long had Mallard known about Rupert and the Noira necklace? He needed money to pursue his passion. Had he decided to insure his own venture capital? Was he a blackmailer? A killer?

Or was it Henry—Henry, desperate for capital?

Henry was the one who'd written the article about Wild Rupert. Or perhaps it was Aunt Maddie, also desperate for money. Was I blinded by my dislike of Godiva? No. No.

"Godiva is in this up to her naked neck," I said.

Mallard glanced at me at the word "naked," snorted, and then went back to reading the screen.

"Godiva had a *close* relationship with my father." I tapped the photograph. The metal frame cracked loud against Mallard's desk.

At the sound Lester looked over at us and frowned. Mrs. McGarrity and Mrs. McDay also stared, both their faces alive with their standard curiosity. I so wanted to stick out my tongue at them, but refrained. Let them have their curiosity and eat it too.

Mrs. McDay broke the spell when she pulled out photos of her myriad grandchildren. One glance at Lester's face and she put them back.

I wanted to pat Lester's shoulder and tell him...what? What could I, or anyone, say? Mrs. McDay reached out her hand as I wanted to. Lester turned away.

"No." Mallard pointed at the monitor screen, at a page of close-spaced text. "According to what Lester found, she's the victim here."

"She is?" I had trouble imagining Godiva as a victim, but perhaps she'd been caught in the Noira's black curse.

"She was set up by Rupert," Mallard said, "not the other way around. She's the niece of the owner. The dead owner."

I gasped.

...*little bit of nothing,* he'd called me.

"Godiva set him up then. And she's setting him up now." Did I speak the truth? Had Godiva put my father up to stealing the necklace? Killing her uncle? Derek?

"No," Mallard said. "She was set up by Rupert. He's the killer."

Anger flushed my face. "It's as logical to say that you're the killer."

Mallard leaned back in his chair, his eyebrows raised.

"You're blinded by Derek being found in Rupert's cabin," I said. "You're not even considering who else might have a reason to kill that man."

"Like who?" Mallard asked.

"Like..." Anyone who might be after the necklace, or the money. Henry, Aunt Maddie, Mallard. Or Nance. Nance, with her fervent face when she spoke of the Noira.

"Who?" Mallard repeated.

"Like Derek's *sister*, Godiva. Who's been here before. Who was looking for Rupert. Who lied about her relationship with my father."

"Rupert got close to her to get close to the necklace," Mallard continued. "Broke her heart, he did." He nodded to himself, as if that crime was as heinous as murder.

Perhaps it was. Aunt Maddie came to my mind. She'd lived her life waiting for the return of love. Was Godiva another hapless casualty and my father the villain?

No, I couldn't believe that. My father ran and Godiva hunted him.

"No," I said. "What would my father do with such a necklace? Dance around naked wearing it in his cabin?" I cringed at the image my words brought up.

I'd been so focused on finding out about the necklace and finding Rupert that I hadn't considered why he would steal the Noira. Was its curse that strong? Or Godiva's influence?

"Godiva could have killed her uncle as well as Derek," I continued. I put conviction in every word, a conviction I wasn't sure I felt anymore. "Godiva tracked Rupert down."

Mallard snorted again. I hoped that frosting came out of his nose. It'd serve him right.

"No. Godiva spoke the truth." He pointed at the monitor screen. "Lester researched the uncle's will."

"What's that got to do with it?"

"Derek got everything in a trust fund after his uncle's death. With Derek's death, the fund goes to a museum. Now, Godiva's destitute."

"That means she's got every reason to—" Oops. I opened my big mouth and almost said "blackmail Rupert."

"Reason for what?"

I stuffed the last bite of cake into my mouth while I considered an answer. "Reason for her to come to Starke and pursue Rupert for the necklace. Twice. She must have missed his return the first time," I said. Stickily.

"Naw, when we recover it, it goes to a museum."

Locked away, imprisoned.

The Noira weighed heavy in my pocket. I glanced down and was horrified to see that the outline of the pendant of the woman showed faintly through the cloth. I uncrossed my legs.

A faint clink.

"I need my gun back, now," I said, to cover. I pointed at the open drawer.

Mallard blinked. He glanced down at the side drawer of his desk and looked back at me. "It's not your gun. It's your aunt's gun."

"Actually, it's Great Grandpa's gun."

Mallard shook his head. "Whatever, or whoever—you can't have it back."

"Why not?"

"It's evidence."

"Evidence? It wasn't the gun that shot Derek." At least I could make that statement with absolute authority.

"No, you're right," Mallard agreed.

"So give it back," I said.

Mallard sweated.

"Would you rather have my aunt show up here and demand it back?"

He shuddered, set his jaw tight and shut the desk drawer. "No. There are too many guns floating around this town."

I tended to agree with him. "Mallard—"

"And there's no telling, your aunt might actually shoot somebody someday."

I shrugged. "Probably not. Us Starke's aren't very good at shooting people. Even when we do we usually miss."

"When you shoot people?" Mallard asked.

Mrs. McGarrity saved me from replying by pulling a large rectangle out of her vast, lace-tatted pocket with a flourish and a "Ta-Da!"

Several people, myself included, jumped.

"It's a check, for you, Sheriff," Mrs. McDay said.

Mrs. McGarrity held out the big check.

Tony grinned. So did I. Us Starkers all donated to that check, although, with a guilty twinge, I wished I could have donated more. Lester deserved a lot. He'd worked hard and well for thirty years as sheriff.

Lester reared back. "I don't need charity." He held up his hand in a stop gesture. "Or your pity."

Mrs. McGarrity clutched the check to her voluminous tatted dress. For once, she seemed at a loss for words.

Mrs. McDay came to Mrs. McGarrity's rescue. "Oh no, Lester dearie, it's nothing of the sort." Only Mrs. McDay could get away with calling Lester "dearie." Mrs. McDay shook her head, the cherries bobbing on her hat. "We Starkers are thanking you for all the years of great service."

"And since this town doesn't have a pension yet for sheriff," Mrs. McGarrity added. "And since you quit anyway, we figured you needed the money." Her mouth slapped shut. The widow must have realized what she'd said. She propped the check face out against Lester's monitor. "There," she said.

Lester stared at the check as if a timber rattler lay there instead.

Mrs. McGarrity looked at Mrs. McDay, dismay all over her face. Mrs. McDay raised her eyebrows and her arms. Mrs. McGarrity smiled and nodded and the two old ladies launched into an off-key and raucous version of "For He's a Jolly Good Fellow." Tony and the other construction workers joined in.

Mallard and I did too. I tried to drown out everyone else to let Lester know how much he'd meant to me growing up. Mrs. McGarrity glared at me. I realized how much I'd miss Lester. Another person who was leaving my life. I thought I'd be used to it by now.

Mrs. McChin burst into the office, one pure white braid loose and flopping on her face. "Henry's on the roof and he's threatening to kill himself!"

TWENTY-THREE

We all clustered around Cam's Auto Shop where Henry stood on top of the building's false front. He balanced precariously on the thick wood cap, above the "C" in Cam's. Behind him, a backdrop of smoke. Surreal. Unreal. Too real.

With a gulp, I remembered the high school nights Henry and I spent on that roof, making out. Why did Starkers always end up on the roofs? Was Nance right when she said, "You mountain people, you always want to go higher," whenever I outreached my jewelry making skills? Maybe. But maybe not for the reason Nance believed. Maybe we only wanted to get closer to our mountains.

Henry waved an object around.

I squinted. That couldn't be—ohm, it was. A gun. Another one. That was the trouble with living in Idaho. Everybody had guns.

"Everybody stay back," Henry said, a cliché. Of course, he was under a great deal of pressure.

I waited for my aunt's voice to ring out with a snappy comeback such as, "Well, duh, Henry." No, that would be my snappy comeback. Hers would be "Henry, get down from there, right now, you idiot." And he would.

Where was my aunt? The Widows Brigade stood next to me, close to the front, as a matter of course. Mrs. McChin had re-attached the braid to the crown of her hair, thereby restoring the signature Chin look. The construction crew, led by Tony, clustered behind Lester and Mallard. Most of the other Starkers scattered around in a loose semi-circle. The doggie developers stood outside the circle, the curs.

Nowhere did I see my aunt. I didn't see Nance either. How odd. They both adored being in the thick of it, whatever it was.

"Now, son, put the gun down," Lester said.

"No." Henry's voice sounded dark and hard. Not like Henry.

"What seems to be the problem, Henry?" said Mrs. McChin.

Henry gazed at Dog Face Mountain. He seemed not to have heard. Across the muzzle of the Dog wisps of cloud floated, serene, detached from human suffering.

"Is it because of your business going bust?" Mrs. McDay said.

Henry dropped his chin. His face twisted in shame.

I caught the Alpha Female of the Sun Dog Developers giving a small, smug smirk. "Shoot her," I wanted to say to Henry.

"Don't worry, Henry," I said instead. "Camerons lose everything. It happens all the time." It did, like clockwork.

Henry looked at the gun in his hand.

"Henry, put the gun down," Lester repeated, with more force in every word. Lester stood, loose limbed, his arms at his sides. One hand rested near his gun, almost as if a casual gesture yet I sensed that Lester could pull that gun as fast as any gunslinger.

"Camerons always come back," I added, "even richer than before."

That, too, was true. Unlike my family who lost everything and it stayed lost, the Cameron's wealth ebbed and flowed, a tide of magnitude and scarcity.

Henry glanced at me. I hated the despair I saw in his face. "A Cameron never lost a dream before, Dora."

"You know that's not true, Henry."

"That's right," Mrs. McDay piped up. "I remember about your grandfather before World War II."

"Yes, yes," Mrs. McGarrity interrupted, "we've all heard that story before, Bitsy, a million times."

"But..." Mrs. McDay started and then subsided at Mrs. McGarrity's glare.

"Put the gun down, Henry," Lester said. Each word sounded carved into stone, stone that matched Lester's face, all his expression gone. "And we'll talk."

Mallard stood silent and still, a statue to match Lester, his eyes focused and flat.

Henry gave a laugh. "I've talked, Sheriff. I've talked to other Realtors, those developers," —he gestured with his free hand at the Sun Dog pack and they edged farther away— "and bankers. I'm done talking." He gave another laugh that ended in a sob.

"Henry, please," I said.

He brought his hand holding the gun up and used the back of his hand to wipe his eyes.

Lester placed his hand on his gun. "Henry, put the gun down, son."

Henry shook his head.

"Henry, come down from there, this instant," Mrs. McGarrity said. I'm sure she tried to sound like her old school teacher, busybody self, but her voice quavered.

I wanted to run until I escaped this nightmare. Until I woke up and none of this—not my father stealing the Noira, nor Derek being killed, or the end of our dreams—had happened.

"I surely do need my car fixed up, Henry," Mrs. McDay said. "And you surely are the best mechanic for miles."

I clutched the Noira in my pocket. I wanted to blame it. Didn't it symbolize all that had gone wrong? Would Godiva have come to Starke and fired up Henry's hopes, only to have them destroyed?

"Henry?" Mrs. McChin said. "Don't you want to come down and have a cinnamon roll?"

Henry waved his hand holding the gun in a dismissive gesture.

"Clear the civilians away," Lester said to Mallard.

Oh, no. It didn't matter what Henry had done or not done, this couldn't happen. This wouldn't happen.

At Lester's words, the Sun Dog Developers scurried away, well-tailored tails down. As they went, the Alpha Female cast a look back over her shoulder. Pity seemed etched into her frown. Perhaps I'd misjudged her.

Mallard took Mrs. McGarrity's arm.

"Young man, unhand me," she said.

"Ma'am, come along."

She looked into his face and went. Mrs. McChin and Mrs. McDay trailed after her, bedraggled lost ducks that followed a defeated leader.

Henry held the gun in a tighter grip across his body.

My mind whirled. Money, it was all about money.

Tony stepped back to let the Widows Brigade pass then fell in line behind them.

"Dora," Lester said.

I didn't budge. He took my arm. "Henry," I yelled, "Nance wants to buy, um…" I couldn't force myself to say "Aunt Maddie's store."

Lester tightened his grip.

"She wants the Cameron Castle," I blurted. Ohm, no she doesn't.

Everybody looked at me. It was getting to be a habit with my fellow Starkers. At least one of the people who stared was Henry. I had all his attention.

"Really?" Henry lowered the gun.

"She's got tons of money." That answer was not a lie.

In a cluster, the Widows Brigade took a few steps back toward Cam's Auto. They knew about stray bullets.

Henry frowned. "Why? Why would she want—"

"Why not?" I found myself saying.

"Because the Cameron Castle ought to be condemned?" Mrs. McChin said.

"No," I said.

"Because the Castle has a nude squatter?" Mrs. McGarrity said.

Henry hung his head.

"Don't help her, dearies." Mrs. McDay nodded at me, the cherries on her hat bouncing. "Go on, Dora."

"Don't bother, Dora," Henry said in a too quiet voice. He raised the gun.

I sensed the police tense.

"Nance can take anyplace and make it pay big bucks," I said.

Henry hesitated.

"For Buddha's sake, she took a derelict house trailer, plonked it down on an empty lot on the outskirts of Boise, and made millions."

Henry stood frozen. The wind picked up a lock of his hair and made it dance.

"She said it's time for a high-class jewelry gallery in Starke. She's right." I gave a tiny gasp of realization. Why shouldn't it be the Cameron Castle instead of my aunt's store? If I promised to go back to work for her, would Nance give me a loan to pay off Maddie's rent? Could it be that easy?

"Could it be that simple?" Henry asked.

"Yes," we all chorused.

"Cameron Castle as a jewelry store?"

"Not a jewelry store alone. It could be all sorts of shops." I was on a roll, now.

"A mall," Mrs. McGarrity said.

"A lot better mall than that dogged mining shaft monstrosity," Mrs. McChin said.

"Hey," Tony said, "that's one of ours."

"A very nice place it is, dearie," Mrs. McDay said.

Henry beamed. "But the Castle Mall will be fabulous." He set down the gun and raised his arms. "Don't shoot. I'm coming down."

Everybody cheered.

My shoulders slumped. Mallard sweated in relief. Lester grinned one of his old full-face grins at me for a second.

Tony looked at his dust-covered watch, grinned, and said, "Quitting time."

I stood aside as the crowd dispersed and the police talked to Henry, who looked sheepish. A catastrophe averted.

Mrs. McChin patted my arm on her way by. "Good job. A shame your aunt wasn't here. She'd have brought him down even quicker."

Where was my aunt? She was still missing from the commotion, as was Nance.

Had Nance tracked down Aunt Maddie? Oh, dear Buddha, don't let it be so...

TWENTY-FOUR

"And this one is?" Nance tugged on a frame and pulled another of Charles's paintings through the small door of our backyard studio. She set the painting on the dead grass and stepped back, placing her hands on her hips so her bullseye breasts thrust forward.

"One mess," she answered her own question.

I stood at the corner of the homestead's back porch, out of sight of Nance and Aunt Maddie.

Aunt Maddie stood to one side of the studio doorway, her mouth part way open. How bizarre. My aunt caused those faces in other people; she didn't make them.

Aunt Maddie stepped closer to Nance. "Charles titled that one *One Life, One Mess*," she said. She gave a store clerk simper.

Oh no, Aunt Maddie must believe that Nance was vetting Charles's paintings to buy. Somehow, I figured she was wrong.

"It's amazing how you knew the title," my aunt continued. "Must be because you're another artist." In full-fledged sales mode. I half-expected her to curtsey.

I stepped off the porch. "Aunt Maddie's always *loved* Charles and *his paintings*, Nance." I hoped she heard me and understood.

Aunt Maddie yelped.

Nance jumped.

Together they stared at me.

My aunt placed her hands on her hips. "You're not supposed to be here. You're supposed to be in Boise"—she pointed at Nance—"with her." She hesitated, mouth still open.

"I got distracted, big time," I said.

"Of course." Aunt Maddie gave a flip of her hand in Nance's direction. "You're evaluating Charles's paintings for sale."

"The Cameron Castle is up for sale, Nance. It's a lot bigger place than..." I almost said my aunt's store.

"Oh, I've heard all about that nudist colony."

"It's not—"

"Way too much bad publicity for it to be viable as a property," Nance said.

Trust Nance to have heard all about it already and to dismiss any idea I had, as usual.

"Publicity." Nance slapped her cheek as she always did when struck by an inspiration. "We'll have a fire sale."

"A *fire sale*?" Aunt Maddie said.

As one Aunt Maddie and I turned and looked toward Dog Face Mountain. A small plume signaled that the Canine Creek fire still burned. Stubborn. Horrifying. In the fall of a drought year, such as this year, a fire could start and never stop until the snow flew. Such a fire took not only property, but all too often, lives.

"Oh," Nance said, "not a real fire sale. Completely different."

"Completely different how?" I asked. I couldn't help myself.

Nance's ideas, despite being off-the-wall, often worked. If she sold Charles's paintings, no matter how, that alone could save the store. Hope fluttered its wings in my chest. Would my path finally hold a little less suffering?

"Well, first of all, we'll remove these wonderful frames," Nance said.

Aunt Maddie opened her mouth and then closed it.

"Then we put the paintings on sale."

Aunt Maddie nodded in approval while I frowned in puzzlement. That was the problem with Nance. I never knew where she headed, just that it would be a wild ride.

"When a customer buys a painting, the money gets donated to their favorite cause."

"Where's the profit in that?" I asked. The hope flew off.

Nance held up an imperious hand. "There's more."

"You mean we donate a portion of the proceeds?" Aunt Maddie said. Even she, as unsuccessful as she was as a shopkeeper, knew better than to donate all the money.

Nance wagged a finger. "Wait."

My aunt frowned.

"Then we have a great big bonfire—"

"Not until it snows," Aunt Maddie said.

Nance made an "of course" gesture with her hand and said, "We'll have the bonfire around Christmas."

There'd be snow by then, I hoped. Oh wait, I wasn't going to hope anymore. That led to more suffering.

Nance's eyes opened wide. "Yes, yes of course, that'd be even better advertising, a Christmas bonfire."

"Now how would a bonfire be advertising?" my aunt asked.

Nance flung out her arms. "When everybody tosses their painting onto the fire, it'll be glorious."

Aunt Maddie and I stood there stunned.

"Toss the paintings onto the bonfire?" I asked.

"On purpose?" Aunt Maddie seemed to be having trouble grasping the whole concept. Me too.

"They'll feed the flames and feed Nance's Innovations."

"Charles's paintings?" Aunt Maddie struggled. "Charles's paintings? You want to burn Charles's paintings?"

Nance twirled.

I could tell she already knew how it'd happen, including the weather. The weather wouldn't dare disagree.

"Nance's Innovations?" Aunt Maddie still struggled.

Nothing stopped Nance in full spate or full twirl. "Yes, yes, Nance's Innovations," she sang. With her arms out, she resembled a large whirligig toy. The bullseyes made her dizzying to look at, or maybe that was just the presence of Nance.

"As the ashes rise," she said again, "as the paintings burn away, it'll be fabulous, tremendous, stupendous advertising for my store right where" —Nance stopped mid-twirl and pointed at Aunt Maddie— "your store is now."

"You want to destroy Charles's life work to advertise your store to throw me out of my own store?"

Oh-oh, Aunt Maddie had caught up.

Nance clutched both her boobs. "It'd be an honorable end, like a Viking funeral."

"Dora, do you have my gun?" Aunt Maddie asked.

I shook my head.

My aunt glanced around.

"What's she looking for?" Nance said.

"A weapon," I said.

Nance looked at her and then back at me. She took several steps away from my aunt.

Aunt Maddie picked up a length of framing, a rather delightful piece of scrolled walnut.

"Run," I said to Nance.

My aunt never followed through on any of her threats of violence. She hefted the walnut and then assumed a baseball batter's stance.

Of course, there's always a first time.

Aunt Maddie seemed to be focused on Nance's chest. Those bullseyes might be irresistible targets.

"Run," I said again to Nance.

Nance thundered across the Looney Jump Creek Bridge with all the grace of a stork jogging.

Aunt Maddie rested the framing length on one shoulder, a baseball player at rest. "You get out of town," she said to me. "And you take that...that bit—"

"I've got a plan for taking care of Nance," I said and realized as I said it that my plan for Nance to buy the Cameron Castle had already turned to ashes.

My aunt moved her hands higher on the wood as if she choked up on a bat for a bunt. "You're leaving. Now."

Aunt Maddie didn't listen. She never listened. She gazed up at Dog Face Mountain, now carved with deep shadows from the setting sun. "That murdering thief Rupert is out there somewhere."

"I'm not afraid of my father."

"You should be. He steals everything beautiful and destroys it."

Fatigue, hunger, and fear for my father and maybe for myself roiled over me in hot waves.

"You're wrong," I said. "If you mean the Noira necklace, he hasn't destroyed it."

Aunt Maddie made a dismissive gesture. "My sister—"

"He didn't destroy my mother. She ran away." The old pain roared into my heart.

My aunt flinched. "No—"

"I won't be like my mother, like Charles, like Rupert. I'm not going to run. Not now. Not ever."

Everyone abandoned me. Even Aunt Maddie with her insistence I leave.

"That evil man drove Patty away," Aunt Maddie said in little more than a whisper. Maybe she didn't believe it herself.

"No," I said. "My mom ran off with Charles."

Aunt Maddie's chin came up. "You can't see the truth about Rupert."

"My father—"

"Yes, he's your father. You can't accept that he'll never love you. No matter what you do. He can't give you the love you want."

Rage flooded my mind. "Charles is never coming back. Never. "

My aunt's face crumpled. "That's not true."

I couldn't stop myself gesturing at the paintings scattered about the yard. "This is all a joke. Charles left because he didn't love you."

"No, no."

Stop, I told myself. Stop. "You're fooling yourself. You've always been a fool."

"Oh, Dora, please." Tears rolled down Aunt Maddie's face.

I stopped. Too late. Oh Buddha, I'd never seen my aunt cry.

"Aunt Maddie, I didn't mean it." I would've given anything to take my words back.

My aunt said nothing. She walked toward the back porch.

"I can make it right." I followed behind, my hand outreached. "Please let me make it right." I touched her shoulder.

My aunt ran into the house and slammed the door.

I leaned my head up against the door. "Aunt Maddie, please. Forgive me."

Silence punctuated by the wind through the pines bordering the homestead. It sounded as if the trees sobbed and underneath, an echo of a broken woman weeping. Oh, no, no, no.

I tried the knob. Locked. She'd locked me out.

"Aunt Maddie, let me in."

Nothing.

I pressed my face into the crack between the door and the frame. "I swear I will make it right. I promise, I promise, I promise."

TWENTY-FIVE

I scrubbed away my tears with the backs of my hands, staggering down Main Street, half-drunk with dismay. The fool wooden sidewalk made me trip and almost fall. I was done falling. I set my jaw, hard. The low rays of the last of the sun reflected off the store front windows and mirrored my red-eyed face.

Mrs. McChin passed me going the other way. She stopped, started to speak, then hesitated and kept on moving. Wise old woman. I needed some heavy-duty meditation time, or maybe some screaming-out-loud time. I stumbled into my one remaining sanctuary and headed for my workbench at the back, my own private altar. And stopped dead.

Godiva stood over my kiln. She held the kiln's electrical cord in her hand and studied the frayed cord as if examining some new species of snake.

"How the hell did you get in here?" I asked, my voice hoarse.

Godiva jumped. "Where is it?" She waved the cord, the head flopping back and forth. A dead snake.

"Put that down."

She dropped it.

"Answer me, how'd you get in?" Any minute, my head might explode like an overheated kiln.

She smirked. "I walked in. The front door was open."

No it wasn't. Was it?

I turned and stared at the bolt. Hadn't I just unlocked the door? No way to remember such an automatic action—too sleep deprived and too upset.

"Now that I've answered your silly question, answer mine." Godiva bent, gave me a view of overstretched spandex, and snatched up the kiln cord. She resumed investigating it. "Where have you secreted it?" she demanded without even a glance my way. I suppose she saw me as only a stupid shopkeeper.

"Secreted? Isn't that something caterpillars do?"

That got her attention. Godiva stalked toward me until stopped by the leash of the cord. "Where is it?" She managed to convey a world of threat into those three words.

I remained locked down in one spot. "Where's what?" Admissions were for the guilty. Such as Godiva.

"You know *what*." Godiva tried to take another step. She tugged hard on the cord. Being attached to a kiln, it didn't budge. The nudist looked down at the cord and then at the kiln. Then at the outlet in the wall.

"Don't," I said. I jogged toward her and the kiln. The floor wobbled beneath my feet as I trod over the top of the trap door leading to the tunnels. Aha.

"Heat. I need heat," Godiva said.

"It's not all that cold. And sure not snowing, blast it," a high trilling voice came from behind me.

I spun around and collided with Mrs. McDay. The tiny little old lady must have sneaked in on her itty-bitty birdy feet. I needed to replace that bell, lock the door, get a security system, maybe a few bear traps strategically placed...

My apron clattered and her cherries bobbed as we untangled.

"Dearie, my hat." Mrs. McDay tottered.

I grabbed her arm. "Sorry."

"It's okay." Mrs. McDay gave my steadying arm a pat. "Mrs. McChin said you seemed a bit upset."

That put it in Mrs. McDay's own tactful terms. Somehow I knew Mrs. McChin had not been nearly so generous in her description of my mental state.

"What is that nudie lady doing?" Mrs. McDay pointed with the hand not reattaching her hat to her white hair at Godiva. Mrs. McDay gave a start. She stared, her eyes huge behind her old lady glasses. "Oh no, don't—" she yelped.

"A kiln is a furnace," Godiva announced, triumph in every word. She plugged the cord into the wall socket. Sparks sputtered. Godiva yipped and fell.

"Pull it out, you fool," Mrs. McDay screeched.

I sprinted toward the socket and stopped short, not wanting to be shocked.

Mrs. McDay, moving fast as a bird with a cat after it, snatched one of my leather gloves off the workbench. She yanked the cord from the wall and gulped big chunks of air.

A tiny curl of smoke wisped from the socket.

"Fire!" Mrs. McDay cried, a world of terror in one word. The Great Starke Fire had happened when she was five. Her father had died.

I kicked at the wall around the socket until the brittle plaster, a patch installed seventy years ago by Henry's grandfather, fell away. The exposed ancient wiring sparked tiny flames.

"Eep," Mrs. McDay squeaked.

I snatched my leather gloves from Mrs. McDay and beat out the nascent fire and tore at the plaster until a huge hole revealed the pieces of old lathe.

"It's out," I cried at last.

Mrs. McDay and I both turned to give Godiva a lesson in living and not dying in fire country.

"Listen up," I started.

"You idiot, dearie—"

Godiva had gone.

TWENTY-SIX

I managed to reassure Mrs. McDay that everything was peachy keen-o, to use one of her own favorite phrases. I don't think she believed me.

As she tottered down the sidewalk, cherries bobbing, I stepped back into the store and into the deep shadows. I tugged the Noira necklace from my pocket. It hung heavy in my hand.

Yup, no problem with any stolen necklace, no problem with my aunt's back rent and rage at me, no problem with a murdered man and my father the main suspect. No problems at all and I wasn't about to pull a Henry-on-the-roof-suicide-by-cop routine.

First, the necklace needed repair.

I laid it on a piece of soft, worn black velvet. I fished the pearl out of my pocket and placed it underneath the Noira's tiny onyx foot, where it belonged.

Or where I believed it belonged. With the two put together, I sat back on my stool and foraged my favorite loupe from a pocket.

Underneath the loupe, the pearl came into sharp and bewildering focus.

Though the pearl added a magnificent finishing touch to the Noira, it had been attached by etching a thin line around the outside of the pearl and then inserting silver wire which looped at the top. The pearl still had its loop, along with a heavy double jump ring to attach it to the necklace.

Over time the solder of the corresponding loop on the necklace had given way and left a gap just big enough for the pearl to slip loose. Sloppy work.

Now I knew why, in such a magnificently made necklace, a piece—the pearl—had been able to fall into the ash trap.

Why silver? Why such shoddy workmanship? It couldn't be the work of a master jeweler.

It couldn't be Pietro. Could it? Was he exhausted by his rage at his ex-lover? Or perhaps he'd wanted one major flaw in the necklace, as she was flawed. Or perhaps, close to suicide, he no longer cared. I imagined him at his workbench in his Paris attic, bent over the Noira, in the last of the winter light, desperate to finish, desperate to be done at last.

No. No master, no matter what, would fall so far. I rubbed my face and then glared at the old laptop computer. "If you don't boot up," I said to it as I pressed the power button, "I'm tossing you out the front window."

It flickered on. Good to know threats worked sometimes.

Surfing the Internet, I came across the articles Lester and Nance had shown me. In the poor, grainy photos the necklace looked perfect, the pearl a fantastic final touch. Crossing my fingers, I delved further into the necklace's history and discovered over a hundred years of despair, desolation, and death.

Desperate Noira arranged herself naked in the same pose as her beautiful, condemning necklace. She wore only the necklace when she slashed her throat. I swallowed back bile at the unbidden image of her heart's blood flowing over the blood rubies.

After her death, the necklace disappeared, stolen, and was recovered a decade later. The police discovered it when they searched a burglar's home, after killing him in a failed burglary. The necklace, claimed by Noira's relatives, was sold after years of legal wrangling.

I pulled up a long-winded, gushing article from one of the old gossip magazines entitled "The Black Necklace of Death." The purchaser, a Greek shipping tycoon named Demeter, found the pearl in a tiny curio shop. In the article Demeter said that his "fortune" to chance upon such a perfect match to the necklace meant that attaching it to the necklace would "destroy Pietro's bloody curse forever."

Huh. I wondered at a man with enough money to buy the Noira, who then commissioned a cheap, bad jeweler to add the pearl. At least, I hoped the job didn't cost Demeter much. It wasn't worth much.

I raised my shoulders to ease the twitch there. Many people believed jewelers were interchangeable. I'd once asked Henry, when he called me a glorified watch repairer, if skill and knowledge didn't matter in auto mechanics either. He didn't speak to me for a week.

The article continued with the tale of Demeter presenting the "cleansed" necklace to his bride, who wore it only once, on her wedding day. As she had walked down the aisle, she coughed up blood that stained her pristine white dress a red as dark as the blood rubies. My hand rested on my own chest, my breaths coming fast and short. When the beloved bride died of tuberculosis mere months later, her lover locked the necklace away with his broken heart.

After Demeter died, the necklace was sold to Godiva's uncle. I stared at the article I'd found. It showed the ruins of the mansion, blackened stumps. To one side, police carried a stretcher with a black bag. I read the words, a jeweler suspected and seen fleeing the burning mansion, the naked niece escaping at the last moment, her white form racing across the dark lawn as the old man burned to death...

"I have to find my father." My voice echoed high and tight in the empty store.

At the press of the off button and with a loud groan, I turned off the computer. The store had darkened during my research and I flicked on a lamp. My reflection stared back at me from the black monitor screen, grim and paste-white with all my blood drained.

I snatched the necklace off the workbench, wanting to crush it beneath my fingers, wanting to destroy all that malignant energy. I couldn't imagine now that I'd ever desired the evil thing.

No way could I sell the necklace to Nance. No way could I give the money to my father. No way could I use some of the money to keep my promise to my aunt. No way would the blood of the necklace stain my soul. There had to be another way. Somehow. Some way.

Why didn't I just leave? I could get a job working for a jewelry manufacturer in any big city of my choice.

I shuddered as I imagined that job. Jewelry fabrication for the big companies meant the same endless repetition of work as in any factory. It would be a just punishment for me if I surrendered.

With my head in my hands, the necklace rested cold and smooth, a dead thing against my skin. I wanted to bury it back in the ashes forever.

My head came up. No. Hiding it wasn't the answer. If I'd done Right Action when Rupert first handed me the necklace, if I'd given it to Lester or Mallard...

I started toward the door. And stopped.

No. I had to see my father first.

TWENTY-SEVEN

Rubbing my aching eyes didn't help. I peered out the front window of Aunt Maddie's store. If I leaned far enough, I could see the sheriff's office down at the end of the block. I congratulated myself that my stakeout was a little more subtle than Lester's had been.

I didn't want to chance getting stuck in the fruit cellar underneath the office. It wouldn't be all that convincing to either Lester or Mallard if they heard me as I insist—encouraged—Rupert to surrender. It wouldn't do either my father or me any good if we both ended up stuck in jail.

When Lester and Mallard left then...if they ever did. It was already past midnight. Maybe they waited for Rupert to recognize their amazing persistence and, awestruck, turn himself in.

I yawned and took another large swallow of cola. I'd bought a six-pack and already drank three. My head buzzed with sugar, caffeine, and exhaustion. Maybe I'd be the first non-alcoholic Buddhist to ever drink herself to death. After I got diabetes.

At long last, Mallard, who moved tired, got in his car and drive away. Lester, moving old, followed in his Jeep. I waited several long minutes, until I trusted that the police wouldn't return. As I threw open the trap door to the tunnels, the Noira necklace twinkled at me from where I'd left it on the workbench. I started to stuff the horrid thing into an apron pocket and paused.

I remembered when I had tumbled off the roof and now didn't want the necklace to fall out again at the worst possible moment. Where was a good hiding place? Where would it be safe from Aunt Maddie's cleaning and, Buddha forbid, Nance's rearranging?

After dismissing various hiding spots in turn, I almost gave up and settled for stuffing it back into my pocket when I stubbed my toe on the old kiln. Of course. Maddie had no use for the kiln. Nance knew it was broken. And now Mrs. McDay, and therefore most of Starke knew the kiln was dangerous.

I kept the pearl separate and secreted it in a bit of felt in my apron pocket. I scampered into the tunnel, following the opposite direction of the arrows on the "Hoosegow Excape" signs.

Once, I caught sight of Fat Freddy's long scaly tail as it disappeared around a corner. "Food, Freddy, food," I cried as I followed. Only to turn the corner and come face to whiskers with not a cute-domestic-albino Freddy, but rather an old-ugly-big-yellow-teeth tunnel rat. I don't know which one of us "eeked!" louder.

This tunnel appeared almost un-traveled. Maybe the only traveler to and from the fruit cellar cell had been my Great Grandfather. Rubble almost blocked the entrance to the cell, save for a Rupert-sized hole. I squeezed through the narrow opening, regretting my diet of Mama Chin's cinnamon rolls.

I tumbled into the tiny fruit cellar and shone my flashlight around the minute space, expecting to see my father's eyes flash at me like a trapped animal's.

Nothing. I'd arrived at long last to find the fruit cellar empty.

An ancient oil lamp stood on a shelf, a box of modern matches next to it. I lit the lamp and looked around at Rupert's refuge. My father always picked tiny spaces to exist in, as if he'd already been arrested, tried, and condemned.

A century ago, someone had whitewashed the packed dirt walls and then had mounted pine shelves. The shelves were stockpiled with someone's canning. Enough food crowded on those shelves to feed a family for a year.

Most of the cans bulged around the seams. I winced at the idea of Rupert opening and eating the contents. I sat upon the seat, a battered stool next to a shelf where there sat a couple of opened cans and scraps of tin, glass and twine, a pair of well-used tin shears, plus a glass cutter and a bottle of epoxy. My father had been here.

The reek of rotten fruit from the opened cans mingling with the stench of old whitewash and dirt made me shudder. I pulled my apron tighter around me and sought what little warmth I could find.

Where was my father?

The grave cold cell made me shiver. Best I could do was wait a while and see if my father showed up. He'd return for his tools, if he could. No jeweler ever abandoned his tools.

Mallard and Lester wouldn't be back for a few hours. I needed to stay awake to get out before they returned. I sighed and leaned my head against a shelf. I'd rest my eyes, as Aunt Maddie always said...

Pain shot through my behind. I yelped and fell off the stool.

I scrambled to my feet. In the light from the antique oil lamp, I ducked my head, as if somebody might have seen my fall from grace. No one saw. No one shared the fruit cellar with me. No one could have squeezed into the minute space without waking me up.

Wriggling around to look at my bottom, I spotted and yanked out a large splinter from the stool lodged in one cheek. "Ouch," I yelped. My voice sounded loud in the tiny space. I hoped a cop hadn't returned.

The trap door flung open.

I yelled.

"Shh," Rupert said, finger to his lips.

TWENTY-EIGHT

I gaped at my father, outlined in the light from the sheriff's office. In one day he had transformed. He'd trimmed what little of his hair remained. I suspected he'd used his old pair of tin shears, for his hair hung in chopped, uneven lengths.

"How do I look?" Rupert asked.

Words failed me. He'd shaved his beard off as well. Large gashes on his cheeks and chin combined with his other injuries for a look of a man who'd been in several accidents.

"Get down here," I said.

My father winced. "I look a lot better, don't I?"

I stared at the array of bruises and cuts on Rupert's face. "Somebody will see you up there."

He gave a tentative tight-lipped smile that concealed his rotten teeth and missing teeth. "I did it myself." Rupert patted the back of his head. "Maybe I should trim off a little more back here?"

Blood pounded in my ears. "You're worried about your hair?" I wanted to pull mine out by my roots. "Get..." I started to say and then realized I wanted Rupert to remain up in the sheriff's office.

I didn't know when Lester or Mallard would return. When they did, my father would give himself up. I'd find a way to keep Rupert here. He wouldn't run this time.

Using the plank ladder press against the dirt wall, I clambered up and crawled out onto the old splintery floor of the office. The brilliant neon light, no longer blocked by my father's body, raked over my eyeballs. I lay there and inhaled a hundred years of dust from a thousand criminal feet and wondered why the cops left the light on all night, in sleepy little Starke.

Oh, right, they left it on because Starke no longer remained a dying mountain town. Now Starke was the brand new ski resort *Aurora* where murderers roamed.

"Rupert, you need to—"

"Did you bring the money with you? Did you leave it down there with my tools?" Rupert swung his body onto the ladder.

"Listen—"

"When can you get the Noira back?" my father asked.

"What?" I tilted my head to one side. Maybe fatigue affected my hearing.

A cotton bag flew out of the tunnel and smacked me in the shin. The tin shears hurt the most. "Ow!"

"Quiet. Oh, sorry." Rupert climbed out of the cell with far more grace than I had displayed. My father scooped up his tool bag and went to Lester's desk. With a twinge, I noticed that the Widows Brigade's check sat on the keyboard. Neatly torn in half.

"When can you meet me with the money and the necklace?" He started opening and rummaging through Lester's desk drawers.

"What are you looking for?" I asked.

"All you need to do is give me the money." Rupert pulled open another drawer.

Why did nobody ever answer my questions?

"Get back the Noira," my father continued, "and all my problems are solved."

"You'll turn the Noira in to Lester. Once you're safe in custody, you don't have to worry about blackmail."

"Custody?" My father's voice squeaked. "You mean in jail? Whyever for?"

I clenched my hands into fists. "Because you stole the Noira."

Rupert slammed a drawer shut. It echoed loud as a gunshot. "Don't believe what Lester, or that piece of lying junk" —he pointed at the computer monitor— "tells you."

So he had been in the fruit cellar beneath us all that time.

"I believe every word." I realized as I said it that I spoke the truth.

Rupert stared at me, his mouth half-open, displaying his rotten stumps. "Dora? But you're my daughter. How could you think—I didn't steal the necklace. Such beauty didn't belong with that mean old man." Rupert's hand fell to his chest and covered his heart. "It belongs to the great beauty who deserves such a compliment."

"Huh?" My hearing was going again.

"A true work of art, for the ages in her true state, naked before God." He stroked his chest. "And one I thought lost to me forever, burned to death along with that old man—"

"Didn't you read the news—" No, no, my father had been on the run. He might not have known Godiva hadn't died. No wonder he'd run from her at first. He'd seen a dead woman.

"And then to think we missed each other by only days that became decades..."

I remembered Mrs. McGarrity's words to Henry. *"Your father, Henry, didn't let that crazy woman and her brother settle in, not for no reason, no way, no how."*

"Godiva and Derek were here, in Starke, looking for you, years ago," I said.

Rupert continued his stroking, still lost in his past. He smiled. "Now, at last, through the glory of the Noira—"

"Which you stole and now need to—"

Rupert hunched his shoulders. "Oh, Dora, I know I've never been a good father to you."

A lump formed in my throat.

"I'm not a bad man, despite what Lester says."

"Father."

"Or despite what that spiteful, evil woman, your aunt says."

I pulled myself up straight and crossed my arms on my chest. "Prove it."

He blinked at me. Tears glinted on his eyelashes. "How?"

"Turn yourself in."

"I told you, Dora, I can't—"

"That's the only answer."

Rupert shook his head so hard that a shaving cut opened and bled. "No. I can't spend the rest of my life in a jail cell."

An image came to me of Rupert huddled in the fruit cellar, and then another image of him crouched beneath his wool blankets, shivering in his tiny cabin, trapped by the snows outside. How would jail be any different? Warmer? Better food? A dentist to fix his teeth?

"You're already in prison," I said.

He ran his hand over his face, smearing the blood from the cut over his jaw.

"You've never escaped, no matter how much you ran."

Rupert hunched his shoulders. "I've done everything in the service of my love." He stepped over to Mallard's desk, pulled open the bottom drawer, and repeated his pillaging of other people's drawers.

"I'll make sure that after you turn yourself in, the cops arrest the real killer," I said.

I had no clue how I would force Lester to do so. But I'd think of a way to make him realize that Godiva killed her brother.

My father ignored me. He yanked on the top drawer. Locked. He removed a needle-nosed file and inserted it into the lock.

"Rupert—"

A click. My father pulled the drawer open.

Rupert withdrew his hand from the drawer. He held a gun, a .38, still wrapped in a thick plastic bag with a red "EVIDENCE" seal.

Mallard burst through the door, gun drawn. "FREEZE," he yelled.

"Don't run," I yelled at my father.

Rupert ran.

TWENTY-NINE

Rupert dashed across the office and leaped down into the fruit cellar.

I heard the thump of his landing and then a yip of pain. I ran to the hole and peered down just in time to see my father crawl into the tunnel.

"Don't run!" I yelled, meaning crawl.

Mallard pushed me aside. "Stop, thief!"

"Stop thief? Oh, please," I said.

Mallard gave me one irritated glare before he jumped and clambered after Rupert.

"Of course, it is better than 'Stop, murderer,'" I said to the empty room.

Rupert took the gun along on his flight. He and Mallard could be hurt—fatally.

I grabbed Great Grandpa's gun and bullets in their own evidence bag out of the drawer. In case I gave in to my current temptation to shoot my father. Buddhist Right Action, my right foot.

From a distance down the tunnel, I heard Mallard yelling, faint and far away. No way to catch them.

The sound of glass breaking came from down the street. Outside in the dim light of dawn, the glass of Mad Maddie's Marvels front window lay in glinting shards on the sidewalk. Rupert sprinted down the street, headed again for the mining shaft mall, the only difference being this time that his beard didn't fly in the wind. Behind him, Mallard jumped out of Aunt Maddie's front store window.

Couldn't my father have picked another tunnel exit, say the one in Mama Chin's? Couldn't he at least have used Maddie's front door? I knew who my aunt would blame for the trashed window.

Mallard rushed by in hot pursuit.

Rupert must not know that the developers had fixed the fence around the mall and padlocked it. "Wait," I called. I ran after Mallard.

He was a few feet behind Rupert when I reached him and grabbed his coat. Mallard stumbled, righted himself, pulled away, stood, and glared in my direction.

I guessed I wasn't in his good graces anymore, either. All I needed was to get Henry and the Widows Brigade angry at me and I'd be lucky not to be run out of town on a sheep. A Starke tradition.

Rupert flung himself at the fence and bounced off. Good one, Dad. He ran toward the gate and right on past. My father must have spotted the padlock. He sprinted toward us.

Mallard skidded to a stop, his shoes squeaking on the pine sidewalk. "Freeze," he managed before I plowed into him and knocked him flat.

Rupert leaped over us both. Maybe he should tout "wild mountain man recluse" as a health regime. He roared back into the sheriff's office.

Mallard and I rolled around for a couple of moments, a bizarre mock-dance, until we untangled. Mallard, breathing hard and heavy, jumped up and followed. Me too.

I arrived at the front door of the office just in time to see Mallard disappear down the ladder to the tunnels. I leaned against the doorjamb and puffed and considered my few horrid options. Mallard would catch Rupert or lose his quarry in the tunnels. I suspected the latter. My father knew the tunnels. Mallard didn't.

When Mallard returned, I didn't want to "discuss" with him what Rupert and I happened to be doing in the sheriff's office. I didn't think he'd believe I had tried to convince Rupert to turn himself in. Nor did I want to talk about my successful attempts to slow his chase of the prime murder suspect.

The trap door to the fruit cellar and tunnels still gaped open. I moved to close it but it didn't matter. Mallard wouldn't forget the tunnels existed, after all. Nor would Rupert dare return.

I sniffed and smelled eau-de-rank-Dora. I needed a shower and a change of clothes, real soon. I needed real food, real soon. I needed sleep, in a real bed, real, real soon.

When I'd gotten a few feet down the sidewalk to Aunt Maddie's store I hesitated, one foot raised. Parked next to my aunt's station wagon was Nance's Mini Cooper. Shards of glass shone on both windshields from the rising sun of another smoky, snow-bereft day.

I sighed, got into the station wagon, crawled into the back, and found the most comfortable position. As I started to fall asleep, I realized I needed to be somewhere else.

It all went back to her. If I could surprise her maybe I could get some answers. Or, perhaps, I could catch me a killer. I slapped myself awake enough to drive. I'd lie in wait and maybe even get some sleep.

THIRTY

Tap, tap, tap. I pulled the blanket over my face. "I'm up."

"No, you're not."

"Five more minutes, Aunt Maddie. Then I'll get up for school, I promise."

"School?"

Wait. I no longer went to school. And that wasn't Aunt Maddie's voice; it was Mrs. McDay's. I peeked out. What was I doing in the station wagon?

Oh. Right. I'd staked out the Cameron Castle.

When I'd arrived, only a faint glimmer of the dawn of another sunny day illuminated the old hotel. The soft early light didn't help the decrepit old derelict's appearance. The huge fir tree still leaned, a dirty drunk, against the Castle's tower.

A good Idahoan, I knew better than to barge into the Castle and demand answers from Godiva while it was still early enough that she could shoot me and claim she thought I was a burglar. As I'd bet she would. Of course, if Rupert had her only gun, the .22 used to kill Derek, I'd be okay. But I wasn't willing to risk it.

I'd parked where I could watch the Castle's front door, crawled into the back of the station wagon, and closed my eyes for a minute.

"Dora, wakey, wakey," Mrs. McChin said now. She'd joined Mrs. McDay. From outside the car window, they peered at me.

I blinked back in the bright light of way-too-early morning. The smoke that softened their features didn't help. Only let me know the forest fire still burned.

Mrs. McDay gave a cheery wave, the cherries on her straw hat bobbing. "Time to get up, Dora. You don't want to miss it."

Miss what? I sat up and stared past her. What I saw made me want to lie back down and pull the blanket over me again. On the Castle's wraparound porch between the two main pillars, a bright pink and purple banner, half-hung, flapped in the icy cold breeze.

Beneath the banner, matching pink and purple arrayed Mrs. McGarrity danced from one foot to another. Her arms waved as she directed her two grandsons, Jeffy and Jamey, in stringing up the other end. When I'd babysat those two they hadn't been nearly as compliant. Or as tall. Or as capable.

Mrs. McGarrity's dog Bark pranced around the porch, as imperious as Mrs. McGarrity.

In between flaps I read the banner: "NO STARK NAKEDS IN STARKE."

Oh Buddha, shoot me.

Not many Starkers seemed to have turned out for this catastro—event. Yet. Still early.

Miss Mary, married eleven years, had all her twelve kids with her, including Billy, the oldest at fourteen. Billy stared at the front door with a hungry expression. Perhaps he hoped to catch sight of a naked female who wasn't a baby sister.

"We figured you slept here to be ready when we started," Mrs. McDay said.

"Started what?" I feared I might hear a "baa" any moment.

Joe and Joe's daughter, Maureen, of Maureen's Bar, set up a table with wine glasses, bottles of wine, and a price list, in the middle of the Castle's dead grass front yard. Tony, the construction boss, helped, or at least hovered, next to pretty Maureen.

I half-expected to see my aunt at the table beside them, selling potato-sack T-shirts. No aunt. I heaved a sigh of relief at my luck.

"Our protest, of course." Mrs. McChin pulled me back to the current disaster.

"No nakeds, no nakeds," Mrs. McDay chanted. She gave a tiny sparrow hop.

Old George, ninety and stopped counting, paused as he hobbled behind Mrs. McChin and Mrs. McDay. He, too, stared at the Castle's front door. Perhaps, like Billy, Old George yearned to catch a glimpse of a naked lady, maybe his first in decades.

"Not yet," Mrs. McChin said, "we haven't got our signs yet."

"Oh, right." Mrs. McDay trotted across the yard toward her Rambler parked on the other side of the circular drive.

"There's only one naked." I paused. "That I know." I paused again. "That's alive."

Mrs. McChin backed away. "One naked is one too many." She sauntered after Mrs. McDay. Mrs. McChin had worked too hard for too many years in Mama Chin's to ever trot again.

I searched the windows of the Castle for any sign of movement and saw none. Had Godiva taken off? No, she wouldn't leave, not this close to getting the money. She must be hiding in the Castle. Not that I blamed her for not showing her face, or any of the rest of herself.

Nance pulled up behind my car. She unfolded from her Mini Cooper. Today she wore a dress with a famous Escher print of two hands drawing each other on the front. The huge Escher hands delineated each breast. Nance munched on a cinnamon roll from Mama Chin's.

"Dora." She gave a little wave with the cinnamon roll.

"That's not vegan," I said.

"This one is. Mama Chin made my specific recipe." Nance popped the last of the roll into her mouth. As she chomped, her earrings, perfect little echoes of the Escher hands, danced.

Crumbs sprayed. I considered opening my mouth and catching some.

Mrs. McDay tottered up to us. In her skinny little old lady arms she held several homemade cardboard signs mounted on broomsticks that proclaimed "NUDE OUT."

"Here's your signs."

"Those are brooms," I said.

"Yes. We need them back after the demonstration."

"What a clever idea," Nance said, with an entrepreneurial gleam in her voice. "We should carry those in Nance's Innovations." She licked her fingers, smacking her lips. Whether at the taste of leftover cinnamon roll or future sales, I couldn't tell.

"Nance..." I needed to disabuse her of the idea of stealing my aunt's store. Maybe if I...

Henry pulled up behind the Mini Cooper.

I grinned. A possible solution had possibly arrived. Henry jumped out of his car. He stared at the banner, then at Mrs. McGarrity, then at the decorated tables. He slumped.

"Private property," he said, loud enough for Mrs. McGarrity to pause and give him a glare, before she turned back to her task.

Henry pulled out his ultra-sleek cell phone and pressed one number. I suspected he called the sheriff's office. On speed dial. The problem of partying on drought-dry grass was enough to send any sane person calling the police.

I needed to talk to Godiva before the cops arrived. Maybe I could even get her to confess. How?

The brooms in Mrs. McDay's arms provided much needed inspiration. "I'll take one of those," I said. Maybe I could sweep a confession out of Godiva.

"Me too," Nance said. "I need a prototype. One will look lovely as a display in the front window, perhaps with a Christmas scene as a sign."

"Oh, thank you, dearies," Mrs. McDay said. "We'll be forming a circle soon in front of the porch." She handed a sign to Henry as he came up to us and then off she went. "Don't forget, it's no nakeds," she sang over her shoulder.

Henry smiled at Nance. His eyebrows rose as he noticed her dress. I thanked the Buddha that she hadn't worn the bullseyes.

I raised my chin and put on my best sales smile. "Nance, this is Henry, the one who owns Mad Maddie's Marvels and..." —I pointed with my hand not holding the broom sign at the Cameron Castle— "this glorious Cameron Castle—"

"Glorious?" Henry said.

I shot him a look that I hoped said *Work with me, Henry.* "Soon to be vacant," I continued.

Henry nodded. "As soon as Lester gets here."

I hoped Lester took his sweet time. I needed to get to Godiva so I scanned the windows for a sign of long blonde hair and saw nothing. I beamed at Nance, showing all my teeth.

"Dora, what's wrong?" she asked.

I dropped the grin. "And then you can start work on renovating the great Castle," I finished.

She looked blank.

"I suggest we start with rat traps," Henry said.

Not helping, Henry. No wonder his realty business was failing fast. I grimaced. "Nance is a Buddhist, like me, Henry—"

Henry didn't look surprised.

"And they're chipmunks. Really cute chipmunks," I said to Nance. "Except for Fat Freddy."

"Fat Freddy?" Nance asked.

"They're vermin...except for Fat Freddy, of course." Affection warmed Henry's tone. "Maybe we can send Bark in," he continued, pointing with his chin at the little dog who had fallen asleep on the Castle's steps, "as an exterminator."

Nance and I looked at him.

He spread his hands wide in an "understand me please" gesture. "Natural selection."

"Anyway," I threw my arms wide in the direction of the Castle, well, one arm, my other hand was hampered by the sign. "This is the perfect place for Nance's Innovations."

Nance placed her finger on her lips and tapped.

"The front entry can be the art gallery," I said.

I could see it, with artwork adorning the old stone fireplace and a display case with my designs shimmering in it where the reception desk now stood. I smiled.

"Oh." Henry scrubbed at a wrinkle on his shirt front. "You're *that* Nance."

"This filthy old place?" Nance asked.

"It cleans up good," Henry said.

"That tower is completely out of proportion."

"We can tear the tower down," I said.

Henry shot me a glance.

I raised my eyebrows and gave him a "sale-is-sale" nod.

"Of course," he said, his voice tight.

Nance flipped a hand back and forth. "Tear the whole horrid mess down."

Henry's face fell. I'm sure mine followed suit.

"You can get right to the renovation of my new flagship store," Nance said.

My vision of a Castle gallery flew off, headed in the same direction as the missing snow. I'd forgotten that once Nance got on a path she stayed on that path. No matter what, not even if the path was cluttered with the bodies of her victims.

"Flagship store?" A faint hope quavered in Henry's voice.

"You can't have a flagship store with only two stores," I said, half to myself, and half petulant.

"I need the whole space gutted and all the fixtures replaced," Nance said. "I need the work done as soon as possible. I can pay cash."

I remembered the sheaf of twenties she had pulled out of her purse. Nance had come prepared. But for what?

Mrs. McDay called out, "Dora, Henry, we're ready to start."

Henry tossed down the sign and took Nance's arm. "I don't see that as a problem," he said as he led her down the driveway path. I didn't bother to tell him that she was already ensconced, that nobody ever led Nance anywhere. I'd tried.

"Henry?" Mrs. McChin sang out.

The Widows Brigade stood in a circle along with Billy and Mrs. McGarrity's grandsons in front of the Castle's porch. All held brooms at the ready. Bark the Rat Terrier Terrorist stood, awake and alert, on the top step, head cocked to one side.

"Henry, Dora, get over here right now," Mrs. McGarrity said. At the sound of her command, Bark hopped down the stairs and joined the circle.

Henry and Nance proceeded down the drive, heads close together, best friends.

With a sigh, I hoisted the sign and joined the circle.

"Fine then." Mrs. McGarrity started walking.

We all followed.

"No nakeds!" Mrs. McDay shouted.

"No nakeds!" we echoed.

How to get to Godiva without anyone noticing? I wondered as I walked. Wait. There was more than one way into the Castle.

I stepped out of the circle, earning a glare from Mrs. McGarrity, and mimed a shiver while pointing at my car, which earned me a nod of permission. I strolled toward my car, until everyone turned back to the business of eradicating nudity for all mankind. Then I took off for the back of the Castle.

THIRTY-ONE

Cobwebs, dead leaves, and other unidentifiable debris clung to my apron and my hair. Ugh. I brushed off as best I could. The kitchen door, half glassed, with one pane long gone, had provided an easy, if messy, access. The cardboard that replaced the pane flapped in the cold breeze. I hadn't even had to break in.

Inside, I walked into a pile of leaves that had accumulated over who knew how long next to the door. The leaves flew everywhere, helped by a gust of wind and something that squeaked as it fled.

I clutched the broom, ready to whack any creature I saw. So not a Good Action. That's why Buddhists practice. What I truly meant in the Buddhist sense was, ready to gently sweep any adorable small woodland denizen out the door.

Another rustle had me raising the broom high. I tensed.

A brown beast with a long scaly tail raced across the filthy floor and disappeared into a hole in the baseboard, too quick for me to strike. I lowered my broom and resisted the urge to sweep all the trash out the kitchen door.

It wouldn't do much good. The rest of the old hotel kitchen appeared as trashed and trashy as the entrance.

In the Cameron Castle's glory days high tea and a full breakfast was served in the dining room, so the kitchen was huge. In one corner an old refrigerator, the kind with coils on the top, still worked. I could tell that by the hum, or roar rather, of it running.

The only modern touch in the entire enormous space: a tiny microwave that stood next to a sink big enough to bathe a football fullback. Empty frozen food boxes sat stacked high next to the microwave. More TV dinner boxes overflowed the trash. All that trash, quite a boon for the rats, um, chipmunks.

My nose wrinkled at the reek of stale junk food. I snorted. What was all Godiva's talk about "my body is a temple"? Maybe Godiva blackmailed Rupert and killed her brother. Maybe not. One thing was certain, she was a slob.

Beneath the refrigerator noise and the faint echo of the chanting outside, a soft rustling sound came from upstairs.

What was that? Bird? Rat? Godiva?

I headed toward the sound and stood at the bottom of the decrepit, narrow servant stairs to the second story and prodded at another leaf pile. Nothing scuttled.

My first foot on a step made it groan. I hesitated. It wouldn't do me any good to fall through a rotted step and break an ankle.

From above came a soft thump. I sprinted up the stairs to the second story. A scratching helped me pinpoint the sounds. They came from a room halfway down the hall. I tore in that direction and flung open the door. The old ballroom of the Castle dazzled me. Sheets drooped in tatters from three crystal chandeliers hung across the vast open space. Gilded mirrors, now stained and cracked, covered two of the walls. Huge windows along the courtyard side let the sunlight stream into the ballroom. The fainter sounds of "No nakeds!" streamed in as well.

On the last wall another enormous stone fireplace reigned. The last embers of a fire still burned within its blackened interior. Despite the warmth radiating from the fireplace, the cold of the vast space made my breaths puff into the air.

Close to the fireplace sat a mattress on the top of which roiled—

I screamed.

THIRTY-TWO

My father's hairy, hideous, horrible behind paused mid-raise. Or thrust. Or plunge.

"Aargh, aargh, ugh," I gargled. I squeezed my eyes tight. It didn't help. I still saw an afterimage of Rupert and Godiva having disgusting, disturbing, dismaying sex.

"Dora," Rupert hollered.

I opened my eyes only to see my naked father leaping from the makeshift bed in a full frontal view.

"Eek." I wanted to plunge the broomstick into my eyes. Instead, I dropped the broomstick and placed my palms over my eyes and rubbed. Hard.

"Give me the necklace. It's the only way to save your father's wretched life," Godiva said into my darkness.

My hands dropped.

"Wretched?" Rupert echoed. He stepped away from the mattress. Closer to the fireplace. My father noticed his naked nearness to the embers and leaped away, bits swinging.

Argh. I kept my eyes fixated on Godiva and blinked at her through the little white and black spots swimming over my vision. She lay beneath the blanket, her limbs spread out in every direction. Maybe, greedy, she wanted to lay claim to the whole bed.

"What would you call it, Rupert?" Godiva demanded. "You and your rotten teeth." She rubbed the back of her hand over her mouth.

Unbidden, my hand snuck up to my mouth. My lips twisted under my fingers. Ick.

Out of the corner of my eye, I caught an inadvertent glimpse that Rupert had grabbed his pants off the mattress and leaned on one leg to put them on. All of him leaned, including a long central section—I flinched away, snatched up the broomstick sign, and held it up as a shield against his aged body. Who knew you could get wrinkles *there*?

"Yes, wretched is the word," Rupert said, "when I believed you, my beloved," —he gazed at Godiva— "perished in the flames" —he looked over at the fire and shuddered— "then I had no life. Only despair. Only death."

Godiva gave a nod of approval at Rupert and his mushy dreck.

"The Noira and the money, too," she said to me. "It's mine. Mine." She propped herself up onto her elbows. The blanket fell away. With her generous endowment and without a bra, the effects of decades of gravity were revealed.

I looked away, toward the windows. Mrs. McGarrity's voice rose above the others. "Out!"

"I'm not going to let those stupid old women run me out of Starke again," Godiva said, rage in every word. "Not until I get what I returned for."

"Me," my father breathed.

"Sure," Godiva agreed, with not an ounce of conviction in her tone. She shivered. "It's always freezing," she said in a tone that insisted somebody fix the weather. Right now. She tugged up the blanket—to my relief.

"You might want to rethink the whole naked thing," I said to her, my voice high and breathy.

"My uncle disapproved too," she said.

I opened my mouth to say I didn't disapprove so much as I hated a preview of my own bust's future.

"And because I was a naturist girl, not a naturist boy like my brother," Godiva continued, snarling out the words. "My uncle stole my birthright from me. He hated me being in my birth state, innocent and free."

"I told you I wasn't a thief," Rupert said to me.

Godiva sat up farther. "And Uncle—may he burn forever—was going to give my beloved away to—to—" she sputtered "—the masses." She spat the last word out with a gob of spittle.

"Beloved? Birth state? Birthright?" I struggled with Godiva's obsessive convolutions. "Masses?"

"The true truth, beauty to beauty, glory to the glorious," Rupert said.

That didn't help.

I peeked over the sign at Rupert. He now, thank the Buddha, wore both pants and shirt. I lowered the broom.

"Did you bring the money with you?" he asked.

"And the Noira," Godiva said.

My hands itched on the broomstick to beat Godiva, or maybe Rupert, about the head. Okay, so not Right Action. Make me care.

"Are you telling me you still care for—for—" I pointed with the broomstick at Godiva. "This blackmailing fratricide?"

"You're wrong, Dora—" My father tipped his head toward the picture windows. "They've stopped chanting."

Rupert and I rushed to the window. Rupert stood behind me and off to the side as I looked out. The Widows Brigade looked back.

Beyond the porch roof, they arrayed below us, their circle now ragged. Mrs. McDay's sign drooped. Mrs. McGarrity stood with both hands on hips, never good. Even Bark stared up at us, his head cocked to one side. Nance and Henry had disappeared. I didn't have the energy to worry about what that meant.

It must have been all the yelling and screaming, Rupert's yelling and my screaming.

Mrs. McChin looked over her shoulder. "There they are," she shouted at Mallard and Lester, who headed up the circular driveway. She pointed at us.

"It's Rupert," Mrs. McDay called out. Even with ancient eyes, she'd spotted him cowering behind me.

My father yelped.

The cops broke into a run.

"Help! Help!" Godiva yelled.

She gave me an evil Mona Lisa smile. I raised the broomstick and her smile disappeared.

Rupert tugged on the window sash. "Dora, help me," he said. He grunted with effort.

Down below us, Lester pulled out his gun. He disappeared underneath the porch roof, Mallard right behind him. The Castle's front door crashed open.

"Help," Godiva squawked.

Together, Rupert and I pushed up on the window sash. The window opened with a squeal. Rupert clambered out onto the porch roof.

"He's escaping!" Mrs. McGarrity bellowed.

Footsteps sounded on the stairs. "Not again," Mallard's voice came from the stairwell.

Rupert skittered across the old asphalt tiles. Several of them gave way and flew off. One of the tiles smacked Bark on the head and he yelped.

"Don't run," Mrs. McDay said. "They'll shoot you."

Rupert leaped off the porch roof corner. He landed next to Mrs. McGarrity. She raised her broom high.

Lester flung open the ballroom door. I turned to see him lift his gun. I turned back to see Mrs. McGarrity whack Rupert with the broom.

"Don't—" I said. Then a thick black curling snake of death rose over Starke. No, rising close to Dog Face Mountain. My home.

"Oh God, oh God, oh God. Fire!" I shouted.

Everyone froze. Mrs. McGarrity stopped, the broom in mid-strike. Rupert stood poised on one foot, hands over his head. Behind me I heard Lester's hard breathing.

"Fire!" I yelled.

As one, the people below looked at me. Then several stared in the direction of Canine Creek.

"No!" I flung my arm out the window. It struck the sash with a thump. Pain shot to my shoulder. I pointed. "In town! In Starke!"

Mrs. McDay screamed and then clasped both hands to her mouth.

Rupert broke and ran. Miss Mary grabbed her two youngest. Billy grabbed the two siblings nearest to him. Tony flew toward his truck, which roared into life and shot down the driveway. Mallard's and Lester's footsteps thundered back down the Castle stairs. Jeff turned to his grandmother, Mrs. McGarrity, and gestured at her with his outstretched hand.

She patted her myriad pockets and looked around herself. Jeff's gesture grew desperate. Jamey yelled, "Gamma, keys, keys."

I grabbed my keys from my apron pocket and leaned as far as I could out of the window. "Jeff!"

He ignored me.

Mallard and Lester raced to their police car. Joe ran to his, his wine forgotten. Miss Mary and Billy loaded up her kids into her old Volkswagen van.

I tried again. "James."

James ignored me.

The police car's tires spit gravel as it tore out of the driveway.

"Jeffy, Jamey," I said in my old babysitter voice.

They both looked up.

I held out the keys and shook them. "Take the station wagon." I tossed the keys hard so they'd clear the porch overhang.

James caught them on the fly. The brothers ran to the station wagon.

I raced toward the stairs.

"All this silly fuss for a little fire?" Godiva asked.

As I passed the mattress I whammed it with my sign. She scuttled away from me, exposing her breasts.

"You need a bra," I said as my parting shot.

Outside, Mrs. McGarrity searched through a voluminous purse, almost as large as Nance's.

I resisted the urge to snatch the purse out of her hands. "Dump it out," I said.

Mrs. McGarrity looked at me with an irritated frown, then nodded. She took the purse and turned it upside down. A profusion of objects tumbled out.

I heard a snort and gazed up at the source of the sound. Godiva leaned out the ballroom window. She waved a large white flag.

Was she surrendering? Then I saw it was an enormous brassiere.

"Remember," she shouted, "get what's mine to me or kiss your father goodbye forever."

I considered flipping her a defiant one-finger bird. Not Right Action. And not in front of the Widows Brigade.

Mrs. McGarrity held up her keys in triumph. "Found 'em."

I snatched them out of her hand.

Mrs. McGarrity clutched her tatted bosom. "Dora, how dare—"

"I'm driving."

Mrs. McGarrity, Mrs. McDay, and Mrs. McChin all opened their mouths.

I started toward Mrs. McGarrity's car. "Come on, now or never," I said in my best Aunt Maddie tone.

They fell in line behind me.

THIRTY-THREE

Charles's paintings didn't burn well. Stacked into a cone, with the small pictures in the core and the larger on top, all the awful things did was smolder and stink. Thirty-year-old oils on canvas, his paintings should have produced a huge conflagration. Instead, only one small painting at the center of the conical stack displayed serious damage. Several other paintings showed singe marks. The burn damage improved Charles's work.

Aunt Maddie never could build a fire. She always tried. But her fires in our fireplace always ended up all smoke. A last wisp curled up from the center painting. James sprayed it again with the garden hose and the painting sizzled. It looked even better soaking wet.

"That's the last," James said.

"What little there was," Jeff said. They appeared almost disappointed. Almost.

Across from Looney Jump Creek, Starke's brand new fire engine waited. Somehow, to me, it seemed a little frustrated. Almost.

Aunt Maddie stood to one side of her failed bonfire. A smudge of black ash covered her forehead and one cheek. Her green gardening coat now resembled a mudpack and Aunt Maddie, huddled, a defeated mud hen.

Lester and Mallard and the Widows Brigade stood across from her.

At least the rest of Starke didn't witness my aunt's humiliation. I knew that Miss Mary, Tony, and Joe and Mo all now raced through town, banging on doors, alerting the residents to the danger. A fire could destroy a drought-dry mountain town in moments. Fire kills.

Dog Face Mountain towered behind the police and the Brigade. The dog's face appeared to snarl in disdain at my aunt. Fire kills.

Mallard's uniform shirt glistened, soaking wet. Not all from sweat this time. Along with Jeff and James, he'd been dousing the last of the few flames when I, and the Widows Brigade, arrived.

Lester stood next to him. Arms crossed in front, not a drop of moisture on him.

We all stunk of the rank, dirty smoke. And fear. The fire had painted us all with terror.

I needed a shower and a change of clean clothes. My skin itched as if I'd never get clean.

"Oh, Margaret, how could you?" Mrs. McDay said.

Ohm, she'd used my aunt's full name. Nobody did that. Ever.

Aunt Maddie didn't even look up. "I thought Charles's love would burn hot and clean," she said in a flat voice.

"And burn down the whole town," Mrs. McGarrity said.

"I don't think it would have done that." Mrs. McChin pointed at the trench Aunt Maddie had dug in our back yard.

A few inches deep and wide, it circled the paintings. Aunt Maddie must have spent all night digging. An image came to my mind of my aunt toiling away through the night and early morning hours on a chore of destruction.

The sun reflected from the water filling the trench and reminded me of the scales on a snake. It reminded me of Ouroboros, the snake that swallowed his tail, a symbol of life eternal.

Aunt Maddie stared at the fire, her eyes dead. I'd never seen her face so blank. I didn't believe my aunt wanted a symbol for eternity when she made the trench. She shook her head and scrunched lower in her muddied green gardening coat. "I thought I could burn it all away."

"That and everything else, if it had jumped that moat," Mrs. McGarrity said.

"Little chance of that." James rolled up the last of the hose and laid it next to the studio. "C'mon Gamma, let's go."

"I thought it would burn hot enough," my aunt said.

"Hot enough for what?" Mrs. McDay said.

"Once again I could feel the heat of his love," Aunt Maddie continued as if no one had spoken. As if no one was there. She reached up and scrubbed at the ash on her cheek.

I gasped. My aunt's hand shone pink and raw, burned as if she'd held her hand into the fire. Had Aunt Maddie intended to make a funeral pyre? For herself?

The Widows Brigade looked from my aunt to the bonfire. Consternation darkened all three faces.

"What were you thinking?" Mrs. McChin said.

"Surely you weren't thinking—" Mrs. McGarrity said.

"Nothing is ever that bad, Margaret," Mrs. McDay said. "Nothing."

Lester took my aunt's arm. "Come on, Maddie, let's go to Doc Byrne's and get that hand fixed up."

She didn't budge.

Lester lowered his head and sighed. "I'll be glad to be out of this damned, crazy town." He gave a gentle tug on my aunt's arm.

She stood immovable, a statue. Too quiet. Too still. Too silent.

Lester looked over at Mallard. "A little help here."

Mallard stared at my frozen aunt. He sweated. Still, he stepped forward.

"Aunt Maddie, please, go with Lester," I said.

She lifted her chin. I took a step toward her. She pointed with her damaged hand. Raw, bloody skin glistened in the sunlight.

"Get out," she said.

"Aunt Maddie—"

Aunt Maddie yanked out of Lester's grasp. "If you'd only gone back to Boise when I told you, none of this would have happened."

"No..." A single tear rolled down the outside of my nose.

She narrowed her eyes. "Get out."

I swiped at the traitorous tear. "Charles will return." Take back your dreams, Aunt Maddie, I silently prayed.

With her injured hand, she grabbed a length of framing that had fallen away from a painting. "And stay out." She flung it at me.

It smacked me in the chest and bounced off my apron.

I gasped. Mallard gasped. The Widows Brigade gasped.

"That's enough of that." Mallard grabbed my aunt's arm. Lester, a few seconds behind, snatched Aunt Maddie's other arm. They half-walked, half-dragged her toward Looney Jump Creek Bridge.

"No, don't. Aunt Maddie..." I ran behind. I reached toward her again.

"That's right. I'm your aunt, not your mother," Aunt Maddie said over her shoulder. "Your mother's long gone. There's no one left."

Mrs. McGarrity gave a little wave. "We're right here, Maddie."

Aunt Maddie stared back at her with that same dull expression. "I'm not." She shrugged her shoulders and Lester and Mallard released her. She started walking toward the police car. "I'm already dead."

She walked to the car and got in, and never looked at me.

I stood there as Mallard and Lester drove off. I stood there as Jeff and James rolled up the hose, gave me a last look of pity, and departed. I stood there as the Widows Brigade tut-tutted reassurances at me and then left to spread the word that the fire was out and we were all saved.

I stood there as Mrs. McDay returned. She grasped my hand, hers only paper-thin skin and bird-bones. She squeezed tight, looked up into my face until I nodded and only then returned to the Brigade.

I stood in the quiet with the taste of ashes in my mouth. A core of blood-hot anger started at my heart and spread throughout my limbs. "Enough," I said into the silence.

The pearl lay heavy in my apron pocket. If only Rupert had never come into the store and given me the Noira horror. I clutched the pearl and raised my hand up high. If only I had turned over the necklace to Lester at the first. I looked for a good place to throw the damned pearl.

My arm, raised, paused. I had destroyed my aunt's world with only my words. I lowered my arm. If I could give Aunt Maddie her dreams back then...if Rupert had enough money to escape then...if I sold the Noira to Nance then...

I stuffed the pearl back into my pocket and set off to pass on the curse on to a friend.

THIRTY-FOUR

A sturdy piece of plywood blocked where Rupert made his last getaway through the front store window. No glass, no pieces of window frame, no destroyed Spuddy Buddies. Who did all that hard work—Tony?

Across the street, he helped Maureen unload her father's fire-panic-loaded truck. Tony spotted me looking at him. I pointed at the plywood and nodded my thanks. He gave me a thumbs up.

I took out my key, bent to insert it in the lock, and stopped. A brand new brass doorknob, complete with a security bolt lock, gleamed.

I swore, and not a nice pretend swear word, either.

Nance. It had to be her interfering meddling officious usual self.

Banging on the door, I yelled her name.

Nothing.

Last I saw of her, she'd been headed off with Henry, all lovey-dovey. I could see her ordering him to change the lock. Henry would be plenty eager to comply with any of Nance's wishes. Money and those Escher hands wielded fast results.

Never mind that Maddie's and my possessions still remained in the store. And the possession of a dead man, the Noira necklace. We hadn't been evicted, which made it illegal to lock us out. Nance never let little things like legality stop her.

I stood on the sidewalk and seethed, while considering kicking the door down. I studied the bolt lock and thick planks of the old door and reconsidered.

My fist pounded the plywood on the window. And then I shook my stinging hand. Tony had mounted the plywood with a profusion of thick, heavy-duty nails. That plywood might never come off. Now both Tony and Maureen stared at me. I gave a casual wave and waited until Tony, with a shrug, bent back to his task and Maureen followed.

Was Nance still with Henry, planning who knew what other insanity?

I slammed down the sidewalk and headed for Henry's. The wood planks reverberated under my feet. I stopped short outside Mama Chin's café.

Parked skewed so it blocked two full places, was Nance's Mini Cooper. Sunlight shone against the always-pristine front window of the café. I pressed against the glass and cupped my hands around my eyes. Inside sat Nance, perched on a box. With a plate of what looked like beef stroganoff on a bigger box in front of her.

She noticed my nose squashed against the glass and lifted her fork laden with a cube of something that dripped brown gravy. My ex-boss saluted me with a come-hither gesture.

How did Nance stay so thin? She never stopped eating. Of course she ate vegan, but it was her special version of vegan and included cinnamon rolls.

I flung open the café door. The old booths had vanished, along with the old stools ranged along the counter. I wended my way through the towers of boxes. There seemed to be more boxes, more dishes, and more chaos.

As I reached Nance's table—er—box, Mama Chin bustled over. She pointed at Nance. "Make her leave."

"I'm not finished," Nance said, all mild-mannered Buddhist.

Mama Chin shook her finger and her whole body shook along. "Starke was burning down and she wouldn't leave."

"One of the Widows Brigade said that was merely a lot of smoke," Nance said.

"You were the last to see him." Mama Chin pointed a sugar-dusted finger at me. "Where's Fat Freddy?"

"In the tunnels where rats belong." I pulled up another box across from Nance.

Mama Chin crossed her arms over her chest. She stepped closer to me. "We're closed."

I looked up at her.

Mama Chin dropped her arms. "Dora?"

I tossed my head in Nance's direction. "I need to talk to this woman."

Nance paused, a forkful halfway to her mouth. She blinked and put her fork down.

"But Dora," Mama Chin said, "we're closed."

"Now," I said.

She backpedaled and bumped into a stack of boxes, which swayed. She held out a hand to steady the boxes. "I'll be in the kitchen." Mama Chin fled.

I turned to Nance.

"This woman?" Nance said. "I'm 'this woman'?"

I didn't say anything.

Nance straightened on her box. The Escher hands shifted. I'd never once seen Nance wear pants. What would she do when snow lay two feet thick on the ground? I supposed I'd find out if it ever snowed. I wondered if I still cared. Or if I'd be around.

She flipped a dismissive hand over the remnants of her meal. "No matter. You've had a rough couple of days."

Ya think? I almost said.

"As a Buddhist I'm trained to be forgiving, whatever the insult." Nance pushed her plate aside. She reached out to pat my arm.

I shrugged away.

"Dora?"

"You came here—"

"I came here to create my flagship store." Nance flung both arms wide. "Nance's Innovations," her voice rang out.

The swinging door to the kitchen moved an inch. I caught sight of a small work-roughened, floury hand. Mama Chin.

I leaned forward. "Bullshit."

Nance's hand flew to her mouth.

"You came here to commit a crime," I said, my voice low.

Nance clasped both hands to her bosom, perfectly over the other hands. "I don't know—"

"The Noira."

"The Noira," Nance echoed.

"You came sniffing around for the necklace."

Nance gave an insulted sniff. "In no way did I—"

"I have the Noira."

Nance reared back on her box. The box creased beneath her. I guess she did weigh a bit, despite always looking as if she'd blow away in a winter wind.

The swinging door opened wider.

"I knew it. Rupert gave you the Noira," Nance yelped.

I thumped my lips with my index finger. "Shh."

Nance persisted. "He stole it and killed that old man—"

"For once in your stupid life, shut up."

Nance's mouth fell open. "Dora?" she asked again. Her lower lip trembled.

"Mama Chin?" I called out.

After a pause, the kitchen door opened a crack and Mama Chin peeked out. "What you want?" she said in a perfect imitation of a clichéd old style immigrant Chinese. One that had never attended Dartmouth and graduated with honors. "I no hear you from where I was, way, way in back."

I ignored Mama Chin's humor and pointed at Nance's plate. "Do you have any more of this?"

Mama Chin snorted. "A bit. But it's gone cold."

"Then you need to reheat it as I would like some."

Mama Chin opened her mouth, looked at my face, and closed it again. She nodded and closed the kitchen door. I waited until I heard the sounds of pots banging to grab the pearl in my pocket. I tossed it on the box Nance used as a table. It bounced.

Nance jerked back. Her body settled farther into her box seat. I wondered what was in the box and if it were fragile.

"There's a taste." I almost added, *you might find it bitter.*

Nance snatched the pearl. "This is the pearl that was added to the Noira."

How long had she studied the necklace, to recognize the pearl right off? I imagined her bent toward her computer monitor screen for hour after hour, scrolling through Google pages.

"You can have the necklace," I said.

"The necklace?" Nance looked at me, eyes wide. Perhaps she didn't dare believe what she'd heard. "I can have it?" She patted her chest as if she checked the space where the Noira would rest.

Her chest didn't look big enough to carry the heavy, noxious weight of the necklace. That was her problem. Not mine.

I noticed her long graceful fingers. She'd be far better off wearing gorgeous rings that highlighted those beautiful hands, than a necklace that emphasized her long, too thin, scrawny neck. I amazed myself that I paid attention to such nonsense now.

"It's mine?" A smile bloomed all over her face. She didn't possess the necklace, not yet. She didn't know the weight of it, not yet.

The kitchen door swung open. Mama Chin stood there, a steaming plate in her hand. She stared. How much had she heard?

"Is that my stroganoff?" I called out.

Mama Chin brought the plate over. Nance placed both hands over the pearl, all innocent and demure.

Mama Chin set the plate in front of me. "Doesn't warrant the name of stroganoff. Not having a speck of meat."

"Thank you. That'll be all," I said.

Mama Chin frowned.

"Shut the door behind you," I said.

"Stolen?" Mama Chin said.

I ran both my hands through my hair. "Mama Chin. Please."

She grimaced. "Okay." She gave me a pat and left.

Nance and I watched her head back to the kitchen. She shut the swinging door tight behind her.

"How much can you hand over for a down payment?" Let it be enough, I prayed.

"What?" Nance stared down at the suitcase-sized monstrosity at her feet.

"I know you, Nance. I know you came to Starke with money. How much?"

"Fifty thousand," Nance said.

"You thought you could buy the Noira for a measly fifty thousand?" Now my voice squealed outrage.

"Like you said, Dora, it's cursed and stolen. It's not like you could sell the necklace on the open market. In fact, I think fifty thousand is too much—"

"Fine." I stood. The box wheezed as air rushed back into it. "I'll turn the necklace over to the police—"

"No, it's mine." Her hand gripped the pearl tight and became a bird of prey's taloned foot around a bloodied dead prize. "I need it to be mine," she said, her voice an echo of Godiva's that made me shudder.

"You want the damned horror?" I asked.

The delicious aroma of the vegan stroganoff wafted around me. I wanted to puke. I wanted to toss it into Nance's oblivious face.

"Then pay for it and take it," I said. "Maybe you won't add your blood to all the other blood. Maybe you're immune."

Nance gazed down at her hands as if she searched for telltale red. "Why are you so angry at me?" Her shoulders hitched once, twice. And then fell.

I passed my hand over my eyes. The images of Noira with a slashed throat, of a woman with a bloody white dress, of an old man burning flashed in my dark. And then of Nance wearing the necklace, open-eyed and dead.

"Don't do it, Nance." I grasped her hands and forced her to look at me. "Don't take the Noira. Please." I gave her hands a little shake.

I didn't know what I'd do if she didn't give me the money. Maybe lose Maddie's love forever. Maybe keep my soul.

She blinked at me, puzzled.

I squeezed her hands until she winced. "The Noira's evil. Everyone who possesses it is destroyed." I released my grip.

Nance bit her lower lip. I watched her stroke, with one fine-fingered hand, the black pearl as if to reassure herself that it existed. Or as if it lived.

She squeezed the pearl. Tears coursed down her cheeks. "Oh, Dora, I know I'm a fool. But I have to have the Noira. It needs to be mine. Mine."

My heart ached. I gritted my teeth until the pain in my jaw overwhelmed my heart. "Then you make your own narrow bed." I stood and reached for her satchel. "Fifty thousand is enough."

"Not so fast." Nance snatched the heavy carrier out of my reach. She stood and with the hand not holding the pearl, brushed at a stain on her dress. "When will I get the necklace?"

I thought fast. "Tomorrow." By then I'd have spent her money.

"Tomorrow? Why tomorrow?"

"When you give me the rest of the money."

Nance grasped her chest and destroyed the Escher design. "I don't think I can get any more than a couple of hundred thousand—"

"Fine. Get whatever you can." I wanted Nance out of my way, not an easy thing to do with my furniture-moving friend. Money could be a big enough distraction. "This will do—for now." I reached for Nance's huge purse.

Swift and sure, she kicked it away from my grasp. "I'll get the necklace no matter how much of the rest I can come up with?"

"I didn't say that. You won't get it unless you give me the fifty thousand right now."

Nance whimpered as I grappled her purse away from her guard.

I unclasped the lion's jaws. Inside, Nance's wallet sat atop neatly bound sheaves of twenty-dollar bills. Underneath the money was a jumble of jeweler's tools. I tossed her wallet on the table box, next to my untouched stroganoff.

"Dora?"

I hoisted the bag onto a shoulder and staggered to the front door.

"Dora, wait, I—"

I ignored Nance's confused and plaintive tone. I had places to go and people to save.

THIRTY-FIVE

The heavy bag shifted on my back and dug into a shoulder blade. I yelped. And then swore.

I'd schlepped that sack-on-steroids the three blocks to Doc Byrne's only to discover no Maddie. Doc Byrne, after scolding me for carrying such a heavy bag on one shoulder, replied with "don't know" to my question of her whereabouts.

I ducked my head as I turned onto Main Street and passed by the front window of the sheriff's office. My aunt huddled in the same chair I sat in not long ago. She cradled her burned hand, now mummy wrapped, in her crossed arms.

The stupid bag banged on the doorframe as I entered. At the sight of Nance's monster purse, Lester gave a small gasp. Aunt Maddie jumped at the sound. Mallard started sweating, or rather sweated more.

"Relax," I said to them, "it's a purse." Whose purse, I didn't say.

"A really, really big purse," Mallard said from where he hunched at his desk. He looked from me to Aunt Maddie. He gave me a tiny nod of encouragement. Then he bent back over his keyboard.

Lester sat across from my aunt. He glanced from me to the open trap door to the fruit cellar cell. Perhaps he considered tossing me into the tunnel. The only thing that stopped him was the yellow crime scene tape strung around the trap door.

I couldn't blame him. It must sting that while he and Mallard searched everywhere for Rupert, he was there, already jailed.

The bag banged on my back with every step as I stomped across to Lester. I stopped and tried to loom over him. I'm too short for that to work.

"Why is Aunt Maddie here?" I demanded.

Lester gazed at me from under his gray, bushy eyebrows.

I told my body to *not* take a step back. It obeyed.

"She set a fire," Lester said.

"Which promptly went out, like all her other fires." I put my hands on my hips. "Didn't do a bit of damage." My body tilted over, toward the bag.

"Yes, but—"

I struggled to straighten and turned to Aunt Maddie. "In fact, Charles's paintings are all the better for being a bit singe—altered."

She responded by shrinking deeper into her old coat.

I reached out a hand to her but let it drop and turned back to Lester. "Aunt Maddie also made sure the fire wouldn't spread. You saw the trench."

"Fire jumps."

"It didn't this time." I pointed at my aunt. "So why is she here?"

Lester rubbed his jaw, looking almost as dejected as Aunt Maddie. He sighed for a third time. "There's the large problem of the ticket."

"Ticket?"

"The citation for violating the fire ban," Lester said.

I stared at him open-mouthed.

"New requirement by the new council run by those new doggy residents." He shrugged and looked over at the computer-altered photo of his grandson. "I'll be glad when I'm out of this Podunk town. I'll be glad to be tracking down the killer of my grandson, instead of a pathetic fool recluse who kills old men over broken bits of jewelry, with missing pearls."

Mallard looked up from his monitor. "We're doing the paperwork to issue the ticket. First one we've ever done."

Lester tipped his head toward my aunt. "Maddie, since you don't have a dime to pay—"

"How much?" I asked.

"How much?" Lester echoed.

"How much is the ticket?"

"A lot," he said, "Fifteen hundred bucks."

"Gaak," I gargled.

"The whole town could have burned down," Mallard said.

I opened my mouth to ream out Mallard. But he was right. So was the Dog Developer Town Council, dammit.

"Wait." With a relieved sigh, I slid the bag off my shoulder. I undid the lion's jaws and reached inside, blocking the bag so no one could see the bills inside. I counted fifteen hundred. Then I paused, the money in the bag clutched tight.

What if Aunt Maddie didn't believe my bogus "enormous, vast, huge loan from Nance" story? I considered my glum aunt. No way would she believe.

The more she questioned, the more Lester or Mallard would ask where I came up with so much money. They might demand to see in the bag. They wouldn't believe me, either, I'd bet. Cops, nothing but trouble.

I looked over my shoulder. Lester loomed over me. He could loom.

Cramming the bills back out of sight, I snapped the jaws shut. "Oops, sorry. I thought I had enough from selling Nance a design, but nope." Wasn't a lie. I had sold Nance a design. Not my design. The Noira design.

"You don't know how much money she gave you?" Mallard asked.

What did I just say? Cops. And somewhere along the way in the past couple of days, Mallard had joined their ranks, big time.

Aunt Maddie sat up and shot me a look of suspicion.

Lester reached for the purse clasp. I gave the bag a kick. "Nance gave me all the cash she had, 'cause she forgot her checkbook," I babbled, "and she gave me this bag as collateral until she could give me the rest and I forgot to count how much she gave me and—" I stopped and took a deep breath.

Police and aunt stared at me.

I grappled the bag back onto my shoulder. "What happens to Aunt Maddie now?" I asked.

Lester ran a hand through his hair. "She can't pay the ticket."

Mallard spoke. "We'll hold her in a holding cell until..." He trailed off.

As one, Lester, Mallard, and I looked at the fruit cellar hole.

"You've got to be kidding," I said.

"Why don't you take her home?" Lester said.

"No," Aunt Maddie muttered, her chin tucked tight into her coat collar.

"Aunt Maddie, I—" I started to insist she come with me when a realization smacked me harder than the bag on my back.

I'd thought to have her accompany me to Henry's, where I'd pay off the back rent with a flourish. If she saw me pay Henry, she'd demand to know where I got the money. And once again, not believe my "Nance loan" story. Heck, *I* didn't believe my "Nance loan" story.

She'd already almost burned down Starke, what would she try next?

"No, I won't take Aunt Maddie home. She stays in custody," I said.

Now I had everybody's attention.

"Why?" Lester asked the obvious and reasonable question.

"Because..." I shifted the bag from one aching shoulder to another to gain time. I amazed myself by coming up with an idea. Maybe sleep deprivation made my brain work. Or maybe desperation did. "Because she's a suicide risk."

Aunt Maddie's face jerked out of her coat. "Am not."

"Maddie? Suicide?" Lester said.

"Don't you remember how she acted at the fire?"

"I remember," Mallard said. He stood. "Dora's right."

I am? I almost said. "I can't be responsible for her actions. You're the police. It's your job."

"Dora's right," Mallard said. Amazing.

"But—where do we put her?" Lester said in a confused old man's voice.

"We could take her back to Dr. Byrne's clinic," Mallard said.

"I'm right here." Aunt Maddie shot me a look that said she'd make me pay for my allegation.

Once I'd paid off Henry and gotten Rupert gone, it'd all be a *fait accompli*. Then my aunt, the loose cannon, could be loose. After...wait. She'd be gone from Doc Byrne's in five minutes.

"Have the Widows Brigade take care of her," I said.

"I'm not killing *myself*," Aunt Maddie said, her tone making it clear whom she intended murdering.

"They'll be thrilled," I said. Or not. It wouldn't be for long, either way.

"I suppose—" Lester began.

"Good, that's settled," I said.

The bag and I banged out the door to a chorus of, "Dora?"

THIRTY-SIX

My back humped as an old woman's, I moved as fast as possible away from the police station. Money sure weighed me down. I hesitated, huffing. I needed a safe place to dump Nance's baggage. But where? The store was locked; the homestead was too far, the car—the car.

I heaved the bag into the back of the old station wagon. I tossed the car blanket over the top, contemplated the lump for a moment, then slammed the door closed and smacked my hands together.

Good, now—I turned around and bumped into Godiva. Or rather Godiva's breasts. She stood on the sidewalk, several inches above me. Even encased in a bra, all that boob made for a soft smack. She wore another sweatsuit, this one snow white.

A definite improvement from her nudity at the Castle. I shuddered at the memory.

"Give over, bitch, or I'll tell the cops where Rupert is hiding," she said.

Heat flooded into my face. I stepped onto the sidewalk. We stood to nose to nose. "First, I'll see you burning in hell."

Uncle, may he burn forever. Her words came to me in a rush. "You burned down your uncle's mansion. You killed him."

Godiva cocked her head to one side. "Oh no, everyone believes—knows—Rupert killed my uncle." She gave a tiny, angelic smile that went with her outfit. "And if you don't give me the necklace and the money, I'll tell them Rupert tried to rape and then kill me," she said in a breathy little girl voice. Her breath smelled of rancid fried meat.

My nose wrinkled. "Lester wouldn't believe—"

"Where your precious toothless father is hiding, I can make certain he's killed during his capture." Godiva crossed her arms beneath her huge breasts. They jutted out and pointed at me.

My hand itched to smack her smug, naked face until she cracked. If Rupert died, he'd be blamed for everything. Even if he survived, there'd still be no proof Godiva killed her own uncle and brother.

The sound of my aunt hollering drew our attention from each other's nose.

Outside the police station, the Widows Brigade was hauling Aunt Maddie off under her vociferous protest while Lester and Mallard watched. Mrs. McGarrity and Mrs. McChin each had hold of one of Aunt Maddie's arms, with Mrs. McDay bringing up the rear guard. Tough old birds.

Lester spotted us looking. Even from that distance, I could see his frown.

"Your time's up," Godiva said.

"So's yours." I realized with a flash of desperate inspiration why I spoke the truth. If my new plan worked, I wouldn't need to find Rupert. If it worked, I could save him without giving him money and him running away, perhaps forever. If it worked I could save them all, even myself.

My appetite came back with a vengeance. I wished I'd eaten that stroganoff.

"Your father's funeral." Godiva gave a little wave at Lester.

He took a step back, shook his head and then headed down the sidewalk toward us.

"No wait." I put a cadging whine into my voice. "All right. I'll give you the necklace and the money."

"Now," Godiva said as if I'd pull both out of an apron pocket.

"I haven't got either with me."

Godiva's lips drew back. "What?" she said through her teeth.

"Nance has the necklace. I'll get it back for you." I tried to sound as pitiful as possible.

"Now," Godiva said. A world of threat echoed in that one word.

Lester had almost reached us.

"I need a couple of hours to find Nance. She might have put it someplace and—"

"One hour. In your aunt's stupid store."

I managed to keep the grin off my face.

"Or else." With that last statement, the cliché of villains everywhere, Godiva gave Lester another little wave, a dismissing one, and sauntered to her Cadillac.

As soon as she left, I let the grin spread all over my face. I skipped the last few steps to Lester and flung my arms around him.

He gave a small gasp, almost a sob.

"I'm going to fix everything," my voice rang out.

"Oh, Dora, my silly girl." Lester squeezed me tight and then released me. He placed a hand on my shoulder. "Dora—that money—at the station—you need to know..." A shadow passed over his face.

I looked up and gasped.

Black storm clouds roiled over Dog Face Mountain, moving fast and furious.

A brisk cold-but-warm-enough-to-snow, wind whistled down the street. It tore away the smoke wisps. I breathed deep of the sweet heavy perfume of the coming storm. "Snow. Thank you, Buddha. Everything's on the right path at last."

Lester looked up too. "No." He ran his hand over his mouth, an old man's querulous gesture. "Whatever you're thinking of, Dora, don't do it." In the dimming light, he appeared gray, washed-out, a ghost of himself.

"I'm going to..." I stopped. I couldn't tell Lester my plan to have him catch Godiva in the store, clutching the Noira red-handed. A great sheriff, he wouldn't go along with my plan for entrapment. He'd demand the necklace, now.

"Meet me in Mad Maddie's in an hour."

Lester gave me a little shake. "Dora, for once, listen—"

I pulled out of his grasp. "Gotta go. An hour. Promise." I didn't wait for his reply, but heard his voice ride the high wind as I ran toward Cam's Auto.

"This is one thing you can't fix."

I turned back to argue but caught a glimpse of a figure on top of Cam's Auto. Oh no, not now, not again. And ran.

THIRTY-SEVEN

Henry sat on the false front cap. His legs hung over the edge. He stared off at Dog Face Mountain where the clouds, now a solid wall of dark, flowed over the dog's face.

I stood on the flat roof about ten feet away. I didn't think he'd heard me climb up the attic ladder. I closed my hand around Great Grandpa's gun in my apron pocket, brought it out, and loaded it with quick jerks of my fingers.

What would I do, save Henry by shooting his gun out of his hand? Both of Henry's hands held the cap tight. Where would he hold a gun? I re-pocketed the gun and stepped across the tarpaper roof.

"I don't think you'd die if you jumped off, just break a bone. Or two." I came up to Henry.

His upper body twisted around, fast. He started to topple. I grabbed his arms and yanked hard. Henry clambered back onto the roof.

"That's twice I've saved your life." I peered over the edge to the sidewalk below. "Of course, if you broke a neck bone like Great Grandpa Starke, you might die."

"Dora—"

"But you might linger. As I recall, Great Grandpa hung around for weeks. He never did do anything half—"

"Dork."

"—rear ended," I finished. "What?"

"I'm not jumping off."

"Not now, you're not." I gave his arm a little shake for emphasis.

"Let go." He tugged at my grasp. "You're going to make me fall."

"Aren't you up here to kill yourself, again?"

Henry snorted. "Don't be ridiculous." He smoothed his hand down his shirt.

Rumpled as ever. But he'd changed into a pair jeans and an old high school sweatshirt, stained and torn. I couldn't remember when I'd last seen Henry wear comfortable clothes instead of those nasty realtor suits.

I wiped both hands over my face. I didn't have time to play with Henry. "Hand over the new key to Mad Maddie's."

"But Nance—"

"I've got plenty of money to pay the back rent."

"You do?" Henry swayed.

I grabbed his arm again to steady him.

He stepped off the cap and gave himself a little shake or maybe a shiver, for the wind blew ice cold, a presage to the snow. "Doesn't matter. Not anymore."

"What?" Was lack of sleep making me hallucinate?

"I'm a lousy realtor. I hate being one. I suck."

"You're not so awful. Not that bad."

Henry raised an eyebrow at me. "I depended on rent from your aunt's store to save my business? Your aunt's store?"

"Okay, but—"

"I'm selling out."

I gulped. "You don't have to do that, Henry." I laid my hand on his shoulder and crouched down next to him. "I've got enough money—"

"No, no." Henry shook his head. "You don't understand, Dora. I want to do this." He chuckled. I couldn't remember the last time I heard him laugh so deep in his chest. "I love fixing cars. I'm the best mechanic I know."

My mind gave a skip trying to keep up.

"There used to be one and only one mechanic, a great one, in Starke. Me. Then there was none."

I rubbed my cold nose. "Too true."

Henry grinned with his whole face, his eyes wide. "Now there is one great one again. Me."

"Oh, Henry." I grinned back. I loved seeing him so happy.

He stood up. "You're the one who taught me to follow my own path. If I sell to the Sun Dogs— "

My grin fell. "What about Mad Maddie's?"

"I'm sure Nance's Innovations—"

"No, no, not Nance." I looked over at the store and saw a tall, stork figure open the door. "Nance."

"I need the key to the store. Now, Henry." I had to get Nance out of there and fast. "The key, the key." I flapped both hands at Henry in a gimme gesture. "For Buddha's sake, give me Mad Maddie's key."

Henry took a step back. "But Nance said—"

His words made me glance at the store again. I froze. Lester leaned against the store's door.

"Oh great Bodhi Tree, let Nance have locked the door behind her," I said.

"Bodhi Tree?" Henry took another step away.

Lester cracked open the door. He tilted his head.

Great, wonderful, tremendous. Now both Lester and Nance would be in the store before Godiva. Terrible timing.

With his free hand, Lester pulled his pistol from the holster. I gasped. Lester crashed inside the store as fast as the first snowflakes now streaking down. He slammed the door behind him.

I ran toward the roof hatch.

"Where are you going?" Henry called behind me.

I slammed open the hatch, jumped onto the ladder and clambered down.

I ran.

THIRTY-EIGHT

I skidded to a halt outside Mad Maddie's door. A high-pitched scream sounded inside.

"I'm coming!" I hollered.

A crash answered, followed by a man yelling.

Another scream echoed from the store. What made me believe I could save everyone with my silly plan? Whose death would I be responsible for this time?

I banged the door open. It bounced shut as I stormed inside.

"Dora, down!" Lester yelled at me.

A shot whizzed over my head and took out one last remaining Spuddy Buddy in the front window display. I crouched onto all fours. A piece of glass cut into my hand. I whimpered but couldn't hear myself in the reverberation from the gunfire.

When I looked up I saw devastation.

Cordite smoke hung in the air. Below it, the jewelry tree lay fallen over in the aisle, its branches crushed. Scattered pieces of glass from a shattered display case were all over the floor. The big oak table lay overturned in the center of the aisle.

Lester crouched behind the oak table, his gun drawn. His left arm dangled. Blood poured from a wound on his upper arm.

"Lester, you're hurt," I cried.

Lester shook his head in warning before he turned his attention back to the shooter at the other far end of the aisle, close to my workbench. Who was the shooter?

"Back off, Dora," Godiva shouted and answered my question, "or I'll kill your little friend."

Little friend? Could she mean Nance?

"Dora, run," Nance called and answered that question.

I hated that answer. I scuttled toward Lester. Without turning around again, he gestured for me to get away.

Instead I kept going. A piece of glass sliced through my jeans into my knee. I ignored the pain and crawled. Miles to the sanctuary of the table.

"Dora, get out of here," Lester hissed as I reached him.

"I told you Godiva was the killer." I couldn't resist.

Lester gave me a nudge with his elbow. "Go on, go get help."

"I am help."

I gathered my courage and popped my head around the far edge of the table. I froze. Godiva held Nance as a shield.

At my workbench, my tools and wax patterns lay scattered. The one of Dog Face that Nance had tweaked for me lay on the floor, flattened by a footprint. Ruined.

I swallowed, hard. What did that matter now?

Nance's face showed one black eye almost swollen closed and a split lip that bled down her chin onto her neck. Godiva fared little better with her long blonde hair snarled into a witch's nest around her face, and a huge bloody scrape on one cheek.

Godiva's hand that trapped Nance in an unloving embrace also held the source of all our misery—the Noira necklace. Godiva's other hand held a .357 magnum that dwarfed her tiny plump hand. She waved the revolver around. Her eyes showed all the white as her gaze followed her wavering gun.

If I ever doubted she killed before and would kill again, I didn't doubt it now.

Nance also grasped the Noira. In horror I watched her tug at the necklace.

"Nance, let it go," I screamed.

Godiva focused on me. "This is all your fault!" She fired.

The shot plowed into the four-inch-thick oak tabletop. I ducked back. My ears rang louder.

"Goddammit!" Lester yelled loud enough for me to hear him over the ringing.

I fumbled in my pocket for my gun.

"Enough!" Lester jumped up.

I followed. I couldn't let him be killed because of my stupid plan.

Godiva swung her gun back and forth between the two of us. Dear Buddha, she held a big honking thing, not a .22, so it couldn't be the gun that killed her brother. Why, when I was about to die, did I worry about what gun would kill me?

Lester fired. The shot went wide and slammed into my workbench.

I squeaked as if it struck me. *Never fire at anyone unless you shoot to kill.* Lester's words echoed in my mind.

Godiva ducked. She released her hold on Nance. Nance slumped to her knees but didn't relinquish her hold on the necklace.

"Let it go," I yelled.

She obeyed, for once. She let go of the necklace. She fell to the floor.

Lester had a clear shot at Godiva. He took aim and fired again. The bullet ricocheted off the far wall, then burrowed into the floor inches away. He missed? Again?

Lester grimaced. The pain from his arm must have destroyed his aim.

Godiva raced toward the tunnel.

"Shoot her." Who yelled that? Ohm, it was me.

She dove down the ladder. Lester ran after her. I followed.

"Dora," Nance said as I passed her.

Something in the way she said my name stopped me. I crouched down beside my injured friend. "It's okay."

Grimacing, Nance struggled to get upright. "I think that crazy bitch broke a rib."

"Stay down," I said.

Nance pressed her hand hard against her side. "She has the Noira."

"Good."

"No, no, it's mine." She pulled a knee underneath her, giving me a view of lacy purple underwear.

"Stay down." I wanted to smack Nance but settled for a gentle hand on her shoulder. "The Noira's not worth dying for."

Tears rolled down Nance's face. "Yes, it is."

"No, Nance. Let Godiva have the cursed monstrosity."

"She doesn't have it all," Nance said. She opened her hand. The black water pearl clattered onto the floor.

I stopped breathing. *...broken jewelry...missing pearl.* The pearl fell off the necklace after Rupert had hidden it in the ash trap. How could Lester know it was missing?

Why hadn't Lester yelled at Godiva to drop her weapon in standard police-speak? Why hadn't he shot her, since she held a gun that she'd fired? Why had he, a crack shot, missed?

"Forgive me, Dora." Nance twisted her body to snatch the pearl.

My mind spun. I needed to make it right. I had to stop Lester.

"Drop it," I said to Nance.

She whimpered.

I slapped the pearl out of her hand.

She gasped.

"Where's your cell phone?" I asked.

"What do you want—I don't know. I don't have it." Nance's voice possessed a passel of panic.

I made an annoyed noise deep in my throat. "Scream until somebody comes." I ran to the tunnel. "Tell them to call Mallard."

"Mallard?" Nance asked. "Call a duck?"

"He's a police officer."

I climbed down the tunnel ladder to the accompaniment of Nance hollering. I yanked my flashlight out of my pocket and shone it on the ground, searching for an indication of where Lester and Godiva ran. At the front of the left branch of the tunnel a tiny wet spot reflected. I stepped closer and touched the spot. It came away red.

Far off down the tunnel came a faint sound of someone yelling in a high voice. Godiva.

"The Castle," I yelled to Nance. "They're headed to the Castle."

"The Castle? What Castle?" Nance's voice trailed after me as I ran down the tunnel.

My heart pounded. Lester must have interrupted Derek beating Rupert up and killed him. Maybe an accident, but Lester killed him. Lester blackmailed my father. Why?

A memory of the computer updated photo of his grandson came to me and Lester's insistence that he would find the hit-and-run driver. For that, he needed money.

I ran. My flashlight beam bounced off dirt walls. My breath came in gasps. I reached the ladder to the Castle. Below the ladder lay a gun. Godiva's gun. I shone my light up the ladder. Smoke curled in the beam.

"Fire. Fire. Fire in the Castle," I sobbed. I turned to race back down the tunnel for help.

My father cried out, "Oh, God. You killed her, Lester."

His voice came from inside the Castle. With the fire. With Lester, a killer.

"I'll kill you," Rupert yelled. The sound of running footsteps followed.

"Rupert, wait, no." I climbed. "No, no."

At the top, in the darkness, heat and smoke roared over me, making me cough. I clambered out and stumbled on something soft and wet and flung out my hands to brace myself. My flashlight clanged as it hit the floor and died. Sudden darkness.

I struck the floor, the wind knocked out of me. I needed air, any air, even hot smoky air. I gulped and hacked, then pushed myself up. Scrabbled for the flashlight.

Found it and turned it on. I played the light over my wet hand. Blood.

I shrieked and then clamped my lips closed, shining the light on the thing that tripped me.

In the beam, Godiva lay dead beside the tunnel entrance. A wound above her generous breasts bled. Blood spread down her snow white front. Blood-matted hair haloed around her head.

I screamed.

THIRTY-NINE

Into the silence, something squeaked. Too shaken to scream again, I squeaked, too, and cast the flashlight around, frantic to find the source. Two pinpricks of red flashed in the smoky darkness.

The red eyes crept into the light. Fat Freddy.

Freddy sat on his haunches next to Godiva. He held his little rodent arms in from of him. His paws pressed together as if in prayer.

I giggled. The giggle turned into a sobbing cough. I hiccupped.

Freddy squeaked again.

I sniffled. "Mama Chin is worried about you."

The fat rat tipped his head at mention of Mama Chin.

I made a shooing motion with my hand. "You go on home."

Freddy ducked his head up and down as if he nodded in agreement. Then he scurried off down the tunnel ladder, perhaps headed for home.

I smiled at his anthropomorphic antics. The spell of my terror broken, I turned my attention back to the dead woman. Smoke wreathed her body. *Oh Buddha, no. Lester must have missed in the store on purpose. He didn't want to kill her in front of witnesses.* I didn't want to believe my unbidden thoughts.

Godiva's hand twitched.

I yelped. "You're alive," I breathed.

Godiva tilted her head in a tiny motion toward me. "I'm so cold."

I touched her icy hand, a frightening contrast to the blazing heat. "Hold on, help's coming."

Under my touch, her hand trembled, a trapped, dying bird.

"What happened?" I asked in the gentlest yet most insistent voice I owned.

"Please. Start a fire. I need a fire. So warm, so lovely." With her dying breath, with fire all around us, still she wanted more. "Like my Noira…" A thick cloud of smoke obscured her face. Her hand stilled.

Silence.

"Godiva? Mary Jane?" I shined the light into her face and into her open, unblinking eyes.

I stood and took several steps and then started choking until I doubled over. I fell to all fours. I peered with tearing eyes but couldn't see twelve inches in front of me through the smoke. Where was the tunnel entrance?

Panic rose in my chest. *Buddha, please help me find a path now.*

A cold, clean wind cut a swath in the smoke. I used it as a guide and wheezing, stumbled on all fours toward its source. My cut knee throbbed as I crawled.

The smoke thinned a little. I felt the Castle's lobby's flagstones under my hands. I crept on, breathing shallow. Heat made my skin prickle. I prayed I didn't walk into flames.

At last, through streaming eyes, I perceived the vague outline of the front door. It stood open and inviting. Air. Safety. Freedom. The wind blew in and with it floated enormous snowflakes.

I tried to run and stumbled on the stone steps. The cut knee cracked against an edge. My lungs burning, I staggered up the rest of the steps and outside.

The glorious air made me gulp.

Then I gasped. The rotund Castle tower blazed.

I stumbled off the porch and slipped into a skiff of snow. Icy cold stung my cheeks. Great snowflakes swirled around me, gusted by the wind. I turned my face skyward. My mouth open, I took deep breaths while the blessed cooling flakes chilled my hot skin.

On my knees, I gazed up at the tower.

Flames from the huge tower, now a torch, flared high into the storm. What remained of the dead fir tree, now an enormous blackened match, leaned against the tower's base.

An ash burned against my face. A snowflake caressed my cheek. Hot and cold.

Past the Castle, beside the fir tree next to the tower, the dancing flames flickered over two figures. They stood several feet apart. Lester. Rupert.

I clambered to a standing position, slipping and slithering over the snowy lawn toward them. "No," I croaked.

Lester stood ramrod straight next to the fir tree, his face lit by firelight. One hand held a gun pointed at Rupert, the other the Noira. Blood from his wound dripped onto the necklace.

The falling snow almost screened my father. He huddled in the stand of fir trees that led to the mountains. He held a gun in one hand, his other arm by his side.

"No," I shouted, loud and harsh. The wind drew out my denial into a scream.

Rupert turned toward me.

Without taking his eyes off Rupert, Lester yelled, "Dora, get the hell outta here." In a wild gesture, he threw out his wounded arm to shoo me away. The Noira flew from his hand.

My father and I followed the arc of its flight through the falling snow. Snowflakes puffed as the Noira vanished into a drift. Lester never wavered from his focus on my father.

Lester raised his damaged arm and grasped his gun two-handed cop-style. Firelight flashed over his face, creating a demonic mask.

Rupert took a step toward where the necklace landed then stopped. "The necklace doesn't matter any more." He brought his gun up and pointed it at Lester. "You shot my love, my Godiva, my beautiful lady."

Lester steadied his point on Rupert. "She deserved to die," Lester screamed. His words roared louder than the fire, raw with rage.

Rupert cringed.

"Oh, Lester, no." I put every ounce of watching Godiva die into my voice.

"Dora, she burned her uncle alive," he yelled. "And Rupert's as guilty as that bitch."

Rupert drew back into the fir trees. Lester tracked him with his gun. I pulled Great Grandpa's gun out of my pocket.

"Rupert never killed anyone," I called to Lester. "He won't shoot you. You know that."

"There's no justice. There's only the dead," Lester yelled. He tipped his head in an old familiar way. He had drawn down a sight on the gun barrel. On my father.

"Don't kill him." I brought my gun up into a two-handed hold, like Lester taught me. *Never aim to wound, only to kill.* "Lester, stop the killing." My voice squeaked on the last word. "Please," I sobbed.

He glanced at me for the briefest of seconds. The firelight illuminated his face full of the old Lester. Shadowed with grief and love.

He fired.

"No!" I fired.

In an instant that lasted a lifetime, Lester dropped his left arm as he fired. His right arm flew upward with the recoil. He twisted his body toward me.

My hands bucked back after I fired. My feet flew out from under me. I fell on my butt. The gun tumbled from my numb hands.

A plume of blood sprouted from Lester's chest as he collapsed backward.

I screeched.

Rupert screamed, his voice higher. He still cowered in the fir trees. Unhurt.

Lester had missed. He must have fired wide. Of course he had.

I scrambled to my feet, and ran, sliding on the new snow and dropped to my knees beside Lester. Blood shone in the firelight on his coat front. He gasped and a raw sucking sound came from his wound.

I tore off my apron and bundled it as best I could and pressed it into the wound. The wet sound lessened, but only a little.

"Let it be, Dora." Lester coughed.

"Hold on," I said.

I looked over at my father. He still stood frozen in the same spot. "Help me."

He took a step toward us.

A siren sounded in Starke.

Rupert and I blinked in the direction of the cacophony. The snow screened the truck. Yet I could see the red lights wavering back and forth as the fire truck swerved on the snow-coated road.

Rupert looked back at me. "I'm sorry, Dora." He turned toward the forest.

"Don't run. For once, don't run."

He gave me one last look over his shoulder.

"You'll die out there," I cried.

Rupert didn't hesitate. He ran into the woods in the thick, falling snow. His leather coat flapped in the cruel wind. He flitted, a ghost. Not a man. Not my father. A ghost.

"Dora," Lester whispered.

I looked down at the man who had always been a father to me. In the red light, his face glowed ruddy, as if in health. The flecks of blood on his lips gave lie to the glow.

"Don't talk. Help's coming."

"I never wanted the Noira. I needed money to find Joey's killer," Lester said, his voice threaded high and too thin.

"I know. I understand. It's okay."

"I never wanted to kill anybody."

"Shhh."

"I wanted justice." A snowflake fluttered onto his eyelid and Lester blinked.

I wiped the damp away. "Hold on." I glanced up to see if help came, but the fire engine lights still seemed years away.

Lester coughed. Blood sprayed from his mouth.

"Please stay, please," I begged him.

Lester gasped, his breath ragged. "Forgive me."

"Don't go. Don't leave me."

"Dora," Lester gasped.

I stared into his eyes.

He looked back and with his gaze asked again. He waited for me to say three words. And let him go.

I smiled at him. "I forgive you."

He smiled back. "Forgive yourself too," he whispered.

I nodded.

I lied.

He stared upward at the falling snowflakes. The wet sound ceased. In the red firelight on his face, snowflakes fell upon his open eyes.

In the still of the falling snow, I crouched over him. To protect my old friend from the bitter cold. Flakes fell past me, for the wet showed on his face. Or perhaps that was only my tears.

FORTY

The snow fell.

Forever, I protected Lester until Mallard pulled me away. Forever, the old fir tree toppled in a red shower of sparks. Forever, a spark seared onto my frozen face. Forever, the Castle tower tumbled after the fir tree. Forever, I watched the burning of Lester's funeral pyre.

The snow fell.

I sat in Mallard's police car. My teeth clattered. Even after Mallard gave me his heavily lined and fur hooded winter coat. The firemen, Jeff and James, won the battle. Doc Byrne came. Lester left in the ambulance. The ambulance arrived without sirens, without lights, without need.

The snow fell.

I sat in my same chair in the sheriff's office and answered Mallard's question after question after question. I clutched a hot cup of coffee. And shivered. I'd never be warm again.

The snow fell.

I spent the little remainder of the night at the old homestead. I'd begged Mallard to let the Widows Brigade keep Aunt Maddie. I lay in my comfy old bed for the first time in days. I didn't sleep. When I closed my eyes I saw images—a burning tower, my father fleeing to a cold death, Lester's blood splashed on white snow. I shivered.

At last, I sat at my bedroom window and watched the snow falling thick through the long night. With dawn, the snowfall died. The sun cast rosy light onto the pristine snow making it appear as the color of blood in snow melt.

In the bright, cruel early morning light, I headed to the sheriff's office one last time.

Mallard, gray-faced with fatigue, sat at his usual desk. He glanced over at Lester's desk when I walked in. Out of habit, I supposed.

I couldn't bear to look at Lester's desk. To see the torn check from the Widows Brigade still laying there. To see the crumbs of our last shared cinnamon roll. To see the altered photograph of Joey, his dead grandson.

Mallard stood. "Dora, what are you doing here so early?" His uniform, rumpled and stained, now seemed tailored to his body. Not a drop of sweat showed anywhere on him, despite the office being overheated.

I dropped my chin down onto my old parka, the pink one with the faux fur hood, from my high school days. Mallard had taken my blood-splashed apron as evidence. Red stains that I suspected matched the stains on my soul. I never wanted to see the apron again.

Mallard came over to me and took my arm. Gently, as if he feared I might shatter. "When I have more questions, I'll call."

I set down Nance's purse on his desk. "I'm here to pay off Aunt Maddie's ticket. Then you can arrest me for killing Lester."

"Dora, that's precipitous." Sheriff Mallard dropped his other hand toward his holster, but never connected. He no longer seemed to need the reassurance of his gun.

"Precipitous? Now that you're sheriff you use long words? I shot Lester. I killed—I—" I swallowed hard. No tears, not now, not ever. Once I began, I'd never stop.

"There are extenuating circumstances," Mallard said.

I made a noise deep in my throat.

Mallard gave a small tug on my arm. "Dora, come sit down."

I pulled away from Mallard's grasp.

He sighed, returned to his chair, and sat down. The new sheriff crossed his arms over his chest. "Dora, Lester shot and killed Godiva. Godiva was unarmed."

She deserved to die.

I pressed hard on my aching heart. I realized I touched the same spot on my chest where a few hours before I'd held my apron to Lester's mortal wound. I dropped my hands. "Lester didn't plan to kill anyone."

"I think he did." Mallard rolled his shoulders in an exhausted motion. "The first lesson Lester taught me was never pigeonhole people. Never judge. Never think of people as right or wrong, criminal or victim."

My mouth quirked. "Very Buddhist."

"Dora, listen to me." He leaned forward in his chair. "Lester forgot his own first lesson. Sometimes grief makes a man go mad. You defended yourself against his madness."

"I still shot him. He wasn't pointing his gun at me."

"At that second? Are you sure? In the middle of a snowstorm? With the Castle tower going up in flames? And Lester set that fire. We found an incendiary device with his fingerprints all over it. He'd planned to kill Godiva and your father and burn the evidence."

"No, I don't believe it. I can't believe Lester—I won't."

Mallard scrubbed an eyebrow. "I didn't want to believe it either. And with Rupert flailing another gun around, it's a wonder you all didn't end up dead."

"Lester fired wide at Rupert."

"If what you remember is true then why was Lester shot in the chest?"

I closed my eyes to squeeze back my tears. A vision of Lester twisting his body came to me. I opened my eyes. I didn't want to see. "He turned around after he fired."

Mallard rubbed his mouth then reached his hand out toward me. "So he committed suicide by Dora? Is that what you want his family to know?"

My hands squeezed each other tight. "No, no."

"Do you want Lester's family to know all the details of his destruction? Do you want the town of Starke to know? Don't you want us all to remember him as before? A good man? A good sheriff? A good father?"

I dropped my chin deeper into my chest. "I killed him, Mallard."

Mallard stood again. He took a step toward me and stopped. "I know, Dora," he said in a quiet voice. "But I figure it was self-defense or justifiable homicide."

"You're not going to arrest me?"

"I won't let you use the justice system to punish yourself."

There's no justice.

Mallard flung both arms wide. "Do you want your aunt to go through the agony of you in jail? Up on charges? If it ever went to trial, which I seriously doubt, she'd lose everything."

"She's already lost."

"Only if she lost you."

I brought my head up and looked Mallard in the eye. "She wants me lost."

"Dora, no."

"Yes." I squatted and opened Nance's purse.

Mallard started at the sight of the stacked and bound hundreds.

"Fifteen hundred, right?" I asked.

Mallard passed his hand over his face until he reached his mouth. Maybe he feared what he'd say next. "Where did you get that? No, don't tell me. I don't want to know."

I peeled off fifteen bills. I stood up and held the money out to Mallard. "Take it. Release Aunt Maddie. Then arrest me for receiving money for stolen property."

He dropped his hand. "No."

"To what? Releasing my aunt or arresting me?"

Mallard reached out and took the money from me. He dropped it back into Nance's purse. "Both. Maybe if the investigation shows— no, no, it's all over." He shook his head. "Lester said being a good sheriff was about knowing people first and the law second. I'm forgiving the ticket. And forgetting the rest."

"What about the Noira?" Not that I cared. I never wanted to see that evil horror again.

Mallard snorted. "That's been resolved." He rolled his eyes. "Boy, has that been resolved."

"I suspected this," I said. "You've turned into a good Sheriff of Starke."

Mallard blushed and a tiny drop of sweat formed on his brow. Nice to see a moist touch of the old Mallard.

I picked up my suitcase and Nance's purse. The purse was the heavier of the two.

Mallard frowned at my suitcase. "Where are you going?"

"Away." I opened the office door.

"Where do I find you if when I need you for questioning?"

I turned back, one foot out the door. "Find me like you're trying to find my father now." A cold breeze lifted my words and chilled my heart.

Last night no one, not Mallard, not a state policeman, not Jeff or James, no matter how I pleaded, had started a search for Rupert. Not at night, not in the middle of a snowstorm.

"Your father's a survivor."

"My father was a fool and a coward."

Mallard took my arm again. "Dora, you can't leave Starke. What about your Aunt Maddie?"

"Let go."

"You need to remain in Starke while the investigation is ongoing." Mallard's every word warned police business.

"I'll be working at the All Jewelry Factory Outlet in Boise. You can find me there. If anywhere."

I left.

"Dora?" Mallard's voice came from behind me.

I kept walking. Away.

FORTY-ONE

A squeak greeted me as I wrestled myself, Nance's purse, and my old suitcase into Mama Chin's. On the old countertop rested a shiny new cage. Inside, Fat Freddy squatted on his haunches. He grasped the cage bars and poked his whiskery nose out through the bars. His nose twitched in protest to his incarceration.

"Did Mallard jail you as a material witness?" I asked him.

He gave a hopeful rat look at the cage door.

Mama Chin roared out the kitchen door. "We're closed." She paused mid-step when she saw me. "Oh, it's you, Dora," she said in a much softer tone. "Dora, I—"

I took a step away from her. "If you're closed, lock the front door," I said in a sharp, angry voice. I slammed my lips shut. Mama Chin deserved better than my dumping my anger at myself on her.

Mama Chin frowned. "I can't," she said in a more normal tone, "the contractors need to come and go."

I raised both eyebrows.

"Mrs. McGarrity outed Freddy to the Dog Developers."

My eyebrows stayed up.

"I got thrown out of the mall." Mama Chin stuck a finger in Freddy's cage and stroked his white head. "Luckily, Henry's saner than those dogs. He said long as I keep old Freddy in a cage away from the kitchen—"

Freddy squeaked at the word "kitchen."

"Sorry old rat," Mama Chin said, "you needed to go on a diet anyway."

I set my suitcase down and perched on the edge. "I'm sorry. I'll be gone soon. I promise." I slumped over and stared at the floor. "I need to meet Nance here and then Tony's picking me up."

I'd blackmailed a ride from Tony on his weekly supply run to Boise. When he'd refused at first, I'd threatened to tell Maureen about a certain bad habit he had at the age of five. Always had a stopped up nose, Tony, and an inelegant way of dealing with the problem.

"For what? To go where?" Mama Chin demanded.

"Away."

"What kind of an answer is—"

"None of your business, Mama Chin." I bit my lower lip.

"None of? Hmpfh." Mama Chin turned and stomped into the kitchen.

I glanced at the old clock cleaned, repaired and re-hung on the wall. Nance always showed up on time and often early, especially if the meeting entailed her getting money. Where was she?

Nance flung open the front door. She wore a vast orange fur coat. Even on her tall figure, it reached past her knees. And so thick it made skinny Nance bulky. That answered my question of what she'd wear during snow season. She carried an enormous purse I'd never seen before, this one in brilliant orange faux fur.

She limped inside. A tiny bandage covered the tear on her earlobe. Sunglasses covered most of her black eye. Her head seemed to float on top of the oversized fur coat.

I sunk lower on my old suitcase. My heart strummed in misery. Everyone I cared about I'd hurt. Nance wouldn't be in pain if I'd only done Right Action when Rupert first handed me the necklace. My actions. My fault. My guilt.

The swinging kitchen door opened. A scent of warm yeasty dough and cinnamon wafted out. Mama Chin followed the aroma and stood in the doorway. She pointed at me. "Talk some sense into her," she said to Nance. She stormed back into the kitchen and started banging pots and pans.

Nance placed a hand on her chest. "As a Buddhist, I would never presume to proselytize."

My eyebrows rose. "You're wearing a fur coat."

Nance stroked the coat. Bits of fur fluttered. "This was my grandmother's. These vicunas have been dead for a hundred years." Nance's logic, an immovable force. "Still has a lot of good wear in it." Nance batted at a large bit of fluff.

"You're late," I said. A touch of anger still colored those two words. I couldn't help myself. I needed to get gone.

Nance limped over to me. "I'm never late. You were early." She pointed at my suitcase. "Oh good, you brought something to put your reward in, how wise."

"What?" I'd miss Nance and how she always held conversations that started somewhere in the middle or the end.

Nance grabbed her old lion-clasp purse beside me. "Ouch." She winced. "Who knew a cracked rib could hurt so much?" She unclasped the lion's jaws and started pulling out bundles of cash.

I sat back on the suitcase. "Nance, what are you doing?" Not that I expected an answer.

"The police didn't find it. I did. Though that sweaty policeman kept yelling at me to get out of the crime scene."

"Found what?" I struggled to catch up.

"The necklace. I found it, in the snow, shining in the sun." Nance counted the bills with quick flicks of her fingers. "The Noira wanted me to find it."

I leaned back, away from Nance and her money and her mad obsession. "Nance, you can't keep the Noira. It's stolen. It's evil. It's covered in blood." *Fresh blood. Lester's blood.*

"I wanted the Noira with all my heart." Nance looked down at her long-fingered hands and the money. Then she smiled at me. "But my soul heard your truth about the karma of the Noira."

"My truth?" Nance had listened to me?

"And, lo and behold, there's a twenty-five thousand dollar reward offered by The National Art Jewelry Museum for recovery of the necklace. Who knew?" Nance ducked her head. "Well, I knew. But I was too nuts about the Noira." With both hands she held a couple of sheaves of bills. "There. There's your reward, all thirty thousand dollars."

Mama Chin chose that moment to open the kitchen door again. She stared at the cash. She shook her head and said, "My cinnamon rolls are going to burn," before she stepped back into the kitchen.

"No." I held my hands up and pushed away the air. "You recovered the necklace."

Nance put the cash bundles down on a box next to me. "Desire is one way of suffering, Dora. You taught me that. Sometimes a teacher becomes a student."

"No." I ran my hands over my face then peeked at Nance through my fingers. "You said the reward was twenty-five thousand."

"The rest of the money is for saving my life, my soul, my spirit. Thank you for helping me on my path."

To my amazement, Nance placed her hands together and bowed to me. Well, tried to bow, her thick coat and busted rib prevented anything more than a small pathetic and courageous attempt.

I didn't acknowledge the gesture. "I'm not a Buddhist anymore, Nance. I never was."

"Everybody's a Buddhist. They just don't know it," Nance said. Her logic again.

I dropped my head and closed my eyes. "What I've done—"

"Doesn't matter. That policeman with the duck name wouldn't tell me what happened, but whatever it was, it's over. You've moved down your path."

I said nothing. A brush of fur caressed my cheek. I raised my head to see Nance, her smile small and sad. "You deserve the reward."

"It's blood money."

"Yes, yes, it is," Nance said. "The Noira curse bloodied everyone it touched. Including us." She sighed. The shoulders of the fur coat barely moved. "It's far better that it is in a museum, safely locked away behind unbreakable glass."

"No." I reached out my hand to knock the money off the box.

Nance caught my hand. She gave me a sharp look. "Dora, it's karma. You can't control lives. The past is gone forever." Nance squeezed my hand. "You can't fix what's happened with guilt."

I gulped down bile. Nance didn't know my crime. I pulled away. "Give the money to Aunt Maddie."

"Give me what money?" my aunt said from where she stood in the open doorway. The icy cold wind blew her old gardening coat out around her. She stopped in the open doorway and stared at the stacks of cash. An icy breeze blew snow inside.

"Shut the door. I have to pay for the heat," Mama Chin called. She poked her head around the kitchen door. When she saw Aunt Maddie she gave a sharp nod. "'Bout time you got here." She disappeared back into the kitchen.

Aunt Maddie slammed the door behind her. It rattled in the frame. She stormed up to Nance and raised a bandaged hand and pointed her index finger an inch from Nance's face.

Nance took a tentative, limping step back.

"Now look you, you wealthy weird person you," my aunt said. "Dora is not your employee and you're not buying my store and you're not giving us a loan or any money so Dora can leave."

Nance took another step away from my aunt's vicinity. "I'm only giving Dora her due."

"You'll do nothing of the sort."

Nance took another step back.

Aunt Maddie picked up a stack of hundreds and flapped the stack at Nance. "You take back your slave money."

"Employee? Store? Slave? Oh, no. I'm buying the Castle. Without that nasty tower, it's a great place." Nance grinned at us. "I'm your competition." With that, Nance grabbed up her purses and scuttled to the glass front door. Outside, she bumped full bulk into Mrs. McGarrity. Behind Mrs. McGarrity crowded Mrs. McDay and Mrs. McChin.

Mrs. McGarrity wore an enormous quilted and embroidered coat that increased her size to that of a small grizzly. Next to her, Bark also wore a be-laced monstrosity. He hung his little head—with ear warmers on his stand-up fox ears—embarrassed.

They all danced a slippery sideways dance until Nance gave in and stepped out into the street and around the Widows Brigade. Mrs. McGarrity looked into the restaurant, saw Freddie in his cage, and opened the front door and her mouth.

Aunt Maddie shook the money at her. "Out."

Mrs. McGarrity paused, mouth open. Bark strained on his lacy leash to reach Freddie, who cowered in the corner of his cage. Mrs. McGarrity glanced from Aunt Maddie to me and back again to Aunt Maddie. She shut her mouth, pulled Bark out, and closed the door.

I stood up. "You're back," I said to Aunt Maddie.

My aunt tossed her few thousand back onto the box. "I never left."

I nodded at the wad of cash. "Take it, Aunt Maddie."

She tossed it onto the box. A twenty fluttered over the edge onto the floor. "I've been looking all over town for you."

"Save the store." I picked up my suitcase.

My aunt placed her hands on her hips. "What's all this nonsense about you leaving?"

I looked outside where the Widows Brigade lined up along the front picture window. Mrs. McDay pressed her face against the window, the cherries on her hat crushed. She gave a little wave. I didn't wave back.

I started toward the front door.

"Dora?"

"I love you, Aunt Maddie."

My aunt grabbed my parka sleeve. "Dora, no, wait."

"I have to go."

Aunt Maddie held me fast. "No, listen—"

"No. I'm done." I tugged.

"Stop your pity party," my aunt snapped.

I stared at her.

She dropped my sleeve. "I didn't mean that. No, yes I did. But I really meant—" Aunt Maddie looked down at her old green coat and fiddled with a button that half-hung off. "Dora, I-I need your help."

My mouth fell open. I could think of nothing to say. My aunt asking for help? From me? From anyone? Her button clattered to the floor. I picked it up and handed it to her. She held it in her open hand toward me.

"You ran the store without me for years," I told her.

"I don't mean that." Aunt Maddie swallowed hard. "I need you. Stay with me."

I blinked back tears. No tears. Not now. Not ever.

Her chin came up. "Just because running away is a family tradition doesn't mean you have to follow it."

"I'm not running," I said and realized as I said it that I told another lie.

"You always had the courage to stay. Not run, like Rupert. Not rage, like Lester. Not give up, like me. Don't run. Stay."

"Aunt Maddie, I can't stay." I shivered. I'd never get warm again. "I'm sorry. I'm being selfish, I know." My chest tightened so I had to squeeze the words out. "But I can't bear to stay in Starke. Not after what I did. It hurts me too much."

"Leaving me won't make it hurt any less," Aunt Maddie said, tears in her voice.

"I'm not leaving you. I'm—" My knees buckled. I dropped my suitcase.

"Oh, my sweet, dear girl." Aunt Maddie threw her arms around me.

I buried my face in her old coat and smelled decades of good garden loam and long winters of smoky attempts at fireplace fires. The heady scent of home. "I did a terrible thing," I sobbed into the old fabric.

"Oh Dora," Aunt Maddie said. "Terrible things happened."

"I killed a man. A friend. A father."

"Yes." She patted my back with a strong stroke I remembered from my childhood, not too soft, not too hard.

"I killed Lester. I can't take that back. I can't make it right."

"No, you can't." She squeezed me tighter. "All you can do is continue. Even with terrible grief. Even with terrible guilt. As best you can. That's why Buddhists call life 'practice.'"

I leaned back and looked at my aunt. "Since when did you become such a good Buddhist?"

"Since I started listening to you." Tears ran down my aunt's face.

In Aunt Maddie's eyes I saw my agony reflected. How could I abandon her? I reached out and wiped the tears from her cheeks. "I guess I've got to get started on better karma sometime." I wiped away my own tears.

My aunt smiled with all of her soul.

"It's about time," Mama Chin said as she banged out of the kitchen, a tray in her arms. "These are best warm."

On the tray, plates of cinnamon rolls and mugs of coffee rested resplendent. I smacked my lips. My appetite twinged.

Mama Chin pushed aside the money and set down the tray. "Vegan. I promise."

Mrs. McGarrity opened the front door again. She'd shortened Bark's leash to where he stood so close to her to be almost hidden under her bulk.

Mama Chin's hands became fists.

Mrs. McGarrity held up a little bag of small brown bits. "Fresh baked homemade rat treats?" she said with a world of question in her voice. She gave the bag a shake.

Freddy sat up in his cage.

"I'm sorry," Mrs. McGarrity said in Freddy's direction. "Truce?" she asked of Mama Chin.

Mama Chin pointed at Bark. "The dog—"

"Will stay right next to my side, under my control, every moment."

Mama Chin rubbed her chin. Freddy gave a hopeful squeak. Mama Chin shrugged. "Why not? There's plenty of cinnamon rolls for everyone."

The Widows Brigade piled in with Mallard bringing up the rear. Mrs. McDay picked up the errant bills on the floor. She started stacking them, humming under her breath.

Tony's car slowed to park outside Mama Chin's. He leaned out the driver's side window, took a look at the party, gave a grin and a wave, and drove off.

I snatched the last roll off the platter. "So," I said to Aunt Maddie, "I figure we can repair Charles's paintings first—"

"No," my aunt said.

"What?"

My aunt shook her head. "You were right about Charles, Dora. He's never coming back."

"But—"

Aunt Maddie shrugged. "It's okay, I've accepted it." She looked at me. "Or as you would say, I've moved farther down my path."

"But—" I took a bite and chewed before I said more.

The front door opened again.

"For heaven's sakes," Mama Chin said, "this restaurant is busier now than when it was open. We're closed," she said to the tall, lean older man who stood in the doorway.

With his long lantern jaw and his long gray hair pulled up into a topknot the man looked familiar. What man wore his hair in a bun on top of his head? What man that I knew?

"Charles?" Aunt Maddie gasped.

Double ohm.

ABOUT THE AUTHOR

Conda grew up in the ski resort of Sun Valley, Idaho. Her childhood was filled with authors and artists and other creative types. She grew up with goats in the kitchen, buffalo bones in the living room, and rocks in the bathtub. Now her life is filled with her cat and dog, permanent boyfriend, and writing.

She's traveled the world from Singapore to Russia and her own tiny office, writing all the while. She delights in writing her cozy Starke Dead creative woman mystery series with amateur detective jeweler Dora Starke. The more Dora discovers cursed jewelry, her aunt digging graves, and a rampant poisoner, the more fun Conda has—although sometimes Dora complains about her plight!

Next up, Starke Raving Dead, in which Dora's mad Aunt Maddie proves the aptness of her name. When she's not writing Dora into her quirky and quixotic mysteries, Conda writes the popular tween fantasy Mall Fairies series. The fairy inspiration for her Mall Fairies came from the sparrows that live in the Boise Towne Square Mall in Boise, Idaho. When not rescuing fairies from humans, cats, and themselves, Conda works on the last title in the Mall Fairy trilogy, The Mall Fairies: Destiny.

Make sure to connect with Conda through her website or social media.
Blog: http://condascreativecenter.blogspot.com
Facebook: https://www.facebook.com/conda.v.douglas
Pinterest: http://pinterest.com/condadouglas/
Twitter:https://twitter.com/Conda_V
Amazon author page:
https://www.amazon.com/author/condadouglas

Now enjoy this excerpt from Mild West Mysteries: 13 Idaho Tales of Murder and Mayhem. You'll recognize Dora and Nance from Starke Naked Dead in this story about the tribulations of the self-employed, especially if they're jewelers. Luckily, only rarely do such trials turn deadly...

Conda's note:

This first story is from my Starke Dead cozy mystery series. Stealing Patterns is all about my main character's, Dora's, world of jewelry design and selling, especially the hard, grinding work of selling said designs. One difficult but effective way to do that: trade shows, as is shown here—and from the point of view of one of Dora's nemeses, uh, friends, her sometime boss, Nance.

Growing up with a jeweler father, I remember many events, all too well, much like this one, without the major crime. However, there is always much of the minor crime of stealing patterns in any trade show or conference.

Stealing Patterns

"If you're going to thieve, you'd better be a little more subtle about it," I demanded of the scruffy locked-in-fashionable young man. The only note of original style I spotted on his torn jean and faded hoodie clad body was his distinctive jewelry.

Every piece of his jewelry suite incorporated elements of a revolver. He sported the barrel on a black leather wristband and the stocks and barrels of two guns strung with more leather made a necklace. Most striking, if obviously heavy, each earlobe wore earrings made out of triple brass shell casings, no loaded bullets, cradled by a gold wire hanging low on his ears.

I could see why the young designer got invited to submit to the jury and then judged good enough to be here at Boise's very first (and maybe last, if this nonsense continued) International Idaho Jewelry Exhibition. I supposed that I should be grateful that Boise grew to the point that it could now support a major exhibition. Grateful that now I only needed to drive three hours—okay three and a half if I drove the speed limit, from my gallery in ski resort Starke Idaho, instead of the many more hours to Portland or Seattle or the two-day long trek to San Francisco. Difficult to do, when the same sneaky stealing happened here.

The thief stood three feet away from my table where my ex-employee and now temporary employee, Dora, frantically placed my presentation pieces. The object of my ire covered his cell phone, held waist high with his other hand as if I hadn't noticed. Too little, too late. Perhaps he believed I was too old, being in my fifties, to recognize what he did. Wrong.

I resisted the urge to snatch the phone away and delete the photos of my award winning designs. "At the very least, be more traditional and sketch 'em out when I'm not looking, sheesh."

At a judged jewelry exhibition like this, sure every designer studied the other award winners' designs for, ahem, inspiration. Patterns, it's all about those, we always searched for new

ways to make our patterns. Or, to speak true, as any good Buddhist such as myself, Nance, we'd sometimes outright copy. Maybe even copy that bracelet—I stepped closer and loomed over my fellow thief to stop us both. I'm six foot three; I can do that so well.

Mr. Scruffy shuffled backward out of my looming, grinned and waved the cell phone. "New times, new technology, and who says I'm taking pics of your great jewelry?" He pointed with the phone at Dora. Or rather at her mid-sized cleavage, the biggest part of my short—petite—assistant and part of the reason I insisted she work the show with me.

I'd also insisted, that instead of her usual heavy cotton jeweler's apron over jeans, she wear a low-cut black velvet dress, with my signature Dog Face Mountain pins attached and my award winning platinum and sapphire necklace in pride of place centered in her cleavage. That way every customer got an eyeful of my designs, no matter where they looked and most of them looked straight at that arrowed portion of Dora.

Dora straightened and glared in the chauvinist pig's direction. Mr. Scruffy shrugged an apology and walked away. He moved to the best table in the room, next to the only glass display case, a monster at eight feet tall and five wide. The case stood next to the only unlocked single door in, affording an automatic sight direction for customers, plus lots more display.

Scruffy slouched into a chair and shared something on his phone with one of his companions, a great hulking overall clad master jeweler while I wondered why and how he got the coveted First Prize place. I mean, his dramatic stuff stood out well in the glass case, but still those pieces couldn't be worth as much as one of my necklaces—maybe a security measure?

After all, the sleepy security guard sitting in the corridor next to the door didn't look like he'd be much use, although the sizeable gun in his holster might. Plus, he might just need the weapon to keep back the sizeable crowd waiting in the corridor for the show to open. I nodded. It'd been worth the thousand dollar entry fee to get into this "invitation only juried" exhibition. The organizers obviously used that money to promote and bring in wealthy, eager customers.

"Good riddance," Dora said of the departed guy, breaking into my musings. "Another moment and I'd have gone against all my teachings and smacked the snot," she continued, just as my gaze floated to the large decorative clock above the door. Uh-oh.

Ten minutes, only ten minutes left. "Never mind him," I said as turned back to our tiny table, perched next to the other exit, a fire door leading outside.

"Darn fool judges," Dora said, interpreting my grimace as she so often did. We sometimes worked great as a team. "Give you Fifth Place will they? When they gave those jerks," she pointed at Scruffy Guy and Hulk, "First Place? No woman would ever buy those earrings. They're too heavy for a woman to wear."

I smiled at her vehemence on my behalf while I took a long, careful survey of my carefully planned display. Platinum and gold rings perched, each snug on a one finger stand in a large heart-shaped pattern on the black velvet. Diamonds and high water rubies sparkled in the settings. In the center of the ring-created heart, necklaces copied the heart form.

The longest chain enclosed a smaller chain, and one more within surrounded my best piece. A rose pin of rose colored diamonds gleamed in the center. Sure, the pin would've been bland, except for the leaf curling around one petal, a leaf picked out in emeralds.

Dora crossed her arms over her chest, obscuring my jewelry. I opened my mouth to remind her she was a walking display when she said, "A touch too sparse and cutsey-wutsey, the display, don't you think?"

She snarked about the display we planned together. Typical. When would she ever learn Right Speech? I tried to teach her all I knew, and that's extensive, about our shared Buddhist beliefs. She should be grateful. Right Thought, all the way.

Well, maybe not.

I couldn't afford to bring more. I needed to sell a few pieces before making more of my high end stock. Platinum, gold, and precious gems cost and too many too expensive pieces could sound a death knell for a jewelry business.

But did the display appear too old-fashioned, too cute? I puffed out a long, tired breath. No, no. And even if it did, the form of the display helped prevent any theft. It'd be obvious if any piece found its way off the table and into a pocket, purse, or, I'd known it to happen, mouth. Should I rethink the whole thing? In three minutes?

"What if we shift the display into concentric circles instead of the heart shape?" Dora suggested.

I agreed. "Brilliant." I reached for one of the ring stands when a screech, bang and crash made me jump and Dora scream. I whirled around to see that the glass case next to the entry had toppled over, shattered glass everywhere. Hulk jeweler stood to one side, obviously the instigator of the crash. The old security guard, on his feet, stood in front of the crowd, pressing in toward the door. Scruffy guy tore his bracelet off and had the barrel released in a second. He reached for the necklace as Hulk headed in Dora's direction, hand out.

I spotted the pattern. Hulk would grab and snatch the best pieces, starting with my necklace while his buddy completed creating the gun. Then, shoot the guard and in the resulting melee, escape out the exit. How to stop—I stared at Scruffy, who was almost finished with putting together the gun. Next, the bullet earrings. Earrings.

In an instant, I whirled around and nodded my head toward the guy, hoping to communicate my plan to Dora. It worked. Petite Dora scuttled around Big Hulk and, with me, sprinted to Scruffy. He reared back as we arrived. Together we each reached and grabbed an earring and yanked. Hard.

"Ouch!" He cried as the wires cut through the tender earlobes.

I turned in time to see Hulk bearing down on me, when a bang resonated through the room. Plaster filtered from the ceiling, where a hole showed.

"Freeze!" I heard through the ringing of my ears. In the doorway, through the frame of the fallen case, the security guard stood, gun aimed in a two handed grip.

Dora nudged my arm and when I looked at her, held up the bloody earring. "Good thing you taught me it's all about the patterns!"

Check out this and the rest of the *Mild West Mysteries, 13 Idaho Tales of Murder and Mayhem.*

https://www.amazon.com/dp/1622060466 print
https://www.amazon.com/dp/B016SDH1KE kindle

www.ingramcontent.com/pod-product-compliance
Lightning Source LLC
Chambersburg PA
CBHW072230170626
46813CB00003B/1163